2

MW00775346

WHAT EVIL LURKS

WHAT EVIL LURKS

*A Lavina London
Mystery*

JAMES R. McCAHERY

KENSINGTON BOOKS

For Madeline and Raymond,
who shared so much of my childhood
and who continue to keep me young.

FRIDAY,
DECEMBER
15

Chapter One

> ⤜ ⤛

Who said you couldn't throw your own farewell bash? He'd just done it, hadn't he? And without a hitch, too. So it had cost him a pretty penny, so what? There'd be plenty more where that came from—he'd made sure of that right off.

Not that it was all that much of a farewell, of course. He was only leaving the States for Canada—Boulder, New York for Toronto, Ontario. But it gave him an excuse, the excuse he'd been looking for to get them all together again—all those who had played key roles in his life so many years ago. Back before he'd retired, certainly, back when radio was in its heyday, before the average Joe had even heard of television. It had been his heyday, too, his and Hildy's—the happiest days of their lives. Henry and Hilda Blaine, their soap opera right up there with *The Romance of Helen Trent, Stella Dallas,* and *Backstage Wife.* Well, maybe not all that far up, but a definite credit to the talented, pioneering Hummerts nonetheless, and most certainly on the way up. Up until their careers were untimely nipped in the bud, that is.

The Buick's headlights caught patches of ice on the snow-cleared blacktop road as the car reached the top of the hill. Blaine's squinting eyes spotted them as well, prompting him to maneuver around them. When he reached the pair of four-foot-high shale gate posts that flanked the entrance to Hemlock Lake off to the right, he turned in, then bore left to head around the lake.

It had been good to see them all there tonight—and just to honor him, too—to see him off, on another of life's ventures. Not one of them had refused his invitation, even if it meant—as it had in a few instances—coming in from the West Coast. It was the crowd in the East, though, that had been his main concern. Some of them knew better than to turn down his invitation. The others, well, they probably showed up because they really cared. It was nice to know he hadn't suffered the same untimely fate as radio itself. Hildy would have been pleased.

Dear Hildy. His wife's passing over a year ago was a bit more than he could handle at the time; he'd never thought it possible. When he finally did come around, he realized how low their finances had sunk. With the money running out and his piddling pension and social security unable to meet his more than comfortable life-style, he found it necessary to fall back on an old, secondary source of income he had stopped tapping decades ago. And then only because Hildy had begun questioning the source of some of their money. She would never have approved. Would have left him, more likely than not. That he could never have allowed.

Now, though, things were different. Hildy's conscience was not his. As far as he was concerned, some people could easily ante up $750 a month, and that a mere 50 percent increase after all those years of nonpayment. Not too bad considering the inflation rate. There hadn't been too much complaining when he phoned with the news either. Maybe he should have gone for a thousand after all. Well, there was always time for that down the road. He'd have to get a handle on the Canadian life-style before he could judge with any certainty. Since he'd only just turned seventy-two, there were plenty of years ahead. The money, the house, and property here on the lake would bring a pittance compared with the anticipated outlay up north. Yes, the more he thought about it, the happier he was with his decision. It was definitely time to recoup.

As the car neared the curve in the road heading around the lake, the darkness closed in, the high beams his only source of light. He stretched his neck closer to the windshield and squinted through his thick lenses. As he thought back on the evening with a grin, he could picture the bunch of them stretched out before him at their circular tables. The banquet hall at the Seventeener had seen many a sumptuous wedding, but nothing to equal Henry Blaine's farewell bash. From his table on the dais, he had felt like Henry VIII lording it over his court. And some of his own toadies were no less real than the monarch's.

A few of the gang had wanted to turn the evening into a roast, but of course there wasn't all that much to say about him, even after all those years together in radio—at least nothing suitable for a roasting. He laughed out loud. If they only knew . . .

He hadn't seen most of them since he left New York in '72. Some had gone on into television as early as '53 once they saw the handwriting on the wall, with a few of them still at it in one capacity or another. Others had retired

long before he'd been able to—the ones who could probably live very comfortably into the next century on their
investment interest alone. Why shouldn't people like that
share? Especially the ones he knew still owed a debt to so-
ciety. And while he didn't like to consider himself judge
and jury, still, in his own small way, he was helping them
make retribution.

The familiar tall blue spruce that graced the front lawn
of his home loomed up ahead, off to his right. It was a
welcome sight. He was tired, and his tearing eyes burned
more than usual. He braked and turned into the partially
shoveled driveway, thumbing the automatic garage door
control on the seat alongside him.

House and garage were awash with the electrified color
of Christmas lights. It made him think briefly again of
Hildy and Christmases past.

The overhead garage light came on as the white-paneled
door rose a quarter of the way up. When the headroom
was clear, he pulled in, nosing the bumper up to the square
of carpeting he had anchored into the cement block wall
of the garage, then killed the engine.

He sat back in the seat, his head against the headrest,
and heaved a deep sigh. Night driving tended to make him
tense. When the overhead light went out again, he pushed
the door open, setting off the car's interior lights. He un-
buckled his seat belt, grabbed his gloves from the seat next
to him, and slid his bony frame out the door. Once outside, he bent in again to retrieve the keys, which were still
in the ignition. Grabbing them up in his hand, he backed
out and straightened up. He shook the key ring, holding it
up against the dim light from the car's interior as he
hunted for his house key.

A sharp, agonizing pain shot up through his nose and into the front of his head as he felt but barely glimpsed the woolen-gloved hand close roughly over his mouth from behind him. An onrush of color—as varied and vivid as the decorator lights outside—flooded his brain. Whatever the hand held brought wooziness, balm, and quick oblivion.

MONDAY, DECEMBER 18

Chapter Two

➤ ➤

"This is great junk, Mrs. London," the little redhead said, brandishing a green and silver cardboard St. Patrick's Day top hat in his mittened hand.

"Yeah," his fair-haired companion agreed as he continued to rummage through one of the large boxes Lavina had set out earlier in the afternoon for the sanitation men.

"Just make sure you boys put everything you don't want back into the boxes," Lavina said with a smile as she watched them near the road that skirted her lakefront property. She didn't tell them there was more "junk" in storage that she still hadn't been able to part with after all these years—souvenirs of a lifetime, of a family gone or grown. Every December when she started her annual unpacking of the Christmas boxes, she made a point to go through the mementos to see what, if anything, she could bear to part with. Some years it was a losing battle. Others, like this one, were more successful.

"What's this, Mrs. London?" redheaded Freddie Stoner asked, puzzled, his little nose crinkling up in the middle of his freckled face. He held aloft a large red plastic hoop.

"That's a hula hoop," Lavina said. "You're supposed to shake your body like a hula dancer and spin it around your middle." She jabbed him in his flannel-shirted tummy, exposed beneath his opened thermal jacket.

"Can you show me?" He held the hoop out to her, squinting against the bright afternoon sun that filtered through the tall branching hemlocks overhead.

Lavina fairly howled. "I don't think so, Freddie, no. Maybe when Susanne comes up for Christmas she can show you." Actually, the hoop had belonged to her daughter, Tracey, who'd had its refinements down to an art when it was such a craze. Lavina could picture her even now. As for herself, she had been at a complete loss to operate the thing, even in her younger days.

Freddie's companion, Kevin Greigson, was crouched alongside the three-foot-high cardboard box, his corduroyed bottom grazing the frozen snow beneath him. He was holding what looked like a strip of crepe paper, about an inch and a half wide, rolled tightly under a rubber band he was having absolutely no success removing.

"Here, that I *can* show you," Lavina said, taking the item in question from the little mittened hands and stretching off the rubber band. "I think it was called a lariat," she explained. Grabbing hold of a length of string that was attached to one end, she shook out the crinkled lime-colored strip that unfurled to a length of eight or ten feet. "Now watch," she said in a louder than normal tone as she stepped back on the snow-covered lawn, careful not to slip in the process. She spun the string in a sweeping circle, first at her side, then above her head. A whistling sound pierced the evergreens above and around them. Then, stepping back farther, she made a series of figure-eights in front of her, crossing the lariat from one side to the other, the whistling shriller as she spun faster, the lime-colored crepe a slash of color against the snow. The two seven-year-olds squealed with joy, their mittened hands providing silent applause.

"Let me, Mrs. London, let me!" Kevin shouted, running forward to retrieve the new discovery. A red knitted cap hid his forehead above bright, blinking eyes.

"Is there another one, Mrs. London?" asked Freddie eagerly as he poked through the wondrous box that had already yielded such a trove, his joy fast turning to dismay at the likely prospect that his friend now owned the only one of its kind in existence.

"I think so," Lavina said with a wide grin. Actually she had finally gotten around to discarding three of them. It had never dawned on her that today's supposedly more sophisticated children might actually find them as wondrous as she had in her own youth, and Tracey after her. She had never seen them anywhere since. Certainly not in Susanne's day. Maybe this was the year of rediscovery. Too bad she didn't know someone in the toy business. A relatively cheap item like this would certainly be welcomed by sensible parents everywhere. And it was certainly better than half the horrors promoted today as toys. The simplest things always proved best, she concluded, not for the first time in her seventy-odd years.

Having relinquished the lariat to Kevin, she bent down, extending an arm into the bowels of the box in search of the two others. When her ungloved hand found them, she lifted them out and extended them toward the little redhead. "Which one do you want?"

After a brief hesitation Freddie chose the bright lavender lariat. "This one," he said as he watched the other, orange-colored, disappear into the pocket of Lavina's insulated car jacket.

Lavina straightened up, drawing the unzipped jacket closed across her chest. Actually it had been one of Kenneth's old jackets, but she found it warmer than anything comparable of her own—and lightweight as well. That it had belonged to her husband, of course, might just have had a little something to do with her preference, too.

It took her a while to get the boys accustomed to the art of swinging the lariats, which, after all, were a bit long for their heights. Undaunted, they refused to give up until they had mastered the technique to their satisfaction.

"We're still not through with the boxes, Mrs. London," Freddie said, just in case Lavina happened to be harboring any such ridiculous notion in her head as she approached the boxes again. She understood the boy's meaning completely and smiled. "Let's go through the rest of this junk, Kev," the boy added. "Doesn't Mrs. London always have the greatest?" He tried unsuccessfully to embrace the box like a newfound friend.

"Yeah," Kevin agreed, for the moment setting down his new toy in the snow lest his friend discover something else inside the box without him.

Lavina shook her hatless, steel-gray head and looked off to her right toward the lake. The afternoon was brisk but sunny, perhaps a bit warm for December in the Catskills, though hardly warm enough to initiate any sort of thaw. The ice and snow, she was afraid, were here to stay for a while.

She turned and started back toward the house to tackle the season decorating—she was already later than usual this year—when Freddie called after her without looking up from his search. "I bet there's a lot of good junk in Mr. Blaine's boxes, too," he said, "but we can't look."

"Why's that?" Lavina asked, stopping in her tracks and looking back over her shoulder.

The two friends stared at each other over the top of the open box.

"Ghosts," Kevin finally offered by way of explanation, lowering his eyes and rummaging around again in the box. Freddie joined him without additional comment.

"Ghosts? What do you mean, ghosts?" Lavina turned and rejoined them by the roadside.

"Ghosts, Mrs. London," Freddie now admitted freely, squinting up at her, overcoming his earlier embarrassment. "Real ghosts. We saw them, didn't we, Kev?"

"Yeah," Kevin agreed. "In the house."

"I don't believe what I'm hearing," Lavina said, mock incredulity on her face, the former radio actress in her coming to the fore. "Big boys like you know there's no such thing as ghosts."

"But we saw them, Mrs. London. Honest." Freddie made a valiant though futile effort at crossing his heart with his mittened hand. "We went over there to look in the boxes Mr. Blaine put out, and when we saw the lights in the window, we went and looked in."

"Yeah," his sidekick agreed.

"And when was this?" Lavina asked. "Saturday morning? Mr. Blaine was probably still there." So much for ghosts.

"No. Saturday afternoon, just before it got dark. And Mommy said Mr. Blaine went away Saturday morning."

"He was supposed to, yes," Lavina said out loud,

though more to herself than anything else, trying for the moment to sort the possibilities in her head. Henry had tickets for Toronto, leaving New York late Saturday afternoon. He had shown them to her the night of the farewell party.

"And it wasn't Mr. Blaine in the house anyway," Freddie stated flatly. "He wouldn't have all his blinds closed like that, would he?"

"Then who was it?" she asked, playing along.

"The ghost." This from Kevin as he shoved up the knitted hat that had started sliding down over his eyes.

"Ghosts," Freddie corrected.

"Yeah."

"More than one?" Lavina asked in feigned surprise.

"We just saw the light moving around inside through the blinds," Freddie started to explain. "And heard the doors and all squeaking. We . . . we didn't stay."

"We was scared," Kevin said honestly.

"And did you tell your mommy and daddy?"

"No," Freddie admitted, his sidekick merely shaking his head in agreement.

"Why not?"

"They'd holler."

"Why would they holler?"

"Because we were peeking through the window."

"We ran all the way home," Kevin added, wide-eyed—not that Lavina had to be told as much.

"Well, I'm sure there's some explanation," she said, as much to convince herself as the boys. The thought of burglars on the lake was not one she particularly cared to harbor.

"Yeah," Kevin agreed. "Ghosts."

The two youngsters broke out into a sudden fit of giggles, then settled down again to their treasure hunt.

Lavina turned and made her way back again across the snow-cleared path to the house. Once inside the little wallpapered foyer, she sat down and removed her boots. She hung the brown jacket in the outer closet, then opened the inner door and proceeded into the living room where she kicked off her flats. The fire in the redbrick fireplace in the left wall was burning nicely. In stocking feet she went over, opened the fire screen, and tossed in another log, sending up a spray of sparks into the chimney. With mesh curtain and screen safely closed again, she headed through the doorway leading into the kitchen at the back of the house.

At the sink she looked out through the small window toward the beach end of Hemlock Lake, then off to its immediate right to the Blaine property. At that distance she could barely make out the rear of the house beyond a thick stand of wild rhododendron. There was no visible movement. Not that she really expected any. She pulled back from the windowpane and glanced up at the clock above the window. Four twenty. Not long until dark.

She padded over to the doorway leading into the living room, where she lifted the receiver off the phone on the kitchen wall. She slipped into the pair of white furry scuffs she had left there earlier under the white antique telephone table set against the wall. First, she phoned Henry Blaine's number, which she found in her little address book. When she got no answer, she yanked out the Monticello directory from its slot under the tabletop and with a moistened finger paged to Real Estate. Once she found the name she was looking for, she closed the tome, lifted the receiver again, and punched out the number. They answered on the third ring.

"Clarke Realty. Can I help you?"

"Good afternoon. My name is Lavina London." She was beginning to perspire in the white wool cardigan that she then proceeded to shed one arm at a time, shifting the receiver as she did so, and explaining the reason for her call.

"No, Mrs. London, no one from here has been down to the Blaine house at all—or not since our visit with Mr. Blaine last week, that is."

"You didn't send any prospective buyers?"

"Not alone, no. That's not our policy. There's always an agent on hand to show our properties."

"I see."

"Were you interested in seeing the house, Mrs. London? If so, we'd be delighted to send someone down at your convenience."

Lavina hesitated. Maybe that wouldn't be such a bad idea. It would give her a chance to look around inside. When she realized the plan she was hatching was tantamount to the youngsters' looking in the windows, she put it out of her mind, thanked the agent, and hung up.

She remained standing a few moments, her hand still on the receiver, before she lifted it again and placed a third call. This time she pulled the chair out from under the table and sat down.

"Is that really you, Lavina?"

"That it is, Tod." Tod Arthur was not only the county's tireless sheriff, but an old friend as well who had known Ken and Lavina London back in the days when their home was a mere summer cottage.

"Let me guess," Arthur said. "You're calling to make sure I don't forget to drop off the Christmas wreaths." It was an annual custom of long standing. That and the fruitcake from his wife, Polly.

"If that's supposed to be some kind of dig to let me know I haven't phoned you or Polly in the past few weeks, okay, *touché.*" At least they had been seeing more of each other over the past few months than they had for a long stretch after Ken's death.

"No, Lavina, not at all. It's just good to hear from you. Did you try to reach Pol at the house? She's down in Middletown, if you did."

"No, Tod, I didn't try your house at all. I—Well—" She didn't quite know how to begin. The last time she had gotten involved on a professional basis with Sheriff Arthur, he hadn't been any too pleased. Initially, at any rate. "This isn't a social call, I'm afraid," she finally managed.

"Something wrong at the lake?" He sounded concerned, which gave her all the courage she needed.

"I'm not sure. That's why I'm calling." It was always a sure bet to make them think they were in charge—and needed. Her mother had told her that many years ago about men—to say nothing of policemen. "You know, of course, that Henry Blaine left for Canada on Saturday." A question more than a statement.

"So I heard, yes. Also heard he had quite a *bon voyage* party for himself on Friday night."

"To say the least." It had surprised even Lavina to see so many people. Judging by the number and size of the tables, over a hundred people, most of whom she knew. What had been even more surprising were some of the faces—people who, she had been led to believe, hadn't been on speaking terms with Henry for the past thirty years.

"What seems to be the problem?" Arthur asked.

"Well . . . it seems there have been lights seen at his house." The way it came out, it sounded as if she were talking about UFOs.

"When was this?"

"Late Saturday afternoon."

"You sure he wasn't still there?"

"He told me Friday night he was leaving here around two to make sure he caught his plane in New York."

"And who saw these lights?"

"Two young lads from the lake here. The Stoner boy, Freddie, and his friend, Kevin Greigson."

"They're only tykes, aren't they?"

"Sevenish, I'd say, yes."

"You sure they saw what they said they saw? You know kids, Lavina."

"Somehow I believe them, Tod, yes." About the lights, anyway, she thought.

"Isn't the place up for sale through some realtor up in Monticello?"

"I've already thought of that, Tod. I just finished talking with them. They haven't been down to the house, and they haven't sent anyone."

"No grass growing under your feet, huh, Lavina?" Secretly she couldn't deny that she was tickled pink to have beaten him to the gun on that one. "Well, I guess we should look into it then. I'll send one of the boys over to have a look."

"You can't come yourself?"

"Miss me that much, do you?"

"It's just a good thing for you that you're already married," she said. "Not to mention twenty years younger."

Arthur laughed. "Well, maybe I can come over," he said. "I suppose you'll want to meet me at his house." It wasn't a question; he knew her too well, especially since their mutual investigation of the recent murders surrounding the Frame Funeral Home out on Route 17. "I'll have one of the boys stop off at the realtor's first for the keys and meet you at the Blaine house in"—he paused, and she could picture him checking his watch—"say an hour, an hour and fifteen minutes."

Lavina glanced over at the wall clock over the sink. "Fine."

"What's the realtor's name, as long as you have it handy?"

"Clarke Realty."

"Check. See you shortly."

"Oh, and Tod—"

"Yeah?"

"As long as you mentioned it, don't forget those wreaths before I head down to New York to finish my shopping."

Chapter Three
➔ ⬅

Nelson Doss bunched up the soiled, long-sleeved white shirt and shoved it into the laundry pouch in his suitcase, which lay open on the bed. He grabbed at the small of his back as he straightened up with a groan, then turned for a final look around the antiseptic motel room, its brown-on-brown decor midway between bland and blah. It was almost enough to set off the heaves again.

He spotted his razor case on the dresser, retrieved it, and brought it back to the bag, where he tucked it down into a front corner. After a final look around, he flipped the soft leather cover closed and tugged at a pair of zippers on either side of the bag, guiding them around until they met in the front, where he fastened them together.

At the bathroom sink he let the water overflow in the glass until it was as cold as he knew it was going to get, then downed the whole thing in a single gulp without coming up for air. The worst thing for a hangover, he'd been told, but the only thing besides the hair of the dog that felt in any way fire-quenching. What the hell are you still doing here anyway, Nelson? he silently asked his re-

flection in the mirror. He knew damn well. The more he
had to drink, the less capable he was the next morning of
driving. Then a few more belts set the circle in motion
again. Dammit, he should have taken the bus up here in
the first place. No, that wouldn't have made sense at all;
he'd needed the car.

Why he'd ever gotten involved with Blaine in the first
place was beyond him. Why his father had ever taken the
man on as a client—way back when—he'd never understand either. Hell, his father had asked himself and the
whole household the same question every time he was on
one of his binges. Nelson hadn't even been a teenager
when it all started. Knowing what he knew, he should
have dropped the man as a client the day his father retired.
The agency certainly hadn't been that desperate. On the
contrary. Damn right he should have cut the strings when
he'd had the chance. Instead, he'd spent half his life as the
guy's wet nurse.

He placed the glass back down on the sink and raked his
fingers through the fleece of dark red, tight-curled hair.
He'd never needed a comb. He was glad he'd taken the
nap after lunch, even if it meant paying for another day on
his motel bill. If he hadn't, he knew he would have started
in all over again. If he left now, he could manage until he
was back in Manhattan. He was still pretty much in control, if a little shaky.

The eyes weren't quite as bloodshot as they'd been earlier either, thanks to the drops. Looking at them now in
the mirror reminded him of the look he'd seen in Blaine's
eyes Friday night, magnified as they were behind those
thick lenses he always wore. The man had reminded him
of a cross between George Zucco and Lionel Atwill in one

of their mad-doctor roles. Or maybe even Albert Dekker's Dr. Cyclops. All he needed were the syringes and white lab coat.

As far as he knew, with the exception of a few who'd come in from the West Coast, all the guests had gone right back to the city—or wherever it was they hailed from—as soon as the fiasco had ended. All except Nelson Doss, that is.

He flicked off the wall switch in the bathroom and headed back out to the front door, grabbing up his leather bag on the way. His hand on the doorknob, he took a quick look around. This, thank God, would be his last trip to Boulder. Henry Blaine was now only an unhappy memory. If he had felt better, he would have had a good laugh.

Chapter Four

➜ ➔

The mortuary hearse was backed up to the open garage door, its own double doors opened out wide to either side, the guerney with its bag-clad body already inside.

Lavina London stood just inside the garage door, out of the wind. The only light came from the overhead bulb in the garage and the low beams of the sheriff's car parked alongside the mortuary vehicle in the wide driveway. Yellow "Crime Scene" ribbons vied with the Christmas decorations clearly in evidence. The usual knot of curious bystanders—weather notwithstanding—milled around on the narrow blacktop lake road. Sidewalks were nonexistent at Hemlock Lake, where front lawns met the lake road head on, except, of course, in the few cases where ambitious and knowledgeable owners had anchored railroad ties as protective or decorative dividers.

It was Lavina who had called Sheriff Arthur's attention to what—to her—was an obvious case of murder. Until she had done so, both of them had been forced to accept Henry Blaine's death as an apparent case of suicide by carbon monoxide poisoning.

"It can't be suicide, Tod," she stated flatly after Dr. Errol had completed his preliminary examination and left. The obvious had struck her while she watched him examining the body in the car.

"Look, Lavina, I feel as bad about this whole business as you do," Arthur said. "I can't for the life of me figure out why the guy would kill himself when things were looking up for him, but let's face it—he was alone in the front seat with the garage door down and the car windows open . . . all of them. The ignition's still turned on and the car's out of gas. I'm not telling you anything you don't already know; we discovered him together. Even the fumes hadn't completely dissipated."

"That's just it, Tod, it's too pat." She tucked her hair inside the brown plaid woolen scarf knotted under her chin, her smooth full cheeks reddened by the cold mountain air. "That's what got me thinking. That and the fact, as you said, that it doesn't make sense."

Arthur heaved a deep sigh and dug the heels of his large hands into his obviously tired eyes. "Come on, Lavina, there's no need to dramatize everything. You know what your problem is—"

"If you even dare to suggest for one minute, Tod Arthur, that I'm writing my own script because of my acting background, I'm going to . . . to . . ."

"You said it, Lavina, not me. And watch your blood pressure. Don't want you in the hospital for Christmas."

Lavina narrowed her pale blue eyes and gave him one of her famous withering scowls—or so she liked to consider them anyway. "I can't believe a man with your experience is jumping to conclusions the way you're doing, Tod. You're too thorough for that. How could you have missed the obvious? You knew Henry Blaine pretty well, didn't you?"

"Sure." He dug a crumpled white handkerchief out of his back pocket and lifted off his high-crowned hat with its purple band.

"Well?"

He shook his head, the balding pate shiny below the glare of the bare bulb in the overhead ceiling fixture. "What is it exactly I'm supposed to have missed?" he asked, running the handkerchief first around his forehead and then around his thick, sinewy neck.

"What exactly *did* we see when we came in?" Lavina asked, leading him back to the moment of their gruesome discovery. "Besides all those things you just mentioned, I mean?"

"He was slumped over the steering wheel still in his white dinner jacket," Arthur said, obviously recalling the scene in his mind. "Meaning he probably died the night of his party." He shrugged his broad shoulders. "Garage deaths like this are pretty common, Lavina."

"I'm not questioning the fact that he died of carbon monoxide, Tod—"

"George would, certainly," Arthur was quick to add. " 'Nothing definite until after the autopsy.' You heard him yourself. And not the first time either, if memory serves me correctly." He wiped the back of his hand across his mouth in an attempt to conceal the grin, a mannerism obvious to anyone who knew him well.

Lavina smiled in spite of herself, but ignored the obvious reference to her past involvement with the medical examiner. "Which only proves George Errol is smarter than the two of us," she added.

"Ouch."

"You mean to tell me your investigation here has done nothing to contradict our original suicide theory?" Lavina said, getting back to the case in point: *What's wrong with this picture?* The common illustrated mystery puzzler.

That Arthur was growing itchy, she could see for herself, as he shifted from one booted foot to the other, but she still didn't want to let him off the hook. Not quite yet.

"Think, Tod. Think."

"What do you think I've been doing, Lavina? Dammit, if you know something this poor slob is too dumb or too tired to see for himself, spit it out for Christ's—"

"Tod!" Blasphemy was one of Lavina's few no-nos, at least with people who should know better—and she wasn't afraid to say so either, regardless of what they might think.

Another sigh from Arthur. "For Pete's sake, Lavina—and I don't mean Saint Peter, either—what are you driving at?"

"You examined the inside of the car, didn't you?" she asked, ignoring his attempt at levity.

He nodded, his head bobbing like a programmed doll. It looked almost top-heavy in the trooper's hat.

"His glasses, Tod," Lavina prompted when the nodding stopped.

"His glasses?"

"His glasses." She dug her hands into her jacket pockets by way of punctuation. "Where are they?"

That had been more than two hours ago, and like it or not, Tod Arthur had learned to sample crow. The lab boys had come and gone, as well as more neighbors.

They had found the glasses all right—but not in the car.

They were on the concrete floor outside, behind a couple of bags of halite deicing crystals, up near the left front fender. From their position it was obvious they hadn't been hidden, so they must have fallen. Which could only mean that Blaine was out of the car when he dropped them or when they got knocked off. And he certainly wouldn't have gotten back behind the wheel of the car of his own accord without them.

"I'm sorry, Lavina," Arthur said in a subdued voice when they were finally alone outside the garage. "I should have known you knew what you were talking about. After all—"

"No need to apologize, Tod. We could both do with a little rest to clear our heads."

Arthur reached in and pushed the tiny button controlling the automatic garage door.

At the sound Lavina turned her head in time to see it descending. In the darkness with the light behind it, it reminded her of a curtain falling in a theater. In this case on the last act of Henry Blaine. It gave her an eerie feeling.

"Where's your car?" Arthur asked when they reached his own.

"Sean dropped me off on his way to the Elks." Sean and Winnie O'Kirk were her next-door neighbors and best friends on the lake.

"Then you'll need a ride."

"I thought you'd never ask."

"I didn't." Score one for Tod Arthur.

It was almost eight thirty by the time they reached her house, and by eleven she was still wide awake, her mind much too alert to let her doze off. Seated at the wood-grained Formica kitchen table, she tucked her full-length lavender chenille robe around her legs, then reached a hand into the large bag of miniature marshmallows. She didn't even bother to count as she dumped them into her hot chocolate. Hamilton had called only that morning with the results of her latest blood work. Her triglycerides were down from over 600 to a low of 220. It wasn't exactly that she was celebrating, but she had missed her sweets these past eleven months. She smiled as she wrapped her long, slender fingers around the hot LOVE mug, a Valentine gift from Ken many years earlier.

She sighed as she stared vacantly across the room to the darkened kitchen window. She was of two minds about her upcoming trip to New York on Wednesday. She was certainly looking forward to the annual Christmas shopping spree with her daughter and granddaughter, but she hadn't even finished decorating at home yet. She also didn't particularly like the thought of leaving Boulder with an unsolved murder on its hands. When she stopped for a few seconds to actually let that one sink in, she broke out laughing; she could just hear what Tod would have to say on that score.

There was another reason for the trip to New York this year, of course, and one she still wasn't all that comfortable with. She had finally, though reluctantly, agreed to tackle the memoirs her former agent had been nagging her to write for the past few years, memoirs dealing with her years in early radio. "I've got at least three editors ready to draw up a contract on outline alone, Lavina," he had told her on the phone the last time around. Which probably meant that one had shown a mild interest but wanted to see the whole manuscript. "They know a sure thing when they hear it. Don't forget that long list of shows and credits to your name over all those years." And how! Almost twenty in radio alone. The way he had worded it, though, made it seem even longer somehow—and her older. "How many people can you think of with as long and varied a career in that magic medium of yesteryear as you, Lavina?" Hundreds at least, she thought, refraining from comment. And thinking back now, she wasn't all that sure about the "magic" part either. Nostalgic, yes, but like anything else, it had meant a lot of hard work, fraught with anxiety, insecurity, and disappointment. She wasn't really sure she was up to retracing her steps, living it all over again, even if only on paper and in retrospect.

As she raised her mug to her lips, she wondered about those vague hundreds. There were certainly a number at Henry's farewell party. One good thing at least about the affair was the chance it had given her to talk with some of them, mentioning the book idea. Every one of them had agreed to help her in any way possible—interviews, clippings, network programming, yearbooks, logs, almanacs, reviews, tapes, back copies of *Variety, Radio Mirror*—you name it. Or at least so they had said. And in one of her more exuberant moods, Lavina had promised to take them up on it, jotting down addresses and phone numbers she knew she didn't have at home. They were a gold mine of source material that she'd be foolish not to take advantage of. She'd already promised Jae Patrick that she'd stop off at her home in Jersey on her way down to New York. So maybe the whole thing wouldn't be quite as difficult as she had imagined.

As with many first-time authors, one of the first considerations was the choice of title, and this even before she knew exactly what direction the book would take. Some of the ones she had come up with initially were downright silly; she and Winnie had gotten a real kick out of them. Things like *Radio London, Dial R for Radio,* and *Out of Sight.* Or, by way of tribute to Arch Obler, who'd done so much through sound effects alone to highlight the drama potential of the medium, his own *Theater of the Mind.* Of course, with her luck, some editor would come along and blue pencil whatever title she finally hit on and change it to something as innocuous as *Radio: a Reminiscence.*

She propped her elbows on the table now that she was alone—something she'd never do in public—and seriously began to consider some of the people at the party. Why had they come? Certainly not out of any great love for Henry Blaine. Cole and Violet Hesson, for example, whose luncheon hour talk show had been a direct takeoff of the ever-popular early morning breakfast shows *à la* Ed and Pegeen and Dorothy and Dick. Or Will Argon, the Blaines's soap opera announcer. Even fellow actors Bran Slattery and Audra Mateer.

Poor Henry surely must have seen the puzzled look on her face when she saw some of them, because he'd told her later that the real reason they had shown up was to see her—Lavina, knowing that she lived on the lake. Somehow she hadn't bought it then, and she didn't buy it now. There had been something in the atmosphere, something intangible, that told her they were there strictly at Henry's behest and for no other reason. Nelson Doss hadn't seemed any happier than he was when he'd been saddled with the man as a client. Or Jae either, for that matter.

It was a shame Hilda wasn't around; somehow her presence had always been a balm. That animosities had existed between Blaine and a number of his former colleagues was indisputable. Whatever the reason, it was unquestionably rooted in the past, and even though Lavina was a part of that past, she was far from privy to all the facts. It was difficult to imagine a connection between that and Henry's death. Had someone suddenly decided after all those years that it was time for Henry to meet his Maker? She shuddered to imagine it as she drained the remains of her now cold hot chocolate.

There had been one noticeable face missing at the party, of course—that of Henry's son, Garrett. Just about everyone had commented on it. To her knowledge, he and his wife were still living in New York, and while there may have been any number of logical explanations for their absence, it was still a bit strange. She had considered asking Henry about it at the time but had decided against it. It was a decision she now regretted.

She looked again across to the darkened window and thought of the two seven-year-olds. She had told them there were no such things as ghosts. Suddenly she wasn't quite so sure, now that she seemed confronted with a host of them from out of the past.

TUESDAY, DECEMBER 19

Chapter Five

→ ←

"Don't start in again, Cole, because I can't take much more of it. You haven't let up since we got back."

"I only said—"

"I know what you said, but for the umpteenth time you know as well as I do that we had no choice in the matter." Violet Hesson set a plate of steaming linguini on the dining room table in front of her husband, then her own at the opposite end facing him.

"If she starts asking questions for that damn book of hers, Lord knows how deep she'll end up digging, and then what?"

"We'll cross that bridge if and when we get to it," Violet said, shaking out her linen napkin and spreading it across her lap under the table. "Actually, I don't see any reason she should even bring the matter up. After all, she's writing about all *her* years in radio, not one year in the life of the Hessons."

Cole slid the clam-sauced pasta languidly back and forth on the fine china plate, his eyes lowered, hypnotically observing the pointless movement of the fork.

"That's easy to say, Vi," he finally added, "but still . . . We don't want to end up with someone else holding that sword over our heads."

"Eat your dinner. She may not even bother to stop by. So there's no sense worrying."

Cole pushed the plate away from him, narrowly missing the crystal water glass behind it. "I'm not hungry." He dug a loose cigarette out of his shirt pocket without removing the pack.

"Don't light that thing at the table while I'm eating," Violet objected, lifting her cocktail glass to drain what remained of her Gibson, tiny onion and all.

Cole made a move to rise from the table, then, obviously changing his mind, set the cigarette down alongside his plate and sat back in the captain's chair.

"Lavina London is the least of our worries," Violet continued in a conciliatory tone, forking her first portion of linguini. "She's enthusiastic now over this project because it's something new and exciting. I give her a couple of months at most before she scraps the whole thing. She's not as young as she used to be, don't forget." She dabbed the bright red lips with a corner of her napkin, then took a sip of red wine.

"And we are, I suppose," Cole said, not without sarcasm.

"Younger than she is, anyway," his wife added, not to be bested. "By a good five or six years at least. She must be at least seventy by this time." A definitive pronouncement. Not even a "don't you think?" Cole was used to them by now; it was a long time since she'd sought out his opinion.

He looked at her raven-black hair in its short, outmoded Dutch cut, complete with bangs. One of her many security blankets against the encroachment of time. His own gray hair, he knew, was a frequent source of embarrassment for her. It was something he couldn't understand, but he accepted it as he did all her idiosyncrasies. When it came down to it, there was nothing he wouldn't do for her. Nothing.

"You don't really think she'll cause a problem?" he asked, rolling the cigarette under his fingers on the linen tablecloth.

"Not if we don't let her," Violet said. Then, pointing with her fork, "And don't get nicotine stains on my good linen." Another tiny forkful of pasta, another dab with the corner of the napkin, another sip of wine.

Cole left her to the dishes after they'd finished their coffee and B&B. For once at least, he was glad to have the dog as an excuse. He had to get out, had to be alone.

Once out of the elevator and past the uniformed doorman and double-glass entrance doors, he inhaled a deep breath of December New York air. At 237th Street he turned, leaving behind the din of the Henry Hudson Parkway, the Irish setter leading the would-be master. He smiled. It reminded him of himself and Vi. That hadn't always been the situation, of course. Back in the early days, when they'd had their daily radio luncheon talk show, he'd been the one who took the lead and Vi who did the following. On the air at least. Had she really played the role of demure loving wife only for the benefit of their radio audience, as some of their acquaintances had hinted even back then? Maybe so, not that it really mattered. Whatever the case they had always stayed together— through thick and thin. That must say something about their relationship.

He cursed himself now, not for catering to his wife—that he could never change—but because he suddenly realized as thick moist flakes of snow began to fall again that he had come out without his boots. It was already sticking fast.

Thank God it hadn't started snowing upstate Friday night. That might have posed a real problem. The snow-cleared roads were a blessing. He could picture Violet again now as he had left her that night in the motel bed, her black hair spread out against the whiteness of the pillowcase, dead to the world. She never even heard him go out. It was bitter cold and windy, the courtyard deserted. Except on his return, that is, when he saw Nelson Doss parking his car in front of what was obviously the door to his room. Their own car had been parked around back, out of sight. The brown paper bag under the agent's arm he'd assumed contained a bottle of liquor.

What was even more surprising, though, was finding Violet missing when he got back inside. When she came in close to fifteen minutes later, shivering and barely articulate, she told him she had awakened and couldn't get back to sleep. She had gone out for a brisk walk, expecting to run into him. Not surprisingly, he didn't question her about it. Nor, strangely enough, did she question him.

They arrived back in New York late Saturday morning. Henry Blaine's murder appeared as a small, almost insignificant item in Tuesday morning's *News*. In his perusal of the paper, he almost missed it. Needless to say, neither of them would miss Henry Blaine.

WEDNESDAY, DECEMBER 20

Chapter Six

→ ←

"...*When the Maltese Falcon laid an egg it hatched a flock of vultures, and they're all circling right around my head...*"

A smile formed on Lavina's pale-glossed lips as it always did when she heard that delicious line uttered by the rich, throaty voice of Howard Duff, alias Sam Spade. It was one of her favorite hour-long *Suspense* broadcasts from '48, called "The Kandy Tooth," and the only tale she was aware of that featured the return of the dyspeptic duo from the original Falcon caper, Casper Gutman, and Joel Cairo, joined this time around by Wilmer's double in the person of his younger brother, Marvin.

The image of the vultures unfortunately conjured up another more recent one, causing her to lose track of the story. She sighed, fixed her vision on the clear stretch of New York State Thruway before her and, without looking down, turned off the car's cassette player. She let her eyes wander briefly to the cloudless winter sky. Not a bird in sight—not even a starling, never mind a vulture. Funny, she had never thought of gossiping women in terms of vultures before. And now here she was—their latest piece of fresh carrion.

It had happened during a brief excursion Tuesday afternoon to the supermarket. It was only by accident that she heard them at all. "Where was that London woman, is what I'd like to know," one of them had said. "With the two of them living alone there on that lake—a widow and a widower." As if they had been cohabiting, for heaven's sake. "They're actors, don't forget," the other had added. That damnable word. It was the inclusion of Dr. Ruth's name in the conversation that had really brought her blood to a boil.

She sighed now as she changed lanes, thinking back. It had been her imagination, of course, that her old friend Hildy had been there in the back of her mind egging her on—even pleading with her—to find her husband's killer. And Lavina had been of two minds about it. Until the two vultures appeared on the scene. That was all the convincing she needed. Her reputation, as well as her dead friend's disturbed rest, were at stake. That so many people outside Hemlock Lake knew her by name or sight was hardly surprising, seeing how often she still appeared in local papers and on local television and radio. And now here she was practically accused of fornication and murder. And in her own town no less. Lord only knew how many others were thinking the same thing.

She wasn't even out of the checkout line before she had made up her mind. She was going to find Henry Blaine's murderer and protect her reputation . . . even if it killed her.

She gave a little start, momentarily easing up on the accelerator as she did so. That ultimate possibility reminded her of the last time she had been so determined. That *had* almost been the death of her. She could still picture that early evening in Evergreen Memorial Park. To this day, driving by the cemetery gave her the willies. After all, it had almost become her permanent address.

She focused her eyes on the road, her clear-framed glasses on their silver chain at her breast in case she had to consult her map. Ken's winter jacket was on the seat alongside her. In the heated car her cardigan was warm enough. That and the gray knitted wool dress that had that wonderful way of stretching with her body. Perfect for driving.

As the green Thruway signs whizzed by with every mile, she realized how impossible it would be to get the murder off her mind until it was solved. She hadn't even hinted to Sheriff Arthur that she intended doing some investigating of her own in New York while she was with some of Henry's former colleagues—a fact that gave her occasional qualms of conscience. Not that it probably would have mattered if she had told him. From what he had said, and from the way he seemed to be approaching the investigation, he obviously suspected someone local. Why, she couldn't imagine. There'd certainly been no robbery or indication of a break-in, "ghosts" notwithstanding. And even Tod had agreed that a stranger was hardly likely to have killed Henry and then bothered to fake a suicide. Especially after Dr. Errol discovered traces of chloroform in the man's system. That much at least she had been able to wheedle out of him on the phone this morning before she left. Why he had called she still couldn't figure out.

The more she thought about it now, with nothing else to clutter her mind but the expanse of road ahead of her, the more suspicious she became. Knowing Tod as she did, it didn't take her long to figure it out. He was using a little reverse psychology. Tod wanted her to think he suspected a local killer. And she had almost fallen for it, too. She should have known better; the man was far too astute to ascribe Henry's death to a total stranger, especially with his farewell party only a few hours old. It was his way of trying to keep her from playing amateur detective again. He wanted her out of his hair. The nerve of the man! And after all the help she'd been to him the last time.

She smiled as she heard herself. Her granddaughter, Susanne, would say she was off playing Nancy Drew again. Well, better that, she supposed, given her age, than Miss Marple or Miss Withers. But if that's what Tod Arthur wanted, fine. Two could play the same game. She would play along completely, pretending an utter lack of interest. She wouldn't even call him once from New York—no matter what she found out.

Now that she thought about it, she wondered if he'd been in touch with the New York authorities, and whether or not he already suspected one of Henry's guests from the party. Not that he knew any of them. All the more reason he should have counted on her. Some of it, though, didn't make any sense at this point. What did Tod Arthur know that she didn't know? There had to be something. His silence was beginning to annoy her now more than anything else—and there he was back home, too far away for her to pump.

When the Tempo reached the state line and crossed over from the rough New York link to the smoother Garden State Parkway, she felt in the beanbag ashtray on the dash for her ready supply of quarters for the tolls. Satisfied, she sat back to resume what she knew would be another fifty minutes driving at best.

Until Friday night she hadn't seen Jae Patrick in over twenty years. Which was strange considering how well they had always gotten along, in spite of their almost totally different personalities. Opposites attracting, she supposed. Jae had been into women's lib and equal rights long before the terms were coined. As a sponsor's agent she could be quite vocal on the subject—and often was. Lavina recalled how turned off the woman had been by what she considered the sugary and chauvinistic theme song of the highly touted and avant-garde—for early radio anyway—*Candy Matson* show. They had both loved the show itself because for its time—back for about three years in the late '40s, early '50s—it was something unique, with Natalie Masters playing a female private eye operating out of her apartment in San Francisco, with a heartthrob— Lavina's choice of word, not Jae's certainly—a SFPD inspector named Ray Mallard. She and Jae had both been out on the West Coast during the early days of the show. Which was when they had first met, the summer of '49. Lavina had been contracted for a few episodes of that very show. They had met again back in New York the following year. At that time the agent was waging a one-woman campaign against the wolf-whistle opening on Ann Sothern's *Maisie* show. Personally Lavina had always enjoyed it, especially Maisie's reaction. It was something that had to be heard to be appreciated. But then, that was true of radio in general. The theater of the mind again.

What Jae had been doing the past twenty years, Lavina didn't know. At one time she had been a highly successful advertising agent in a business that, during radio's golden years, just about ran most of the programs. Agencies were responsible for hiring and firing, and in general for setting up the whole audio star system, radio's equivalent of Hollywood's own. They actually developed, wrote, and pre-packaged shows, selling them off to potential sponsors. Jae had joined a splinter group early on and rose to the top along with it, carrying many an actor on her coattails—not to mention the ones that couldn't quite hold on during or after their meteoric rise. Lavina herself had almost signed up with her at one point.

It was Jae, Lavina recalled, who had been responsible for the creation and subsequent rise of Henry and Hildy's soap opera, which originated from New York, starting back in '45. That's how the three of them—Henry, Hildy, and Jae—had fast become friends, though rumor had it that Jae and Henry had been an item even before that. That Lavina didn't know. Nor did she know the woman's age; somehow time seemed to stand still for her. A veritable female Dorian Gray.

Almost an hour later she stood facing the other woman at her front door, and the notion she'd had at Henry's party was reconfirmed. Jae looked no more than fifty-five. It was incredible. When Lavina jokingly asked her secret, all she received by way of an answer was a chime of laughter. Almost as tall as Lavina's five-foot, nine-inch height, she was as svelte and regal as Lavina remembered her.

The home, too, was extraordinary, with furnishings that Lavina knew—even with her limited knowledge of antiques—had never touched an assembly line.

"Is this your first time in Chatham?" Jae asked from her easy chair, facing Lavina across the Duncan Phyfe coffee table.

"Yes." Lavina took a hanky from her shoulder bag, slid

closed the zipper, and set it down at her feet on the Aubusson carpet.

"It's been far too long," Jae said, nostalgia in her voice as she looked beyond Lavina in the direction of the huge unlighted evergreen in the corner by the bay window. When she looked back, she laughed, a laugh like a run of tiny chimes that echoed in the high-ceilinged room. "Never mind your family! Patricia was only about three the last time I saw her. How she loved to run up and down the length of the studios. You remember?"

Lavina remembered very well, and it was strange to hear someone call her Tracey by her real first name. "I certainly do. She loved it whenever I brought her to work with me."

"So what's happened in the last twenty years?" Jae asked, laughing again. Her dirty-blond hair had the body and sheen of a teenager's and hung just below her shoulders in a cascade of combed-out curls, with the disheveled look that was so fashionable. The eyes, too, sparkled with the same deviltry Lavina remembered from the past. The high spirit, the energy—nothing seemed to have changed. Her dress was solid black, another "in" thing among so many fashion-conscious young women—something Lavina couldn't understand for the life of her. As far as she was concerned, black was just not the color of youth.

"You've heard about Henry, I suppose," Lavina said, broaching the topic for the first time.

Jae nodded. "I read about it in yesterday's *Times*. They gave him a nice write-up, considering . . ."

. . . that his contribution to the world was so long ago, Lavina completed in her mind, not at all sure it was the same unspoken thought Jae Patrick had entertained. "I'm glad to hear that," she said. "Hildy would have been pleased. Was it an obit or a news item?"

"Both."

"It mentioned his murder?"

"They mentioned suspicious circumstances and an investigation. Ironic, isn't it? The very night of his farewell party. The article said they found him in his garage."

"Yes." Lavina tugged her cardigan closer together across her breast. "You've never been to his house on the lake?" She'd never stopped by to see Lavina if she had.

"Never. Though I intended to visit both of you several times over the years."

"The best-laid plans, right?" Lavina said, then proceeded to fill her in on the circumstances surrounding Henry's death.

When she was done, Jae shook her head. "They have any idea who did it?"

"I'm sure our sheriff has some ideas of his own," Lavina grudgingly admitted, "but I haven't heard anything. Probably someone on drugs." The clichéd conclusion pained her, but she didn't want to appear any more knowledgeable or interested than she had to.

"Sad."

"When did he and Hildy leave your agency?" Lavina asked, unable to recall whether it had been before or after their soap opera had gone off the air.

Jae looked off in the distance again toward the tree, then back. "In 1950 or so, I think. Round about then."

"Before or after they'd been canceled?" Lavina asked, circling in like a vulture.

Lavina didn't know quite how to interpret the look on

Jae's face. It might have been fear or then again just plain uncertainty.

"Oh, after, certainly," Jae finally said, looking down at her lap and brushing off her dress with the back of her hand. The voice was sure and unshaken. "That was one of the reasons he gave for leaving us. He all but accused me of sabotaging his show. But I thought you knew that whole story."

"Not really," Lavina admitted, though of course she had heard all the inevitable rumors.

"Henry apologized later, of course. Probably Hildy's doing."

"Any reason why he chose the Doss Agency after that?" Lavina asked.

Jae shrugged her narrow shoulders. "Hilda knew Nelson's father. That might have had something to do with it."

"She knew old Simon? I didn't know that." She regretted the "old" as soon as it was out. The man was no older than she was.

"Yes."

"I see you're going to have a lot of useful information for my book," Lavina added, changing the direction of the conversation so Jae wouldn't become suspicious of her prying.

"Look, I'm glad I can help."

During and after a quick lunch Lavina filled her old friend in on the major events of the past twenty years—on Ken and their life together at the lake, his sudden and fatal cerebral hemorrhage, on Tracey and Damien and Susanne, her volunteer work at the hospital, her friends.

"And what about you?" Lavina asked when they found

themselves in Jae's bedroom, where they had gone so Jae could pack an overnight bag for her stay in New York.

"Well, like I said, I never quite got around to marrying," Jae said with her characteristic laugh, tossing an unopened package of black pantyhose into the bag. "What you'd call more best-laid plans, I guess."

"It would have been foolish to marry if you weren't in love."

"That's what I kept telling myself. What I still tell myself. Still, it gets lonely sometimes. But with Ken gone, I'm sure you know what I mean." She forced a little smile and closed the top of the canvas bag.

"And you're actually still working?" Lavina said, sidestepping the question of loneliness completely.

"Free-lancing, Lavina. I pretty much set my own pace. I have four regular clients who are pretty much in demand, and two on the rise."

"Television or what?"

"Just about everything, you name it. Television, radio, records, Broadway, off-Broadway, films . . ."

"Anything in the borscht belt?" The Catskills, Sullivan County, New York, Lavina's neck of the woods.

"Not really, no. Not the club circuit. I don't handle entertainers—stand-up comics, I mean."

"And no writers." Lavina wasn't sure whether she'd intended it as a question or not.

"No, I wouldn't feel qualified to handle a writer. That's a different ballpark altogether."

"Well, more power to you, Jae," she said. "Lord knows, I've still got plenty of energy, but I could never go back to acting at the pace you're agenting."

"You'd be surprised at what you can do, Lavina, if you

want to. Or have to." She stood and looked down at Lavina, who was sitting on the bed. "You know, of course, that we've been hemming and hawing all afternoon, skirting the real truth about Henry's death. You don't really think he was killed by some hophead in need of cash for his next fix anymore than I do."

Lavina swallowed hard, not sure what her reaction should be. Jae Patrick, after all, was nobody's fool. Least of all Lavina London's. If Jae had seen through her charade, there was nothing she could do about it.

"Henry was killed by someone who knew him, wasn't he, Lavina? By someone at the party." The woman's voice told her that she was as convinced on that score as Lavina herself was. Maybe Jae had more information than she'd hoped.

Lavina checked her watch, then got up and smoothed the wrinkled bedspread. Her compulsive homemaker instincts satisfied, she turned to face her host. "Let's talk about it in the car."

Chapter Seven

> → ←

Ghosts.

Sheriff Arthur lifted off his gray trooper's hat and set it on the desk, shaking his bald-pated head with a smile. The two boys had certainly stuck to the story they had confided to Lavina. Even in the presence of their parents. He'd certainly never pictured himself in the role of ghostbuster before.

He smiled again as he picked up the long sheet of yellow lined paper off Henry Blaine's large desk. He examined it more closely this time. Guests, not ghosts. The first eight names had been highlighted with a narrow-tipped yellow marker. Not exactly a dying message, certainly, but it might be worth noting. Especially if what Lavina had said about Blaine's relationship with some of the Friday night guests was true.

He read the list out loud to himself, though why he couldn't say: Will Argon, Nelson Doss, Cole Hesson, Violet Hesson, Lavina London—that was interesting—Audra Mateer, Jae Patrick, Bran Slattery. Even in alphabetical order. Spotting the Rolodex on the corner of the desk, he pulled it over and lifted the plastic lid. A more expansive version than his own, certainly.

He flipped to A. Found Argon, Will. Then to D and Doss, Nelson. He slid a sheet of typing paper out of its holder on the other corner of the desk and started jotting down the names and addresses. They were all there, and all, with the exception of Lavina, living in New York City or New Jersey. An earlier Brookfield, Connecticut, address had been blacked out for Audra Mateer. You can take the woman out of the city, he mused, but . . .

He'd need the addresses if and when he felt it necessary to call his colleagues in New York. He smiled again. It was a lousy trick, there was no getting around it, but by far the best way. Lavina was certainly not about to pay him any mind, no matter what. Anything he might have said about interference in police business would have gone in one ear and out the other. And, of course, he had no doubt that she'd be doing exactly that while in New York. Fortunately—in this case at least—it was just as well. After all, she did know all these people, and had intended seeing them sooner or later in the course of her book research anyway. She had told him that much herself. And had already mentioned three of the eight individuals, each of whose presence at the party surprised her. So why not let her do the spadework? It was only logical.

He could have asked her help outright, of course—and had even considered it. This way, he decided, was better. She'd feel free to go about it any way she wanted—just as she had done the last time on her own—without feeling she had to answer to him. Little did she know that when the time came, he'd just politely ask her what she had unearthed that might be pertinent to Blaine's murder.

She'd be his secret deputy, his mole, her role unknown even to her. She wouldn't like it once she found out, of course, but he'd cross that bridge when he got to it. In the meanwhile the unofficial undercover work might prove invaluable. And while he didn't actually consider her nosy, he knew she had the knack of finding out anything she set her mind to. And what was equally important, he could trust her. His only fear was that the impromptu plan might backfire and put her in jeopardy. It was something that worried him until he managed to convince himself that she was going to do her own thing anyway, Tod Arthur or no Tod Arthur.

One thing he could do, though, just to be on the safe side. Get in touch with the NYPD and fill them in on the whole business. Let them know where she'd be staying—he'd been surprised to learn it wasn't at her daughter's—and who she was, in case she got in touch with them herself for some reason.

He glanced at the electric clock on the desk. Almost ten thirty. But first, the addresses, in case the New York cops asked for them. He didn't want to come across like some country bumpkin. Dammit, why did some people equate small towns with small minds anyway? If that wasn't stereotyping, he didn't know what was. It was something that always got his dander up. Fortunately his record could speak for itself; he'd hold it up to any cop's any day.

"Sheriff . . ."

He was just finishing the entry under S and looked up across the clean, if cluttered, country living room off toward the kitchen area that was separated from the larger room by a service bar. No formal walls, just spacious and airy country living.

"What is it, Chad?" he asked, looking at the still jacketed figure on the other side of the bar. Chad St. James was his new partner and driver. He was still in the process of breaking him in as a matter of fact. He'd gone about as long as he could riding solo in the police car after losing his last man. Actually "boy" was how he'd always thought of him, and how he thought now, too, of Chad St. James. The memory of the younger man still haunted his nights, and days sometimes, too, especially when, as now, he was doing investigative work in a clear-cut case of murder.

He had interviewed quite a number of young men before settling on St. James. After all, if they were going to become bosom buddies by day, he wanted to make sure they were as compatible as possible. He was also thinking down the line in terms of a future deputy. The one little innocent-seeming item that had eliminated most of the job applicants touched on their taste in music. Once he learned Chad didn't care for rock—hard or otherwise— the boy was a virtual shoo-in. That he still lived at home with his parents hadn't hurt his chances any either.

"You'd better come inside and hear this for yourself, Sheriff," St. James said.

One thing you had to say for Chad St. James—he was a stickler for rank and the respect he deemed went with it. "Sir" and "Sheriff" were about as familiar as Arthur could get the boy to be. For someone of Arthur's easygoing temperament, it was somewhat disconcerting. He'd even mentioned it to the Chad's parents. "When he earns a promotion—and your respect—Sheriff," Chad's father had said, "well, maybe then . . ." Chad St. James was obviously a chip off the old block, with plain, old-fashioned upbringing. Arthur just wasn't accustomed to seeing much of that anymore.

"Okay, Chad, lead the way . . ." Arthur pushed himself up out of the chair behind the desk and joined the young man in the dining area. Below his outer winter jacket, Chad's trouser legs had a crease about as sharp as a paper fold. The purple tie that protruded from the open neck of the uniform jacket was collar-tight, and the collar itself spotless and wrinkle-free. Arthur didn't have to see the rest of the shirt or the black, laced shoes. If women still went by appearances, this twenty-four-year-old bachelor didn't stand a chance. His application, Arthur knew, stated that he had a BS from Manhattan College, with a major in physical education. What it failed to mention, however, was the amount of time Chad spent helping the kids at the local youth center. It was a fact probably none of his colleagues were aware of either, and certainly something they'd never hear from Chad himself.

"What is it I'm supposed to listen to?" Arthur asked, as he followed Chad into the larger of the two bedrooms beyond the dining area.

The rookie rounded the full-sized bed to the side nearest the short double window facing out onto the winter-bound lake. The late-morning sun grazed the evergreens, its rays reaching through the uncurtained windows to brighten and warm the unheated room.

"The telephone answering machine, sir," Chad said, sitting down on the neatly made bed by the night table.

"Oh, one of those contraptions." Arthur raised his hands to his hips and stared down at the machine as if it were some sort of lethal weapon he didn't trust. "What's so important about it?"

"There are a couple of messages on it," Chad said. "They seem to have been left Friday night sometime. Listen . . ." He made a move with his strong corded right hand to press one of the little buttons at the base of the machine.

"Hold it," Arthur said, restraining him with a grip on his arm. "Let me get settled here first." He sat down on the bed alongside his new partner, who seemed uncomfortable in his bulky winter jacket. "Okay, let 'er roll," he finally said, stretching his thick neck across the younger man in order to get a closer look at the machine.

A tiny red light in the lower left-hand corner blinked intermittently like some sort of Morse code.

"What does the blinking indicate?" Arthur asked, pointing to the light.

"It tells us there are two messages on the machine, Sheriff," Chad said.

Arthur sighed. "You have one of these gadgets?"

"Sure."

"Your parents use it?" Arthur was sure that, like himself, they didn't.

"Now they do," Chad said. "Now that they know how simple it is."

"Afraid you'll miss one of your lady friends calling while you're all out, huh?" Arthur said, regretting the banality of the remark as soon as it was out.

Chad just smiled. "Ready?" His finger was already on the PLAY button, the heavy gold college ring standing out on his finger. Arthur had noticed it several times before in the car while the younger man was driving. The stone was emerald green.

"Yeah, go ahead," he said.

Chad depressed the PLAY button. The cassette tape inside rewound, stopped, came on. *"Dad? This is Garrett. Sorry I missed you. I just wanted to tell you not to expect us tonight. Something's come up and we can't make it. I'll explain when I see you tomorrow. Don't forget . . . noon outside Downey's. We'll have lunch and talk, just the two of us. Enjoy the party . . . and say hello to everybody for me."* A click, a pause, then a beep.

"That's the end-of-two-minute beep," Chad explained.

A second message followed on the heels of his brief explanation: It began with a burst of eerie organ music, then a sinister laugh. *"The weed of crime bears bitter fruit. Crime does not pay. The Shadow knows!"* Another burst of sinister laughter then more eerie music. A click, a pause, another warning beep. The tape came to a halt, and the blinking lights resumed as before.

Arthur stared at the machine, then at Chad next to him. The boy was watching him.

"The Shadow," Arthur said. "Is that the whole message?"

"That's it," Chad said. "What do you think?"

"Either we're dealing with a looney or someone with a very nasty sense of humor."

"Who is this Shadow, anyway?" Chad asked.

"Lamont Cranston," Arthur said without hesitation. Then, realizing what he said, he laughed. "Sorry, Chad. I didn't mean to be cryptic. It's an old-time radio show. I used to listen to it all the time as a kid on Sunday afternoons."

Chad motioned in the direction of the answering machine with his thumb. "You think it was intended as some sort of a death threat?"

Arthur followed the direction of Chad's thumb. "Or maybe what it was originally—a moral pronouncement. It looks like someone wasn't happy with something our Henry Blaine had done, and was telling him he wasn't going to get away with it."

"An avenger."

"Or Everyman's guilty conscience," Arthur said, slapping Chad on the knee. "That's the Shadow."

Chad smiled. Arthur wasn't sure, but it looked like some sort of pronouncement of his own. Whether on him or the show—or both—he didn't know, but decided it more than made up for his own earlier gaffe.

"That was the show's closing, by the way," he said. "The opening was different. 'Who knows what evil lurks in the hearts of men . . .' "

"Maybe it was just a prank, Sheriff," Chad said. "What with the farewell party and all."

"What do *you* think, Chad?" Arthur asked. No sarcasm. Just part of his teaching process.

Chad shook his head. "I don't think so, no." He rewound the tape, then when it stopped, ejected it. "Just wanted to touch every base."

"Good. Keep thinking that way, Chad. Investigate every possibility at the outset and save yourself a lot of backtracking later." He smiled and rose from the bed, still looking down at the younger man. "We'll make a sheriff's deputy out of you yet."

Chad smiled again, this time obviously pleased.

"And this Garrett, sir? Blaine's son?"

"His only son, as far as I know. I can't say I really knew any of the Blaines all that well. They didn't socialize much—even with Lavina."

"Sir . . .?"

"Lavina London. Another former radio star from Hemlock Lake. She's the one—"

"Oh, Mrs. London, sure. The first name threw me for a minute. She was the lady here with you Monday night, right?"

"Right. And quite a lady." Chad had obviously been brought up to know the old meaning of the word, as well as how to treat one.

"You think she might be able to throw more light on this Shadow message?"

"She might at that," Arthur admitted grudgingly. There might be some special association with the show in Blaine's past, come to think of it. If there was, Lavina was sure to know. It would mean phoning her in New York, of course—something he hesitated doing, especially so soon. But if it meant getting answers, then he'd just have to swallow his pride. And who knew, it might even give her a new direction for her investigation down there. If the motive for this murder was somehow rooted in the golden age of radio, as he suspected, she was the logical one to help him unearth it.

"Garrett's the one coming up today to make arrangements for the funeral, right?" Chad said when Arthur made no move to pursue the subject of Lavina London.

"Right."

"I wonder what he thought when his father never showed on Saturday."

"Probably figured he was mad," Arthur said, turning and making his way back outside.

"I wonder what his excuse was for not showing up at

the party," Chad said when they reached the living room. "Or what their relationship was."

"You've got a point there, all right. Maybe two." Arthur had stopped alongside the floral-upholstered armchair where he'd left his outer jacket. He picked it up and shrugged into it, leaving it unzipped.

"If I pulled a stunt like that with my father," Chad went on as the sheriff sauntered over to the desk to retrieve his notes, "he'd have my hide. Even now."

Arthur returned and joined him at the front door. Obviously the rod hadn't been spared in the St. James household, he thought. Maybe the adage still rang true. Not having had kids of his own, he couldn't say. "Mrs. London might have an answer to that, too," he added. "But you're right; it is strange. Unless, of course, it was only a blind. Maybe he did show. Later on that evening. Maybe his whole taped message was staged just to throw us off the scent."

Chad opened the front door, and the wintry wind swept in, eddying around their trousered legs. "Are you saying he might have killed his own father?" he asked. The pain and disbelief on his face told Arthur the young man had a lot to learn about the real world.

"Everything's possible until it's been eliminated, Chad. You know that. You've taken enough courses."

"Theoretically, Sheriff, sure . . . but his own father! Sh—" He caught himself before it was out, but even at that Arthur was surprised. In a way, though, maybe also a little pleased. It showed a little human tarnish on the halo.

"Sorry, Sheriff," Chad was quick to add, lowering his eyes. "It's just so hard to swallow." He turned and preceded Arthur out the door.

"You know what Sherlock Holmes used to say?" Arthur said behind him.

Chad turned around outside to face him, adjusting the wide-brimmed hat on his head. "When you have eliminated the impossible, whatever remains, however improbable, must be the truth."

"That's it," Arthur said, pleasantly surprised. "So even the improbable becomes possible."

"I suppose so, Sheriff, but between you and me, I'd much rather find the answer in the impossible."

"You and me both." Arthur raised his wrist and checked his watch as Chad closed and locked the door to the Blaine house behind them. "Almost noon. You want to stop at Al's for a bite before we head back to headquarters?"

"Okay with me," Chad said.

In the police car Chad started up the motor and backed out of the driveway onto the still ice-patched lake road.

"Chad, you suggested earlier that the messages were recorded on Friday night before the party," Arthur said when they were under way. "Any special reason? Was the time recorded by the phone machine?"

Chad slid his sunglasses out of their leather case, which was clipped to the overhead visor, and put them on against the glare of the winter sun and snow, then headed around the lake until they reached the shale gate posts. From there, the blacktop road meandered until it ultimately fed into Route 17. "Not on that model," he said. "I was just going by what the son said. But, like you said, that could have been planted anytime. Even after the murder."

"If anyone had gotten into the house, could they have played back the messages?" Arthur asked.

"Sure, but there's no way of knowing."

"That *would* be asking too much, wouldn't it?"

Chad just smiled.

"Can you get me a copy of the tape without my having to phone around?" the sheriff asked.

"Sure. I can do it at home."

Arthur had guessed right in assuming Chad would have the necessary equipment. "Great."

"Say, Sheriff, why don't I drop you off at the diner and take it home to copy now?"

"What about lunch?"

"I can fix a sandwich at the house."

And probably make sure your own dad is all right while you're at it, Arthur thought with a smile.

Chapter Eight
➤ ◄

Their plans to eat at Bogie's were frustrated when they arrived and found the New York restaurant and showplace of the mystery world was no longer in business.

"I'm sorry, Gran, I didn't know," Susanne said forlornly as they proceeded east on Twenty-sixth Street. Susanne had discovered the restaurant a few years earlier, and all she had done was rave about the place and its owners, Bill and Karen Palmer. Lavina was sorry more for the girl's sake than for her own.

"Don't worry about it, Susanne," she said, her arm around her granddaughter's waist.

Before reaching the corner of Twenty-sixth and Seventh, Lavina turned to look back over her shoulder to the black and yellow banner that still hung above the entrance to the closed restaurant. It was flapping in a sudden gust of wind. The silhouette of the Maltese falcon got her to thinking again about Howard Duff. She had known him from his Sam Spade days back at CBS in the late '40s—until the paranoia created by the House Un-American Activities investigations led to the show's being dropped. She had even appeared in a few of the weekly episodes. Humphrey Bogart, unfortunately, she'd never met. Seeing this lovely tribute at what was once Bogie's Restaurant filled her with unaccustomed nostalgia—both for what had been and what would never be. *The stuff that dreams are made of,* indeed.

In order not to waste time, they settled on a nondescript restaurant on Seventh Avenue and sat down at one of the tables. At least it was decorated for the holidays, Lavina noticed, looking around. It was something that, no matter how old she got, always gave her a warm inner glow.

"Mother, you're absolutely incorrigible." The exasperated voice of her daughter sitting opposite her jolted her out of her reverie. "Here we are with a huge apartment in New York and what do you do? Put up at a hotel. Now I ask you . . ." Patricia (Tracey) Halliday—*née* London— shook her dark blond head in disbelief.

"You're not still at it, I hope, Tracey," Lavina said.

"C'mon, Mother," Susanne said, elbowing her mother at her side. "Let Gran have her own space, will you? If she feels more comfortable at a hotel, what's the problem? It's not like she trying to avoid you or something." The twenty-year-old smiled across the lacquered wooden table at her grandmother. Her hair was lighter than her mother's and cropped closer.

Lavina smiled to herself. It hadn't been that long ago, as she recalled, that she had told Tracey much the same thing about Susanne when the girl wanted to go away to Boston to college. Now here was her granddaughter treating her like a teenager. She liked the feel of it somehow.

"All right," Tracey said, resigned to the inevitable, outnumbered as she was by mother and daughter alike—not to mention traitor husband, Damian. "There's no use trying to get you to change your mind and stay down here for the holidays for a change either, I suppose?"

"Absolutely not!" Lavina said, shaking her head and lifting her reading glasses preparatory to checking the menu. "It's Christmas Eve and Christmas dinner at the lake as usual. When I'm gone, you can make whatever changes you want. Until then we maintain family tradition." She slipped the glasses onto the tip of her nose and stared across at her daughter over the tops of the frames. Family tradition, of course, meant exchanging and opening gifts at Lavina's for the immediate family—Lavina, Tracey, Damian, and Susanne—beginning around nine on Christmas Eve, followed by midnight mass up in Monticello, then Christmas dinner the following day. It had been established while Patricia was growing up and continued ever since as the family grew, the only difference being that Ken was no longer with them. "Whatever made you think things would be different this year?"

"I can hope, can't I?" Tracey said, smiling ruefully at the obvious hopelessness of the situation.

Susanne just laughed. "I told you, Mother."

Tracey sighed.

"Any chance Uncle Mark and Uncle Sky will be here this year, Gran?" Susanne asked, using her childhood titles for her grandmother's brothers.

"I'm afraid not, dear." Lavina's two older brothers were as permanently ensconced as she was, one in Ft. Lauderdale and the other in San Francisco.

"Let's order so we get can out of this place, shall we?" Tracey said, picking up her menu. For Tracey, unfortunately, a good restaurant meant expensive. Lavina often wondered where she had gone wrong. It had to have been the early influence of some of her teenaged girlfriends from the posh suburbs. Thank God for Damian. Without sarcasm, he always knew how to squelch the snob in his wife as the occasion demanded. Nothing pretentious about him.

They placed their orders with an attractive dark-haired waitress Lavina guessed to be Greek, then ordered a round of white wine.

"Where *are* you staying anyway?" Tracey asked, lighting a menthol cigarette. Something else Lavina could have seen her daughter do without. There, too, Damian and Susanne sided with her.

"The Southgate," she said.

"You've stayed there before, haven't you, Gran?" Susanne said, tearing off a heel from the French bread in the basket on the table. "I seem to remember the name."

"Oh, certainly. Several times. Your grandfather and I always stayed there whenever we came down to the city. It's only a few blocks from here, Thirty-first and Seventh."

"I bet you hit Macy's first thing," Susanne said, chasing away the drifting smoke from her mother's cigarette.

"Not today, I'm afraid, dear, no. We didn't leave Jae's until almost two thirty and I had to drop her off downtown. I just had time to check in, unpack, and freshen up before I left to meet you two." She had forgotten her cardigan, as a matter of fact, in her rush. Fortunately the dark blue wool knit was warm; it was a mate to the gray one she had worn down.

"You'll be here until Saturday, won't you, Gran? We have a lot of catching up to do. Not to mention shopping."

"Saturday morning, yes." Actually most of her own Christmas shopping had long since been finished. Since October, as a matter of fact. The annual shopping spree in New York was more an excuse to get together with Tracey and Susanne than anything else.

"Who's this Jay person you mentioned, Mother?" Tracey asked. "I don't think I've heard you mention him before."

"Not *him,* dear, *her*—Jae Patrick. She's an agent. I've known her for years. You know her, too—or knew her, I should say—only you were probably too little to remember."

"Wait—," Tracey said, gazing in recollection through the cigarette smoke curling up between them. "She used to come to the apartment when I was little. When we lived in the Fifties, right?"

"Right."

"And she always came alone. And always on a weekday night after work."

"You amaze me," Lavina said. "You couldn't have been more than five at the time."

"She always used to call me Patricia."

Lavina kept nodding her head at the on-target recollections. "Right again."

"And she always brought a cake with her," Tracey added. "In a box from the bakery."

"Never failed," Lavina said, remembering the weekly visits of her old friend to her and Ken's first little apartment in New York.

"Where did you see her, Mother? You said you dropped her off. I'd love to see her again."

"She was at Henry Blaine's party Friday night. I

stopped off at her home in Chatham on my way down. She was coming into the city to see someone, so she came with me." She popped a bite of French bread into her mouth and took a sip of wine.

"How lovely, and after all these years."

"Gran, what about Mr. Blaine?" Susanne asked at the first gap in the conversation. "Was he really murdered?"

"I'm afraid so, Susanne."

"It's absolutely dreadful," Tracey injected, stabbing out her cigarette in the glass ashtray. "A poor, helpless old man like that."

"No older than your mother, certainly," Lavina said with an unsuccessful pretense at pique.

Susanne giggled silently behind her upraised wineglass.

"You're another one," Tracey said, sitting upright in the wooden chair. "All alone up there on that godforsaken lake in the dead of winter. Anything could happen and we wouldn't know for days."

"Nonsense. Winnie would be over pounding on the door the first time I didn't answer the phone," Lavina corrected with a little laugh, her granddaughter joining in.

Tracey shook her head. "There's no way of winning with the two of you ganging up on me like you always do."

"Just be grateful I have such good friends and neighbors, that's all."

"How come you stopped off at this Miss Patrick's, Gran?" Susanne asked around her mouthful of bread.

"I arranged to meet with her to discuss my book. I renewed a lot of old acquaintances at Henry's party, and many of them graciously offered to help me out. There's a wealth of invaluable information in their heads and tucked away in old trunks. Henry's party turned out to be a godsend—for me, at any rate." She raised her glass by way of a personal toast. "God rest his soul."

Susanne followed suit, her glass poised in front of her lips. She narrowed her eyes. "Any chance one of them killed him, Gran?"

"Susanne, really!" Tracey scolded, reaching again for her cigarettes.

"Anything's possible, I suppose," Lavina said, lowering her eyes and setting down her glass.

"You'll be seeing some of the others besides Miss Patrick while you're down here, won't you?" Susanne said, narrowed eyes unchanged. She was staring over the rim of her glass. "And asking them a lot of questions."

Lavina was too close to her granddaughter not to recognize the teasing accusation behind the statement. "Yes, of course." The faint smile was a clear giveaway. That, and the way she tried to avoid Susanne's eyes.

"Your questions wouldn't touch on Henry Blaine's murder though, would they?" The smile the girl tried to hold back broke through, as did her grandmother's when the latter caught sight of it out of the corner of her eye.

"What in heaven's name are the two of you talking about, will you tell me?" Tracey asked, unaware of the full extent of Lavina's earlier foray into sleuthing—or her daughter's role therein.

"Nothing, dear, nothing at all." Lavina looked off to her left to see her rescuer in the form of their waitress returning with their food. She caught Susanne's eye again as she helped make room on the table for the dishes. The girl was just shaking her head, a wide smile on her lips. *The sneaky know-it-all.*

* * *

Will Argon and Audra Mateer were sitting on a sturdy maroon-colored sofa in the hotel lobby opposite one of the two goblet-shaped fountains with their mini *jets d'eau* and base of lush, potted plants.

"I hope I haven't kept you waiting," Lavina said as she approached them. "I was having a bite to eat with my daughter and granddaughter."

"No, Lavina, we're early, is all," Argon said, propelling himself up with the aid of a solid wooden cane poised between his long legs.

Lavina planted a little kiss on his cheek, then bent over to do the same with the woman on the couch. Her light brown, though obviously dyed, hair was tied back severely, somehow managing to emphasize the wrinkles that pulled at the corners of her eyes and mouth. It was difficult to believe she was about the same age as Jae Patrick.

"Give me a tug, will you, Lavina?" she said, extending a liver-spotted hand. "I need a breath of fresh air." Once she was up with Lavina's assistance, she turned to pick up her coat, which Argon helped her slip on with his free hand. "Will and I have just been sitting here reminiscing. We haven't exactly been in touch, even though we do both live in the same area." She smiled up at the tall pole of a man at her side, his thick white curly hair a sharp contrast to the flushed face. When Lavina had first met him, he had just signed on as announcer for Henry and Hildy's soap opera. Lavina didn't know the reason for the cane, and didn't want to ask. It was his voice that disturbed her more than anything else. Once so deep and full, it was now faint and croaky. The change in the once auburn hair was understandable; this, though, bothered her.

Audra, too, had been connected with the Blaine show at

the time, but in her case, in a minor acting role. Never one with big dreams, Audra Mateer had always been satisfied with minor parts, provided they were steady ones. One of her favorite expressions, Lavina recalled, had been "It's regular, and helps keep me the same way." Not the most ladylike of her earlier acquaintances, perhaps, but certainly an honest one. Audra's bluntness, in fact, was proverbial.

"Anyone joining us, Lavina?" Audra asked as Lavina steered them through the open iron grill toward the rear of the hotel.

"No, just the three of us."

They headed past the concierge's desk opposite the bank of elevators and off toward the pair of wrought-iron stairs that curved down to the lower level and the Thirty-first Street side entrance.

"I've got a load of anecdotes for your book, Lavina," Argon said as he preceded the two women down the flight of stairs. "Wrote them down, so's I don't forget them." He lifted his hand from the railing and patted his breast pocket, the other gripping the sturdy cane. Once outside on the sidewalk, he reached into his coat pocket and dug out a bright red beret, which he yanked on over his thick head of hair.

"Right now, Will, I'm just too upset over Henry's death to even think about the book," Lavina said. It wasn't a complete lie, but the only way she could think of to get on track.

"Isn't that something?" Will said, shaking his head.

Audra grabbed his arm for support as they turned unthinking to head west. "It's horrible, isn't it, Lavina? I couldn't believe my ears when you phoned and told me. I hardly ever read the papers anymore, and never would

have heard otherwise." She gave a little smile. "I'm glad
you're here tonight. I feel as if a shadow has somehow
crossed my path—like a black cat."

"Don't think like that, Audra," Argon said, patting the
hand locked around his arm. "Death's a part of life."

"And is murder a part of life, too?" the woman asked.
Lavina couldn't tell whether the visible shiver was from the
cold or from fear.

"Que será será, as they say," Argon said as they reached
the corner. Looking first right, then left, "Which way?"

"Let's just walk around the block," Audra said. "Then,
if you want, we can go back in."

Without further discussion, they turned south, Lavina
on Audra's left, Argon on her right.

"Someone at that party killed him," Audra said before
they had gone a block.

Argon stopped in his tracks at the pontifical pronouncement, halting the progress of the trio. "What in God's
name made you say a thing like that, Audra?" He was
using his cane to accentuate his words.

It obviously had no effect on Audra whatsoever, because
she just resumed their walk, pulling her two companions
along with her. "It makes sense, doesn't it?" she said. "Not
that I'm surprised, mind you. He just pushed someone too
far once too often, that's all."

Before Lavina could get a word in edgewise, Argon cut
in again. "It seems to me that his going to Canada would
more than have gotten him out of anybody's hair, don't
you think?"

"Obviously Canada wasn't far enough for someone,"
Audra added.

"Hold on, both of you!" Lavina fairly shouted as they

reached Thirtieth Street and rounded the corner, heading back east. Still three abreast, they kept close to the curb. "What's all this about Henry pushing someone around?" It was just the sort of inside information she was hoping for—a possible motive for murder, unbelievable as it still seemed.

Audra looked up into Lavina's red-cheeked face, her chin all but buried in her thick wool scarf against the periodic gusts of wind. Both women were hatless. "You knew Henry, Lavina. Probably better than any of us."

"In recent years, maybe," Lavina corrected. *Or so I thought, anyway.*

"Well, he'd been up to something of late," Audra insisted. "No one can tell me otherwise."

"What 'something'?" Lavina asked, her frustration beginning to show.

Audra pulled the little group to a halt, stopping to look up at the taller woman to her left. Lavina's five-foot-nine height often embarrassed her, as indeed it did now in the middle of Thirtieth Street with Audra gawking up at her in disbelief. "Lavina, Henry Blaine was a son of a bitch of the first water. Always was. You mean to tell me you didn't know that?"

What Lavina didn't know about Henry Blaine could have filled another book. Their paths in the past had crossed only when she happened to be broadcasting in New York at the same station where he and Hildy had their soap. After that, they had lost contact until he retired and moved up to the lake. And even then it was Hildy she saw more than Henry.

"I can't say that I did," she finally admitted.

"Lucky for you," Audra said. "I guess he never discovered any of the skeletons in your closet."

"I'm not sure I have any," Lavina said, taken aback. Was that why Henry hadn't bothered with her all that much? It was a strange discovery, if it was so. And had Hildy known?

"Better dig up a few then," Will said, "if you want to spice up those memoirs of yours." He laughed as they resumed the leisurely pace they had set earlier.

"Exactly what sort of things are you talking about, Audra?" Lavina asked, dismissing the man's attempt at humor with a faint smile.

"Lavina, please . . . Don't ask me to dredge up muck from the past."

"But you hinted it was something recent."

Squeezed in between her two companions, Audra just shrugged her narrow shoulders. "It would still be connected with the past, Lavina, believe me. And I'd be no better than Henry was if I started talking about everybody else's foibles, now would I?" She had to be talking about more than little foibles, Lavina realized, if it was something that had eventually led to murder.

"Audra, we're talking about murder, for heaven's sake."

"I know. And as I mentioned to a few of the others earlier in the week, there's a thing or two I could tell if I had a mind to."

"Then maybe you should," Lavina said. "To the police, I mean." She raked back strands of gray hair from her eyes. "I mean, what sort of thing would make someone furious enough to want to kill him, Audra?"

"How about blackmail?" Audra said, her bluntness coming to the fore. It was a possibility Lavina had considered, of course, especially since she knew all the parties Henry might have been blackmailing. But for what reason? The more she thought about it, the less she wanted to know. It ultimately would mean learning something awful about one of the people she thought she knew so well. Or something that they considered awful enough to want kept quiet.

"I don't know, Audra," Argon said when they reached the middle of the block. "You must stay awake nights dreaming up things. I can't for the life of me remember anything nasty Henry ever did to me over the years."

"Nothing you'd care to mention anyway," the woman snapped back without turning to look up at him.

Argon didn't answer, and Lavina wondered what, if anything, Audra Mateer knew that she wasn't mentioning.

"I've got to think it out first, Lavina," the other actress said. "I've got to be certain before I do anything I might regret."

Lavina was going to say something about the woman's doing nothing, which she might regret even more, but decided against it. Instead, she shifted the direction of the conversation. "Where did you all stay, by the way, when you came up to Boulder for the party?"

"Nowhere," Audra said. "Bran Slattery drove me up, and the two of us came back to the city right after the party. I had to be back to feed Sheena. You don't know how ornery she can get when she's not fed on time." Audra's Siamese, She-of-the-Jungle.

"I stayed at the motel where the party was," Argon said. "The Seventeener, is it?"

"Yes."

"I went up Thursday night, as a matter of fact, and

came back Saturday morning a little after five. Checked out and paid up the evening before, before I went over to the banquet hall. That way, I avoided traffic coming back."

"Anyone with you?" Lavina asked.

"No, just me."

"Anyone else stay at the motel, do you know?"

"I saw the Hessons talking to the clerk there Friday night. Whether they had a room or not, I couldn't say."

"And Jae Patrick made it up and back on Friday, too," Lavina said out loud, recalling what the agent had told her.

"Did Nelson Doss drive?" Audra asked. "I mean he looked pretty far gone at the party." Lavina hadn't been mistaken, unless . . . Would anyone fake being drunk to give himself an alibi? It was possible, she supposed.

"I don't know," Lavina said. "What time did you and Bran leave?"

"Early. About eleven. Bran knew I was tired and wanted to get back to feed the cat. He's such a gentleman."

Lavina recalled the man she had spoken to briefly at the party. He was still as handsome as ever, even with the added years. And still with that faint hint of a brogue she recalled from the distant past. They had acted together on several occasions, but nothing more. She didn't even know if he had ever married.

When they had completed their circuit around the block and reentered the hotel, the warmth was a welcome relief, even to an easily overheated Audra. Settled at a table in the cocktail lounge, they ordered drinks.

After two Scotch on the rocks, Argon started brooding, complaining about the fate that hadn't seen fit to make him another Harry von Sell or Don Wilson, announcers

whose names had become household words, names remembered fondly even today by the myriad survivors of
early radio's vast listening audience.

"You should have written more scripts when you had
the chance and gotten into that area of the business,"
Audra finally said in exasperation when she'd obviously
heard enough. "You might have become another Irna
Phillips or Elaine Sterne Carrington. Maybe even gone on
to bigger things, like Herman Wouk or Irwin Shaw."

"I didn't think there was enough money to be made in
the writing side back then," he admitted forlornly, staring
down into his glass. That Will Argon had actually written
for the soaps was something Lavina had never heard
before. It was a whole new side to the announcer.

"And besides," Argon added, "Henry never particularly
liked my scripts—to put it mildly."

"Hilda did though, didn't she?" Audra picked up her
Pilsner glass and stared across at him over the rim, then
took a little sip.

At that point in the conversation, everything went
downhill and eventually ended pretty much on a sour
note, which was far from what Lavina desired. Thank
heavens for Tod Arthur's phone call, which came through
about five minutes after she returned to her suite. It was
the uplift she needed. She grinned to herself at the confidence in her that the long-distance call indicated. It also
told her Tod wasn't all that convinced of his earlier suspicions as he had claimed to be.

The melodramatic *Shadow* message left on the telephone answering machine she found intriguing, to say the
least, even if she didn't have the ready answer Tod was obviously hoping for. Maybe something would come to

mind later. And Garrett Blaine's last-minute beg-out, while less intriguing, was interesting nonetheless. Before hanging up, she remembered to ask Tod for the son's address and phone number. "As long as he's coming right back from the funeral, I can extend my condolences personally down here." His "Sure you can" comeback merely confirmed what she already suspected, so she didn't bother to comment on it. Tod was perfectly aware of her little investigation—what he'd call snooping. What he wasn't telling her, though, grated; there was something he was keeping to himself—she was sure of it.

Her hand was still on the cradled receiver when the coincidence struck her. Tod's mention of the Shadow, and Audra's presentiment of a shadow crossing her path. It was eerie. She lifted the receiver again and, after checking the little address book she'd left out earlier, placed a call to the actress. She let it ring eight times. No one answered.

THURSDAY, DECEMBER 21

Chapter Nine

> ← →

The bow sliced through the calm, icy waters with sheer determination, sending up a fine salty spray. Out beyond the vessel the black-green waters of the bay rippled serenely, shimmering in the morning sun. No choppers because there was no wind, except that stirred up by the speed of the ferry itself.

He pressed the green woolen scarf tight against his nose and mouth and closed his eyes, letting the oncoming rush bathe his brow in its icy freshness. Rime formed on his brows. It was exhilarating. He was, he knew, the only passenger outside on the upper deck. The others inside the glass-enclosed cabin undoubtedly thought him crazy, and maybe he was—but riding the Staten Island ferry in December was crazy in itself when he didn't have to.

But he needed to think, needed to be alone—away from crowds and noise. Here—except for the hypnotic wash against the boat's hull and the hum of the engines—he was spared both. In spring and summer it was something he frequently did when he just wanted to get away, but never before with the temperatures in the twenties—and that up in Central Park. What it was out here on the open bay, he had no idea—and didn't particularly care. It felt good, and that was all that mattered.

His gray-blond hair, long and thick, was at the mercy of the wind, but he wasn't foolish enough to try keeping it down. His ears would probably have been frostbitten by now, too, if he hadn't thought to bring along his earmuffs. They were the kind he hated—the only kind they seemed to sell anymore—with the narrow metal headband that invariably caught in his hair when he tried to lift it off.

He opened his eyes again, this time with obvious awareness of the hoarfrost that had formed on his lashes. He wiped it away with his free gloved hand.

They were fast approaching the world-renowned green lady, which loomed off to his left. He moved across the slippery deck, with careful attention to his footing. The thought of a broken hip was not his idea of the ideal way to spend the Christmas season—or any season, for that matter—especially at his age. When he reached port side, he leaned out against the wooden bulwark to get a clearer view. Incredible as it always seemed to out-of-towners when he admitted it, he had never actually visited the Statue of Liberty, in spite of all the years he'd spent in New York. As with the Empire State Building, she was taken for granted, something he'd get around to eventually. He smiled at the thought that in this, as in so many other things, he was probably a typical New Yorker.

He shifted the slipping scarf, careful to inhale only his own warm, stale breath. Arctic air never failed to induce unpleasant chest pains, a natural concomitant—or so he had been told—of bundle-branch block, his minor heart condition, which otherwise caused him little trouble. Cold and overexertion were his only concerns.

As the New York skyline expanded up ahead he wondered whether the round trip to Staten Island had served its purpose. If anything, it merely seemed to reinforce the plan he had envisioned before leaving his apartment. Since Lavina intended meeting with some of her former colleagues during this trip to New York, now seemed the ideal time. That she would be contacting only the ones who had been closest to her during her acting career meant the move was up to him. Audra had told him as much after Blaine's party. According to her, Lavina was working on a book of some kind dealing with her years in radio.

That had to be his in. Why not? He could certainly help her, couldn't he? It seemed a natural enough approach. Why wouldn't she meet him?

The ferry cut its engines as it neared the inviting berth, cutting back the wind as well.

Henry Blaine's death was somehow always before him. Audra had phoned him as soon as she'd heard about it from Lavina up in Boulder. He'd already seen it in the papers, of course. It was just a shame the little woman brooded so much over the whole business, an unfortunate part of her having nothing constructive to help fill her retirement years. Too much time to think. She also had some ideas of her own about the murder itself, ideas that might very well prove dangerous. He had suggested meeting her several times, but she had always begged off. Even yesterday, he had wanted to see her before her scheduled meeting with Lavina, whom she probably had worrying and wondering now as well.

Brandan Slattery didn't like the sound of that at all. The

thought of Lavina getting all sorts of crazy ideas into her head because of the ramblings of an idle woman with an overly vivid imagination wasn't good. If Lavina was still the headstrong woman he remembered from their acting days together, she might well get herself into trouble. Serious trouble.

The drifting vessel bore left as it entered the dock, inadvertently ramming the tall, weather-beaten wood pier, thick now with algae. The unexpected impact and its accompanying dull thud jolted him back from his musing. Gray-white scavenger gulls that had greeted the boat as it approached the shoreline continued their cawing and circling overhead. Bran released his hold on his scarf and tucked it back inside his gray goosedown jacket, raking back his hair for the first time since leaving the Island.

The ferry recoiled at an obvious shift of gears on the part of the pilot, then rumbled forward again, heading straight toward the berth. As it glided forward, there was a sudden roar of its breaking system, which churned the waters in its bed. The vessel froze momentarily, then eased gently into the berth. Chains and heavy hooks completed the mooring as experienced dockhands carried out their assigned tasks.

By this time Bran found himself surrounded by the flow of late-morning commuters, ready and eager to challenge him up the descending metal gangplank to the upper level of the terminal. Since he was in no particular hurry, once the gate was opened, he let them pass. Not a few of them fairly knocked him out of their path in their inexplicable haste. He'd met them all before on the country's highways—them or their ilk.

Once inside the terminal he looked around until he

found a public phone. After a quick check of the directory—he was surprised to find one—he lifted his Pentel
pencil and notepad out of the pocket of his flannel shirt
and jotted down a number, then deposited his quarter and
waited.

"Hello." The voice was unmistakable. He could tell it
anywhere, and not at all that different from the way it
sounded on radio years ago.

"Lavina?"

"Bran Slattery, you old reprobate!"

"How did you know it was me?" He teased.

"Now who else do I know with a lovely touch of a
brogue?" Even in just saying her name, she had detected it.
He wondered whether he should consider it a compliment. He wasn't quite sure.

He just laughed. "I recognized you, too, Lavina. Your
charming voice hasn't changed any over the years either."

"Then it's the only thing about me that hasn't," Lavina
said with a little laugh of her own. "What are you up to?"

"Well, to tell the truth . . . I was wondering if you might
be free sometime while you're in town. I mean, I'm sure
you've got a million and one things to do, what with the
holiday season and all, but—"

"Say no more. Where are you?"

He hesitated, not sure whether to tell her. Maybe she'd
think he was crazy, too. Honesty won out.

"You haven't moved, have you?" she asked after he told
her.

"Lord, no. Me leave Manhattan?"

"I didn't think so."

"Did you see Audra yesterday?"

"Yes. And Will Argon. I guess Audra told you we were

meeting. It was delightful spending time with the two of them again, even if I did drink a bit too much wine. I'm just not used to it."

"You never were, as I recall." Not that many women were into drinking in those days—or so it seemed in retrospect.

"I'm supposed to meet my daughter and granddaughter for lunch and shopping," Lavina continued, "but I can put off the lunch and—"

"Don't let me interfere with your plans, Lavina, please. I can—"

"Nonsense. I'll be with them the rest of the week. I can still meet them for shopping later. So how about lunch— just the two of us?"

"Terrific. Where?" He paused, waiting, then added, "How about I meet you at—" The name came out of his mouth at the very same moment it did Lavina's: "Rockefeller Center." They both laughed.

"I love it this time of the year," Lavina said, as if telling him something he didn't already know.

"Yes, I know," Bran said.

"How—?"

"I remember your saying the same thing years ago. You liked to bring your little Patricia there for the lighting of the tree."

"Little Patricia, indeed." Lavina chuckled. "You've got a good memory. And a lot of catching up to do."

"That I do."

"And a lovely turn of phrase. The Irish in you again."

"Thank you."

"Anyway, it's settled," Lavina said. "Suppose I meet

you at one of the benches in the promenade? Say the group facing the French bookstore."

"The *Librairie de France.*"

"Your French sounds almost as good as your Irish," she teased.

"That's the Celtic roots," he said with another little laugh. "What time?"

"Is an hour too soon? It's almost ten now."

"I can make it in plenty of time, subways permitting."

Bran hung up the receiver and heaved a deep sigh. He was actually perspiring. The warm jacket in the heated terminal, he told himself. Anyway, it was done. Step number one. Now it was only a matter of keeping calm so he didn't louse up a fine start. He'd just have to be careful, that's all. Very, very careful. Everything depended on that. Everything.

Chapter Ten

→ ←

"They didn't have all these lovely trumpeting angels back then either," Lavina said, looking up at the lavish holiday display set up in the wide flower beds flanking the pool behind them. They ran the length of Rockefeller Promenade between the benches, leading to the Lower Plaza and Manship's flying Prometheus.

"True," Bran Slattery said. "But grand as the Channel Gardens are this time of year, it's still the tree that's the big attraction."

At his words, they both looked off to their right to the huge decorated evergreen towering over the plaza, which, below street level, was now converted into a winter skating rink.

"We should really come back at night," Bran said, "when we can enjoy the lights."

"If I didn't know better, Bran Slattery, I'd think you were asking me out for a date," Lavina said, turning back with a smile to face him beside her on the bench. "And you know," she quickly added, "I always meant to ask about that name of yours, but never got around to it."

"We never spent enough time together, Lavina."

"I guess I was too embarrassed to ask. After all, we were never really that close."

"Feeling closer now, are you?" he asked, a smile on his lips.

His phrasing delighted her. That, and the slight brogue. "Older and wiser—with fewer inhibitions, that's all."

They both laughed.

"Is it asking you are, then?"

"Yes."

"Did you never hear tell of *The Voyage of Bran?*

"I guess not," she said, wrinkling her brow.

"Sure and you've missed something grand, Lavina." He unzipped his gray goosedown jacket. "My father—rest his soul—loved it probably even more than I did. An ancient Irish tale it is, written in the seventh century. The story of the hero, Bran—often equated with Saint Brandan, or Brendan—and his adventures during his voyage to the Happy Otherworld." He was looking at his reflection in the distant bookstore facing them, then turned back to face her. "Today on the Staten Island ferry I somehow felt very much like that seafaring saint in quest of the Earthly Paradise."

Lavina was seeing for the first time a man she'd never really known, a warm, sensisitive, introspective man. "And what is it *you're* in quest of, Brandan Slattery?" She just wanted to hear the sound of the full name on her lips.

"Who knows, Lavina. Youthful dreams, maybe."

"The best kind. Fortunately for us, youth doesn't corner the market on them."

Bran smiled. "Nicely put, Lavina."

"Was your father a sailor?" she asked, the ancient tale still on her mind.

"No, just a dreamer. And storyteller."

"Irish through and through." She slipped her black crocheted bag off her shoulder and set it down on the bench between them, squeezing her paperback copy of Jane Haddam's latest mystery into one of the side pockets.

"Remember when we first met, Lavina?" Bran asked when she looked up to meet his deep blue eyes. Maybe the song was right when it spoke about Irish eyes.

Lavina tried to think back. They'd done so many varied things together in the course of their respective careers. She felt embarrassed, realizing that she had forgotten. Bran obviously had not. "No, Bran, I'm afraid I don't."

"Let's Pretend."

"What?"

"The *Let's Pretend* show. Remember? You were helping coach that young pimply faced teenager who was to play the role of Cinderella, and I was doing the same with the pubescent young prince. We were consultants that week."

Lavina threw back her head and broke out laughing, passersby smiling at her obvious pleasure. "Oh, I do remember that. Was that the first time we met? What fun that was."

"I think your Cinderella had a serious crush on Prince Charming."

"Funny, I seem to remember it the other way around."

They broke out laughing again, something, it seemed to Lavina, that they were doing quite often.

"Let's Pretend. What a wonderful show that was," Lavina said, wiping at her eyes with a gloved finger. She

laid a hand on Bran's arm. "I bet, like me, you still remember the words to the Cream of Wheat theme song."

"I do. 'Cream of Wheat is so good to eat—' "

This time she slapped his arm, interrupting his bass solo. "Please, Bran, not here." The mutual laughter began again. "We'll have an audience in a minute, if you don't watch out. This is New York, don't forget."

"And isn't that what every actor worth his salt craves, Lavina? And actors we still are, don't forget, retired or not."

This time there was no stopping him. He started again from the top and didn't stop until he had reached "For all the family breakfast, you can't beat Cream of Wheat," with Lavina powerless to restrain her laughter. She hadn't enjoyed anything so spontaneous in a long time. Susanne was probably the only other person who could get her going like that.

"Do you realize it lasted some thirty-three years?" Lavina said. "It was known as 'Radio's Outstanding Children's Theater.' Thank God for people like Nila Mack. She made that show."

"Not to mention all those Pretenders."

"How could I forget? Some of them grew up on that show and stayed on as adults."

"I'm not sure I ever grew up, Lavina," Bran said, lowering his eyes to his strong hands in his lap. "I just got older."

Lavina canted her head and looked at him seated there at her side. Maybe it was just what he had said, but he looked like a little boy, his thick gray-blond hair a plaything for the occasional gust of wind.

"I'm sure we all still have that child inside us, Bran. I

know I do." She laid a hand on his. "How old is yours? Seven, eight?"

"Nail on the head, Lavina," he said, looking up with a smile as he took her hand in his own. "Though sometimes I think there's another one in there as well, about seventeen." The dark blue eyes, Lavina noticed, were downright impish.

Strains of "God Rest Ye Merry, Gentlemen" and an accompanying languid hand bell started up somewhere on Fifth Avenue. A Salvation Army Santa. Lavina looked up and around the promenade. A Thursday morning and the holiday shoppers were already in full swing.

"A penny, Lavina," Bran prompted, shaking her out of her reverie.

She turned back to face him with a little smile. "I was thinking about Henry," she lied, realizing that she'd been thinking of no one but herself since she'd met this delightful man again after all these years. She had completely forgotten her self-imposed mission to track down her colleague's murderer.

"Why Henry?" Bran lifted out a roll of mint Life Savers from his flannel shirt pocket, peeled back the foil, and extended the open end in Lavina's direction.

The actress shook her head. "It just seems so sad. Especially this time of the year."

"Were you close?"

"No, not at all." She shook her head again. "With Hildy I was somewhat close, I suppose, but not with Henry. It's just that it all happened so fast." She looked down unseeing into her open shoulder bag between them, then, realizing that her hand was still in Bran's, lifted it away. "What really worries me is that we might know the murderer."

When she looked up again, Bran had compressed his lips, his jaw tense. His pleasant gaze had become a cold, penetrating stare.

"Audra tells me you're playing detective," he finally said, thumbing one of the white mints out of the roll and popping it into his mouth. "That true?"

She couldn't quite interpret the look. Was it concern for her or fear for himself? "Audra's dramatizing, I'm afraid," she said in self-defense, a faint smile on her lips.

"I don't think so, Lavina. Audra's not like that, never was. So there must be something—"

"I'm just keeping my ears open, that's all," Lavina said, lowering her eyes. She knew the gesture was a sure give-away, one that Susanne would spot in an instant. She didn't know whether Bran would see it for what it was or not.

"And your eyes, too, I suppose," Bran said, just about answering her question.

"Look, Bran," she said, "the man was killed in my own community. There are actually people up there who think I had a hand in his death." She zipped open the collar of her jacket, loosened the scarf, then tugged off her suede gloves. "I also happen to be a very good friend of our county sheriff."

"You're working with the police?" He furrowed his brow.

"Not working with them, no." She turned her eyes away again.

"Free-lancing." He smiled.

Lavina nodded, satisfied with the comparison. "Yes, in

a manner of speaking, I suppose that's exactly what I'm doing."

"And this sheriff of yours approves? Lets you run around loose questioning possible killers?"

"Well, no, I wouldn't say that." He was beginning to sound a little like Tod himself. If he only knew. "But we worked together before on a murder case," she said, turning back to face him, "and he knows he can trust my judgment."

"Lavina, if you're playing real-life Clue with a murderer, you're playing a deadly game. You could get killed."

Lavina dismissed the suggestion with a wave of her ungloved hand. "I could be killed in my tub, for that matter, Bran. That doesn't mean I shouldn't bathe."

"That's a ludicrous analogy, Lavina, and you know it." He combed his fingers through his hair, momentarily taming it. "And what kind of man is this sheriff of yours anyway? I mean, is he young? Old? Married? What?"

Lavina shrugged, not exactly sure where he was leading with the questions pertaining to Tod's personal life, and hesitant to draw any rash conclusions. "He's in his early fifties. Married, no children. Why?"

Bran shot her a broad smile, then rose from the bench. "Let's go over and have a look at the skaters." He extended his hand to help her up. Lavina—after scooping up her gloves and shoulder bag with one hand—took it with the other.

"I don't want you doing any more investigating on your own, Lavina," he said when they had reached the wall that overlooked the rink in the plaza. "Stick with questions pertinent to your book and leave Blaine's death to the police."

Lavina stared across at him in disbelief, pulling away her hand that was still in his. "I'm not sure I like your tone, Bran. As a matter of fact, I know I don't. That's something not even Ken ever—"

"I'm sorry, Lavina. Forgive me. I didn't mean it the way it sounded. It's just a request, honest. A personal favor to me, okay?"

Lavina sighed. "Why?"

"I don't want anything to happen to you."

"Or see me discover something I shouldn't." She regretted it as soon as it was out.

He met her gaze. "If you mean something about me, Lavina, I can only say that hurts. But now that you mention it, yes, you may well discover something about somebody—something that might very well be dangerous. That's the whole point."

"Exactly. Don't you see? I may be the perfect one to investigate. Tod—Sheriff Arthur, I mean—wouldn't know where to start. And for that matter, I don't even think it's within his jurisdiction."

"Then give him, or whoever's in charge, what they need. Tell them everything you know that might help. Let them take it from there."

"I can't. I don't know anything yet. Which is why I've got to ask questions."

"Then by rights, you should be asking me questions as well." He gave her a little smile.

"I fully intended to until you threw me off my stride." She was becoming more and more confused by the minute about Brandan Slattery. Was he what he seemed to be or not? How much of that brogue and phrasing were just for her benefit, to throw sand in her eyes in the form of stars?

"As long as I'm asking questions, when did Audra tell you about this so-called detective work of mine?"

"Last night. She called when she got in after seeing you." He smiled again. "I asked her to."

"I see." It was possible, of course. She had tried to reach Audra only once before retiring. Audra could very well have come in later and phoned him. There was no earthly reason to think otherwise, even if Audra hadn't mentioned it this morning when she'd finally gotten through to her. "I'm going to see her again this evening, as a matter of fact," she added. "At her apartment."

Bran merely nodded.

"I suppose you have no idea who might have killed Henry?" she finally asked. "You're not hiding any skeletons you'd be willing to share with me?" This in as lighthearted a tone as she could manage. If she had hurt him before, she didn't want to do it again.

"I'll just keep my personal skeletons where they belong, thank you, Lavina," he said with a grin. "At least for the time being."

"I can live with that," she said with a smile of her own.

Bran looked down into the sunken rink, his arms stretched out on the wall to cushion his chest. After a few moments, without looking up, he said, "Henry had a number of enemies from what I hear."

"Do you know that as a fact, or is it something Audra told you?" The woman seemed to be a mine of information. She should prove a definite asset in more areas than one.

"I can't say I actually recall where I first heard the rumors," Bran said. "Audra and I spoke about it from time to time."

"You and she seem to be quite chummy," Lavina said, seriously wondering if she was experiencing the onset of jealousy. She smiled at the thought. After all, she had barely met this man again after all these years.

Bran shrugged. "She seemed in need of a friend."

"She said you drove her to and from the party Friday night," Lavina said.

"That's right. And left to come home a little before eleven." Again, precisely what Audra had told her.

Lavina shifted the strap of her bag on her shoulder. "Our friend Audra seems to know more than she's willing to share at this point."

"Really?"

"So she claims. And you're the one who says she doesn't dramatize. Any idea what she may be referring to?"

"I really can't say as I do, Lavina. Unless it has to do with Garrett Blaine. For what it's worth, she said he was recently cut out of his father's will."

"Well, that's something anyway," Lavina said. "You have any idea why? If it's true, I mean?"

"No. Do you think it matters? I mean Henry was hardly a wealthy man, as far as I know."

Lavina nodded. "True. Unless, of course, he had more than he let on. Garrett and his wife didn't show at the party, don't forget." She decided not to mention the message Garrett had left on the answering machine.

"Your sheriff should be able to find out easily enough, I imagine," Bran said, stretching his neck to get a better view of a mishap on the ice below.

"I suppose so," she agreed. "There also seems to be some indication—at least according to Audra—that Henry was blackmailing someone."

"It wouldn't surprise me."

"He wasn't out after you, by any chance, was he?" Lavina asked, barely managing to keep a straight face. "Over one of those skeletons of yours?"

"I'll let you mull over that one by yourself, Nancy Drew." Just like Susanne.

Lavina inched back the elastic cuff of her jacket and looked at her watch. "Would you mind if we just sat and postponed lunch?" she said, looking up.

"No, not at all. Provided, of course, you take a rain check."

She gave him a big smile. "You've got yourself a date."

They made their way back to the still vacant bench in the promenade and sat down again, the sun warm on their upturned faces.

"Anything else you can tell me?" she asked.

Bran shrugged. "I suppose you already know Henry was quite a ladies man in his day?"

That much she had always known; some things were impossible to keep secret. "I knew him when, don't forget," she said with a nod. "As a matter of fact, I'd find it much more believable if someone had been blackmailing him rather than vice versa."

"He and Hildy were living together during their show before they got married, you know," Bran said.

Lavina nodded awareness. Back then, cohabitation had been something of a sensation. Indeed, if the fact had been known—or even suspected—the Blaines most certainly would have found themselves without a soap, given the tenor of the times. If the film industry had its Hays Office to wield the scissors of censorship, the FCC was certainly no less unyielding with radio's airwaves. Not to mention the impact such goings-on would have had on the Hooper and Nielsen ratings.

"And you know, too, I suppose, that Garrett was born before they tied the knot," Bran added.

That she hadn't known. "No, I didn't, but only because I don't know when they actually did get married. That was kept very hush-hush, too, as I recall." She slipped the strap of her bag off her shoulder and set it back between them on the bench. "But none of this had anything to do with their finally losing their show, certainly." It was a statement looking for confirmation.

"No, that came later. And at least a year before the boy was born. I still don't know why their contract wasn't renewed. From everything I've heard, the show was a commercial success."

"Jae claims Henry blamed her, which was why he and Hildy switched agencies."

"Could be, but who's to say at this late date?" He rubbed a finger back and forth across his square jaw.

"What about Hildy?" Lavina asked, remembering something Audra had said. "Was there ever anything between her and Will Argon?"

"I don't know. Will was always pretty closemouthed even back then." As he had been last night, Lavina thought—until the alcohol loosened his tongue. "At the party, I couldn't get more than two words out of him. It was like talking to a wall. He seemed to be thinking of something else."

"That could very well be," Lavina said. "I wish I could conjure up in my mind all the little goings-on that night. I might see something that would help."

"Why not view the videotape?" Bran said with a little laugh.

Videotape. Of course! The camera that was her mind began its own selective rewind back to the night of the party. That's what those cameras had been. At the time she hadn't been sure, unaccustomed as she was to the new technology. And while she still extolled the virtues of radio over television, she couldn't withhold her gratitude for the new discovery.

"Bran, you may well have saved the day without even realizing it," she said, seizing him by the wrist. "You think it was Henry who had it taped?"

"Probably," Bran said. Something else Tod could look into, she thought. As soon as she could summon up the nerve to call him. "What do you expect to find on the tape?"

"I have no idea. Probably nothing at all. But then again, maybe somebody looking extremely uncomfortable. Maybe downright guilty looking."

"Thinking about his plot to murder, you mean."

"Exactly." She smiled again, realizing how silly it probably sounded to him.

"It really might be worth looking into," Bran said, setting her mind at rest.

Lavina released her hold on his wrist and turned to follow the pungent odor of roasting chestnuts wafting across the plaza. "Henry and Jae Patrick had been an item at one time, too, you know," she said, turning back to face him.

"Before Hildy's time?"

"Yes." Unless the relationship had resumed at a later date, she thought. It was getting more and more difficult to keep track without a script.

"What about the Hessons?" Bran asked. "They were never overly complimentary to the Blaine soap back then either, Lavina. They often made snide remarks on that luncheon show of theirs, as I recall."

Lavina nodded. "I remember. Yet when the four of them were together, butter wouldn't melt in their mouth. I hope to see them while I'm here, as a matter of fact. Up at their apartment in Riverdale. Violet insisted we get together. She wants to help with the book."

A sudden gust of wind snapped the U.N. flags that decorated the walk above the Lower Plaza, causing Lavina to turn her head. When she turned back, she heaved a deep sigh. "I realize you don't know Nelson Doss," she said, remembering what he'd said at the party, "but how about his father? Surely you know Simon."

"I know we're about the same age, Lavina—but no, I can't say that I know him. Or not all that well, anyway."

"Funny, I thought you'd been with his agency at one time."

"No, never."

Was the protest a bit too sudden? Too vehement? Or was she reading into things again? So far she had found herself being pretty open with him, on the one hand confiding, and on the other accepting what he said at face value. It was difficult to do otherwise.

"I understand he's in a nursing home," Bran added. "Had a bad stroke a few months back that left him partially paralyzed."

"So I've heard," Lavina said. "Jae said Hildy knew

Simon fairly well. And that that was the reason she and Henry went over to his agency."

"Your imagination's working overtime there, Lavina," Bran said with a smile. "You think there was something between them, too?"

Lavina laughed. "You're right. So let me stop while I'm ahead."

They spent the better part of the next hour reliving happier moments from their mutual past and filling each other in on the gaps. When they finally rose to part, with Lavina off to FAO Schwarz to meet Tracey and Susanne, and Bran to see his accountant, it seemed as if they had only just arrived at the promenade.

Bran took both her hands and stepped back, holding her at a distance. "You haven't changed all that much, Lavina, you really haven't. And what a shame we never got together sooner."

"That sounds like the ol' Blarney Stone talking, if you ask me," she said with a big smile, reluctantly disengaging her hands from his.

"I've never kissed it in my whole life, Lavina. Nary a once. Cross my heart." Which he did. "And that's no B.S. either, if you'll pardon my Irish."

Lavina threw back her head and laughed. "Bran Slattery, you're too much. And, come to think of it, those are your initials, too."

Bran groaned. "I was hoping you hadn't noticed." This time they both broke out laughing.

When he was on the point of relinquishing her to her family, Bran raised his still blond brows in playful fashion. "And what about that date you owe me, woman?" he said.

"To see the Channel Gardens and tree here at night? Not to mention the meal you reneged on."

Lavina hoisted her bag strap closer to her neck and smiled. "Pick me up at seven forty-five. The Southgate on Seventh and Thirty-first."

Chapter Eleven

➜ ←

Sheena widened the slits in her brown-masked face that were her eyes, straightened her arched back, and dropped unheard to the carpeted floor from atop the mantel of the wooden fireplace. From her new position in front of the clump of artificial logs, she waved her whiplike tail in a slow arc, staring across at the stranger in the heavy old-rose brocade armchair.

"Lavina is nobody's fool," Audra Mateer said, "even if you think I am."

"That very well may be," her visitor said, "but I still don't see what it has to do with me."

"Why do you think I phoned you?"

"I have no idea."

"I wanted to see you privately to try to get you to go to the police."

Her visitor laughed. "And why would I do a foolish thing like that?"

"Because if you don't, I will."

"I see." The visitor looked down and met Sheena's narrowed blue eyes. The Siamese let out a long, low hiss.

"Sheena, stop that, you naughty girl." Audra got up off the sofa. "Shoo." She chased the cat into the small adjoining bedroom with a couple waves of her apron, which was tied around her waist. Then, turning back to the aged, deep blue brocade sofa she had vacated, she straightened a clean but discolored crocheted antimacassar on one of the arms. Satisfied, she padded across the little apartment in stocking feet to the kitchenette. "I'm quite serious, you know," she said to her guest without turning her head.

"And what exactly is it you plan to tell them?" her guest asked as Audra puttered around in the small alcove. "I mean, why should they believe anything *you* might have to say?"

Audra lifted a battered metal percolator off the low gas flame on the stove and brought it over to the linoleum-covered countertop by the sink, where she had laid out a pair of delicate china cups, both in slightly chipped, gold-rimmed saucers. She filled both cups, then set them on a highly polished silver salver alongside a matching sugar bowl and creamer. "Tell them?" she repeated, setting the pot back on the stove. "Why, that you killed Henry Blaine, what else?"

"Is that what you think?"

She turned from the stove and looked across the short distance that separated them. "Please, no games, all right?" She caught a wisp of dyed brown hair in her wrinkled hand, twisted it around a finger, and tucked it in behind her ear.

"And why should I kill Henry?"

"Because of the child." With this simple explanation, she turned back to the counter near the sink, lifted the tray, and brought it into the living room, depositing it on top of a stack of magazines on the oval coffee table. Lemon wax and fresh coffee vied with each other in the dry, heated air of the room.

Audra's guest lifted the cup about six inches off the tray, then with a shaking hand set it back down again in the spillage in the saucer.

"Here, let me get you a napkin," Audra said, returning to the kitchenette.

"So you know—or think you know," her visitor said with an attempt at a wan smile that Audra was unable to see behind her turned back.

"Oh, I know all right," she said. "There's very little that escapes Audra Mateer, let me tell you." She came back with a batch of blue paper napkins, which she dropped into her guest's saucer under the cup.

"Why did you wait all these years to say anything?"

Audra shrugged her narrow, bony shoulders. "I always wanted to give you the benefit of the doubt, I suppose," she said. "Something Henry obviously didn't believe in. But with his death, well, it's all quite out in the open, isn't it? Any doubts I may have had are quite gone."

"*You* seem to think so," her visitor said.

"Answer me something, will you," Audra said, proceeding around the little table and sitting on the sofa to face her visitor. "He was blackmailing you, wasn't he?" When her visitor didn't answer, she went on. "I sort of suspected as much from something he'd said years ago. What I don't understand is why you waited until now to kill him."

"I did *not* kill Henry Blaine," the visitor said, attempting to raise the coffee cup, again with little success.

Audra shrugged. "Have it your way." She lifted the lid of the sugar bowl, and with a liver-spotted hand dumped three spoonfuls of the sweetener into her cup, followed by a splash from the creamer.

"Henry had the same misconception at one point that you probably have now, Audra. And yes, if you want to know, he did try blackmail. I told him he was off his rocker, and he never broached the subject again."

"He just dropped the whole business? Why? Because he didn't have any evidence? That doesn't sound like the Henry I used to know." She shook her head. "He was a better actor than that. Even if he had no proof."

"And you do, I suppose."

"I didn't say I did, and I didn't say I didn't."

"And am I suppose to guess how good an actress *you* are, Audra?"

"No. I was never anything great, as you well know. So whatever I say is for real. We were all pretty close at one time, don't forget. And even if people weren't as suspicious about such things back then as they are today, what with the media coverage and all, the fact remains that I'm not as naive as you'd like to think. The facts speak for themselves."

"And what do these facts say to you, Audra?"

"Don't patronize me, dammit! You know very well what they say—you're in hot water."

"You actually think you can prove what you're hinting at?"

"Laboratories can do marvels nowadays," Audra said, calming down. "Just look what they discovered about that Egyptian mummy a few months back. Incredible."

"Sounds to me like you've been reading too many medical thrillers," her visitor said.

"No, no, this isn't fiction. They could even tell how

many children she—it was a female—had given birth to. And after thousands of years. Medical detectives, that's what they are." She took a big swallow of her coffee, then set the cup down in its saucer with a little clink. "Oh, they'll be able to determine the truth all right, once some- one points them in the right direction."

"Which is where you come in."

"Precisely. Unless, as I said before, you tell them every- thing yourself."

"There's nothing I can do or say to get you to change your mind?"

"I don't know, is there?" she asked, getting up and crossing to the stove to refill her cup.

"Don't you believe in accidents, Audra?" her visitor said from the chair in the room behind her.

"Is that your defense?" Audra asked, turning her head, a scowl on her face. "You'll have to do better than that."

The visitor gathered up the pair of black leather gloves lying on the coffee table alongside the stack of magazines and slipped them on. Then, picking up the coat thrown over the arm of the brocade chair, the figure rose and pro- ceeded across the room to stand behind Audra in the kitchenette. "Accidents can happen to anyone, you know, Audra."

Audra gave a little laugh as she turned back and re- placed the pot on the stove, shutting off the gas. "If people are careless or stupid, I suppose," she said.

"Yes," her guest agreed. "Then especially."

Chapter Twelve
➔ ←

As soon as she set eyes on the little apartment in Stuyvesant Town, Lavina understood why Audra had hesitated inviting her over. Not that it wasn't clean; it was—spotlessly so. Even after having been ransacked. It was the poverty that got to her.

She stood inside the little apartment to the right of the doorway, where the young detective sergeant had directed her to "stay put" after she arrived and identified herself. It was an ideal spot from which to survey the apartment.

The Siamese—Sheena, she now recalled—had deserted the top of the mantel and practically dashed across the room to greet her—or more likely, seek out her female companionship. She recalled Audra's telling her how the cat hated men. The sleek little thing sniffed at her dress Totes, poking her tiny nose into the opening at the top of the boots, first one, then the other. When Lavina stooped down to rub the feline behind her dark brown ears and then scoop her up in her arms, she was enchanted by the deep blue eyes that stared up at her. After a long, drawn-out purr, the cat nestled in the open neck of her partially unzipped jacket.

Audra's body had already been removed before she arrived, and the windows of the apartment were still wide open. The sergeant had explained right off about the open gas jets on the stove and in the oven. The cat had been fortunate enough to have been locked in the bedroom where a window had been left open; they had found her stretched out on the sill. "You're a smart little kitty, you know that?" Lavina whispered to the little head under her chin. The Siamese snuggled closer.

The reality that faced her in the apartment was stark and unalterable. That she had feared for Audra's safety from the outset only added to the nausea she felt in the pit of her stomach. If only she had followed through on her instincts sooner. The big *If.*

The sergeant was busy addressing two other plain-clothesmen over by the kitchenette, just this side of the chalk outline on the floor, part of it traced on the cracked linoleum, part on the threadbare, dusty-rose fringed carpet.

What the ransacking meant, she could only guess. Drawers in the kitchenette were still partially open, as were the ones she could see in the chest through the open bedroom door. The spread and bedding had been thrown back, with books, papers, and magazines everywhere on the floor. She wondered briefly where Audra stored her collection of old radio tapes, the ones she had promised Lavina access to earlier. Those, and her collection of once popular old radio magazines and digests. Probably in the bedroom in an area she couldn't see.

"And tell the lieutenant not to bother," she heard, causing her to look back around to the three detectives who were headed in her direction. "There's nothing he can do here now anyway." The sergeant in charge ushered the other two men out the door past the uniformed policeman standing in the hallway.

"Now, Miss London," he said, closing the door and turning to face her. "It is London, right?"

"Right. Mrs."

"Mrs." He had his notepad and silver ballpoint out, jotting diligently. "Thanks for your patience and cooperation, by the way. Sorry to keep you standing here so long. Can't take the chance of having anything touched until we're finished."

"I understand," Lavina said with a smile.

"Our fingerprint men aren't even here yet." He shook his sandy-colored head, his eyes bloodshot and visibly tired. Late nights, most likely, she surmised. But he was young and probably dating. Ken, she remembered, never got home before midnight when they were courting. Even on weekdays. But then, she hadn't always been in New York to begin with, because of her crazy broadcasting schedule. And even when she was, it was usually only for a day or two at a time before she had to catch a train or plane for another city. "Here today and gone tomorrow," Ken used to say. Audra, she now recalled, had a more colorful expression for her erratic comings and goings: "Like a fart in the wind, that's you, Lavina. All over the place." The long-ago memory made her smile, even under the present circumstances. Letting her eyes wander back to the chalk mark on the floor, she said a little prayer, all the while stroking the orphaned feline.

"Now, what was it you were trying to tell me earlier?" the policeman asked, looking up from his pad. "You said you saw your friend here last night."

"Yes. Well, not here in the apartment, but in the city. I'm from upstate." Lavina went on to fill him in on everything she knew that might be of help, including the recent murder of their former colleague.

"That's quite a story," the sergeant said when she was through. "You want to give me that sheriff's name again."

She gave him Tod Arthur's name and the Boulder area code, even suggesting that the sheriff may already have been in touch with the New York authorities.

"I'll certainly look into it," the policeman said, completing his notation.

"And your name, Sergeant, is . . ."

"Packard, ma'am. Detective Sergeant Vince Packard."

"Sergeant Packard," she repeated, making her own mental notation.

"Any idea why your friend might have wanted to take her life?" he asked, motioning with his streamlined pen in the general direction of the chalk line.

Lavina stared at him, wondering if he had understood her. "Surely you don't think she committed suicide, Sergeant. Not after what I just told you."

"What I think isn't all that important, Mrs. London. But I'm sure you realize we have to check out all possibilities—if only to eliminate them." He stretched across a rough hand and patted the cat's head, only to be met with a muffled hiss.

"She's an ultrafeminist, I'm afraid," Lavina said with a smile. She thought the word she was looking for was misandrist, but wasn't sure. Man-hater.

Packard smiled. "Just between you, me, and little kitty here, no, I don't believe your friend killed herself."

"You've restored my faith in human nature," Lavina

said with a little sigh, then nodding in the direction of the coffee table, added, "I see someone was having coffee." Somehow she couldn't picture Audra using the china just for herself. "A little careless of our murderer, don't you think?"

"Maybe," the sergeant said. "Or maybe just very clever. The lab boys will learn anything there is to learn. There's another one over in the sink ready to be washed." So she had been right about the china. There had been a guest.

The fingerprint detail had arrived during the course of their conversation and was already at work in the living room and kitchenette.

"Audra always used a lot of sugar, if that will help you," Lavina said, surprised by the silly recollection.

"It might at that," Packard said. He made another notation in his pad, then without looking up added, "I'm afraid I'm going to have to ask you to drop over to the station to sign a formal statement, Mrs. London."

"That's all right. I understand. But can it wait until morning?" When the sergeant hesitated, she added, "I have a da— an appointment tonight that's rather important. I'll be at the Southgate until Saturday morning. You can check my driver's license while I'm here." With the cat still in her arm, she shifted her shoulder bag around to the front of her body, unzipped the center partition, and dug a free hand inside to fish around for her wallet. When she found it, she yanked it out and flipped it open adroitly to expose her New York State driver's license. "There," she said, extending it in the policeman's direction. "Now you even know my age." She laughed as Sergeant Packard accepted the sacrificial offering.

The policeman examined the license, jotting again in

his notepad. The smile that had formed remained the whole time. Returning the wallet to her, he said, "Tomorrow morning will be just fine, Mrs. London."

After the fingerprint detail had moved off into the bedroom, he motioned her across to one of the wooden chairs against the wall near the kitchenette. Lavina sat down with a sigh of relief. "You don't know how good that feels." If she had been alone, she would have kicked off her shoes as well.

"You have any idea of what this killer might have been looking for?" Packard asked. He was standing over her now, his arm extended in a sweeping motion in the general direction of the cluttered floor. "He's left quite a mess."

"I wish I did," Lavina said. While she had some ideas of her own, she had no intention of incriminating anyone specific without a little more evidence. She owed them that much, at least. After all, they had once been colleagues, if not actual friends.

"Could I have a look in the bedroom when they're through in there?" she asked, shifting the cat slightly. She was beginning to feel pins and needles in her right arm.

"I don't see why not," Packard said with a shrug.

His trust, she noticed, after the two others left, went only so far, because he was close on her heels when she entered the tiny bedroom.

Lavina spied the tapes right off—or at least the eight-drawer metal cabinet she assumed housed them. She deposited Sheena on the ruffled covers of the single twin bed and proceeded over to examine it. The cat raised her head, watching her with narrowed eyes—then obviously satisfied, lowered her dark brown head and drifted off again.

As she was about to open one of the drawers at random, Lavina suddenly remembered and turned to the policeman, who was standing at the foot of the bed. "May I?" she said, feeling for a moment as if she were back on the streets in the Bronx playing Simon Says with her friends.

"Be my guest. The boys are finished in here."

Lavina slid out the wide top drawer. It was packed neatly with six rows of plastic-cased cassettes, about twenty-five deep, each labeled and numbered in black ink. She dug out three or four at random and examined the titles, then proceeded through the remaining seven drawers, not even knowing what, if anything, she hoped to find.

"Anything missing?" Packard asked behind her as she straightened up and stood staring at the cabinet.

"I have no idea," she said. There were no empty spaces in the rows of filed cassettes. It seemed pretty farfetched to think anyone would have taken any and replaced them with substitutes. Or at least until she remembered the audio clip from *The Shadow* left on Henry Blaine's answering machine. She sighed, wondering self-consciously if the policeman was having second thoughts about the mental capabilities of this nice old lady whose age he must surely have noted on her license.

In the opposite corner of the room by the door, she spotted the filing cabinet, a typical four-drawer affair, dark olive and prewar. Without consulting the sergeant, she went over and with difficulty pulled open the sturdy top drawer. It was crammed from front to back with old magazines and newspapers, each filed by title: *Billboard, Radio*

Mirror, Radioland, Radio News. . . . She pushed it shut and sampled the other three as well. More of the same, in continuing alphabetical order: *Radio Stars, Radio Varieties, Tower Radio, Tune In, Variety.* If there was anything missing, she'd never know.

"I hope I'll be able to have access to these in the future," she said, smiling again, as she pushed closed the bottom drawer and straightened up from her crouch.

"I guess that depends on the disposition of the estate, Mrs. London," the policeman said.

"As far as I know, Audra has no living relatives." Lavina looked over at the cat curled up in a ball against one of the pillows. "Some of her closer friends might know for certain, though."

"Like this Slattery fella you mentioned?"

"Possibly." She checked the time. It was almost seven. She still had to get back to the hotel to bathe and change. The investigation was already altering the plans she had for her short stay in town. She hadn't even called her agent yet; could she subconsciously be holding back on that one?

Outside again in the living room, she gave a final look around. It was then that she noticed it. On the coffee table where the cup and saucer had been before the plainclothesmen had labeled, bagged, and removed them.

She went over and sat down on the edge of one of the brocade armchairs and slid it across the table toward her. She groped inside her open jacket, found her clear-framed glasses on their chain, and slipped them on. It was an eight-page section of newspaper, yellowed but not quite brittle, opened back to page five. The hole left by the scissors was straight and neat, and took up a column in the lower right-hand corner about six inches long. She unfolded the paper back to the front page. It was from the *Chicago Tribune,* Tuesday, June 6, 1950. She dug her wallet out of her handbag. When she found a folded scrap of paper, she took it out and jotted down the information.

She slipped the paper back into the wallet, and the wallet back into her shoulder bag, and then turned to look over her shoulder. Sergeant Packard was at the door speaking with the uniformed policeman outside. She folded the newspaper back the way she had found it, only this time set it on the table with the clipped page five facedown. While anyone watching her might have suspected that she was attempting to conceal evidence, she was personally convinced otherwise. If her own personal investigation belied her intuition, she promised herself to make amends accordingly. As it was, she might be saving the NYPD a lot of unnecessary time and money. After all, it had been Sergeant Packard's passing remark that had alerted her to the possibility in the first place. And she liked Sergeant Packard. He was sharp; they thought a lot alike. Still, to be on the safe side, she preferred to wait and pursue her hunch on her own.

"Well, Mrs. London," Packard said, returning to the living room. "If there's nothing else you need here, I think I'd better lock up. You'll be wanting to get ready for your da— I mean, your appointment." He smiled and she could spell *tease* in every feature of his bright, youthful face. Maybe he was too sharp, she thought, and then, unable to help herself, smiled as well.

After gathering up what looked like an imitation World War Two navy blue pea jacket—it was too new-looking to be real navy surplus—from the back of the sofa, Packard went over to the stove where he checked the gas jets, shrugging into the pea jacket as he did so. Then obviously satisfied, he returned, and with a wave of his hand ushered Lavina ahead of him toward the door.

The actress reached into the outer pocket of her bag for her gloves, then stopped in her tracks, almost causing the sergeant to collide into her. "Oh!"

"What's wrong?"

"Sheena," she said. "We almost forgot Sheena."

Chapter Thirteen

→ ←

Garrett Blaine tugged at the leather of his gloves, one finger at a time, until the gloves were both off, then tossed them aside onto the passenger seat of his Cougar. He extended an open palm to the heater vents testing for signs of hot air.

". . . *with fifteen-mile-an-hour winds, reaching gusts up to thirty miles. Snow is ex—*" He punched the last button on the dashboard radio, switching stations. "The Little Drummer Boy" temporarily replaced the meteorologist until he clicked off the dial and sat back, the seat belt tight across his broad chest. He never thought he'd find the Christmas season depressing. How wrong he'd been. Even the brightly decorated shop windows and twinkling, colorless lights that foliated the young trees along some of the city sidewalks did nothing to perk up his spirits.

So he'd have to wait it out. What choice did he have? And those country hicks would probably take forever before they released the body. Ashes. What else they wanted to examine now, he couldn't imagine. If they didn't know who killed him by this time, they'd never know.

The lawyer was something else again. Him and his probate crap. Legal Stalling 101. Another parasitic shyster out for the almighty buck. It made him sick just thinking about it. The way he'd felt all day, as a matter of fact.

Rho, of course, had started the whole damn thing. She wouldn't even go up to Boulder with him yesterday to claim the body. Didn't even have the decency to stand by him when he needed her. Oh no, that would have been asking too much. "I had nothing to do with him when he was alive, and I want nothing to do with him now." Only because there was nothing coming to her. If his father had been well-off, she would have been there kissing his dead feet. Crocodile tears and all. Probably even in black. Hypocrite.

As it was, they weren't even getting the house and property on the lake—which, he'd learned on Friday, the old man was leaving to some old crony of his. He could have hauled off and killed the old coot right then and there in the men's room when he'd told him. That he had actually gone to the party the last minute on Friday night—after vowing he wouldn't—and sucked up to the old man was enough to make his blood boil. Talk about humiliation.

He lowered the heater fan as soon as he noticed the condensation receding on the windshield, then lowered his window. After straightening his rear-view mirror, he inched out into the street, adjusting his lights from parking to high.

He'd been afraid to face the sheriff yesterday—so what? Who wouldn't have been afraid under the circumstances? What he had done could only be described as stupid. If anyone had seen him at the house Saturday, he would have been worse off than if they'd spotted him at the party on the videotape. And shit, he wasn't even on the damn thing after all his trouble. What did the whole fiasco get him? Nothing. And after the way the old man had laughed about the property, it was hardly likely he'd be getting any of his other assets—whatever they might amount to. God, he could use the money. And in the bargain, he was probably heading the list of suspects in his father's death. The old man still had the last say, even in death.

As he turned at the light to head downtown, he thought again of the hick sheriff and his young sidekick. They had given him a couple of uneasy moments, that was for sure. Maybe he should have reported finding the body in the garage Saturday in the first place. It would have been natural for him to be there. He wouldn't have had to mention the tape. After all, those kids might have seen him and been able to identify him. The truth of the matter—much as he hated to admit it even to himself—was that he'd been afraid. Afraid and stupid. He'd just wanted to get out of there. Now it was too late. To own up now would only make him look bad. Better to leave well enough alone. Or was it? He sighed. Maybe his father and Rho had been right after all—maybe he was wishy-washy.

The dashboard clock said almost 9 P.M. A heck of a time to be meeting anybody, especially when he could have been home in bed. But he had to go through the motions of the bereaved son; how would it look if he didn't? And it was easier coming down here than having her up to the apartment. Especially with Rho around.

She had seemed nice enough the few times he'd met her at the lake after his mother's death. What had surprised him then was how much younger she looked than his father. He wondered if they had ever been lovers. Maybe she was the one he was leaving the property to. Bitch. What right did she have to it? He tightened his grip on the wheel, then just as quickly let it relax. He was projecting again. She was probably just what she seemed, an old friend. She had certainly been pleasant enough on the phone. Why, though, did she insist on seeing him? She could have expressed her condolences on the phone. Was it possible she knew something? Or thought she did? Just as well Rho wouldn't be around.

He sucked in his expanse of stomach and groped for the button to inch back the driver's seat, then caressed his thick full beard in a sweaty hand.

It was almost eleven by the time he got back to the apartment. One of Rho's inevitable notes was propped up against the sugar bowl on the kitchen table: "Some *woman*"—even when she wrote she had to shout—"named London called. Call her if you get in before midnight." Then followed the hotel name and number, and "Don't wake me coming to bed." Good night, Sweet Prince.

London, he knew, too. Another of his father's old cronies. The one still living up on the lake. It was like old home week. People he hardly knew were crawling out of the woodwork to call him. Like long lost friends.

In the den he turned on the TV light and settled himself in the leather lounge chair. When the hotel switchboard put through his call, she answered on the second ring.

"Of course I remember you, Mrs. London," he said.

"Lavina, please," she corrected. He could hear her little laugh. "You sound like the teenager I remember." He could picture her, too. Tall, genteel, full of life. And always with a smile.

"I just wanted to let you know how sorry I was about your father's death."

He was surprised she didn't say "passing." "Thanks, Lavina," he said, finding it difficult to use the Christian name. He stretched his stocking feet across the footrest and wiggled his thick toes. Both heels, he noticed, were fast becoming threadbare.

"Maybe I shouldn't bring it up," Lavina added, "but you know I was there when the police found your father."

"In the garage?"

"Yes. It was all pretty much of a coincidence, actually. A couple of youngsters from the lake told me they had seen someone at the house, so naturally I phoned the sheriff."

"I see." So the kids *had* seen him. And here she was pussyfooting around. What did she want?

"By the way, why didn't you come to his party, Garrett?" Was she trying to trap him? Did she already know?

"Rho wasn't feeling up to it and I didn't want to leave her alone. Dad understood."

"You spoke to him?"

"I phoned." He loosened the tie still around his neck and yanked it down to one side. Was there a hesitation on the other end of the line? "Actually," he quickly amended, "I didn't talk to him directly. I left a message on his machine." Maybe he was being stupid about this whole thing; after what the Patrick woman had said, what did he have to worry about, anyway?

"Did you see Sheriff Arthur yesterday?" Lavina finally asked.

"Yes. I had to identify the body and, of course, make arrangements for the burial."

The sigh at the other end of the line was unmistakable. "There'll be two of those now, I'm afraid."

"What do you mean?"

"Do you know Audra Mateer?" Lavina asked him.

"I don't think so. Another friend of my dad's?"

"Yes."

"What about her?"

"They found her body earlier today in her apartment in Stuyvesant Town."

"I'm sorry to hear that. She wasn't murdered, too, was she?"

"I'm afraid it looks that way, yes," Lavina said, her voice forlorn. Lavina was a lot like his mother had been. For a brief moment, he had the crazy impulse to unburden himself, tell her everything. The feeling passed as quickly as it had come.

"I was just talking to another friend of yours," he said. "Just saw her downtown."

"Oh, and who's that?"

"Miss Patrick."

There was no doubting the silence at the other end of the line. "Jae?" she finally asked.

"Right. She was very nice, but I really don't remember her all that well. I only met her a couple of times at the house after Mom died."

Another brief silence at the other end. "You don't mean at Hemlock Lake."

"Yes. I was there only a few times myself, so it's not something I'm likely to forget."

"No, of course not. And where did you meet her to-night?"

"We had a few drinks down in Chelsea. A place on Seventeenth."

"She was a very close friend of your father's at one time," the actress said, quickly adding, "before he met your mother." He couldn't tell whether she was hinting at something or trying to whitewash one of the old man's scandalous escapades. Not that he cared.

"Tell me, Lavina," he said, "Do you know people by the name of Hesson?" He lifted a slip of paper out of his shirt pocket and unfolded it with his free hand. "Violet and Cole?"

"Yes, certainly. They used to have a very popular radio luncheon talk show way back when. Why do you ask?"

Garrett hesitated. Again, the thought of opening up to her crossed his mind. Maybe if she had been physically present, he might have. Instead what he was faced with was the glossy eight-by-ten of Rho staring, unsmiling, from her frame on the TV set.

"Did Jae—Miss Patrick—mention them?" Lavina asked when he didn't respond.

"No, no." He hesitated. "Just something I remembered my father saying, that's all." It wasn't a lie—or at least not completely.

"You sound like you're keeping something back, Garrett," Lavina said. She was even beginning to sound like his mother. "I wish you'd tell me; it might be important. As much as I hate to say it, Audra refused to tell me something yesterday, too, and now she'll never have the chance. I can't—"

Garrett cut her short with a little laugh. "Don't worry,

Mrs. Lon— Lavina. It's nothing like that. What with all these people from the past suddenly appearing and all, their names just naturally came to mind. My father . . . well, he never spoke about them very openly. And whenever he did, it always seemed to be in innuendoes. Not that I understood at the time. I was only a kid." He stuck the slip of paper back into his pocket. "Were they at the party?"

"Oh, yes. And I was hoping to see them again today myself, but I couldn't reach them the one chance I had to phone after I left Audra's apartment."

"You were at her apartment?"

"Yes."

"You didn't find her body, too, did you?" The woman certainly seemed to be in the thick of things.

"No, thank heavens," Lavina said. "The police were there when I arrived." He thought he detected a shiver in her voice. He wavered again, wanting desperately to trust her. To trust somebody.

"It must have been hard on you," he said. "First my father, then Audra." He paused, then added, "You're not afraid for yourself, are you?"

It was Lavina's turn to laugh. "I'm hardly a threat to anybody, Garrett," she said. "Henry and Audra apparently were."

"Are you alone at your hotel or did somebody come down with you?"

"Oh, I'm alone. But don't you start worrying about me. You've got enough on your mind. I'll be fine."

"That's probably what your friend Audra thought, too," he added.

"So you don't remember anything your father actually

said about the Hessons," she added, steering away from the topic.

"Not really," he said, trying to remember. "Though I seem to recall mention of their little boy."

A third silence at the other end. Dammit, he wished they had been face to face. What was her antenna picking up from his seemingly harmless tidbits?

"I didn't know they had a little boy," Lavina finally said, her voice hushed now, almost solemn. Maybe Miss Patrick had been right after all. And his father.

"Maybe I misunderstood," he said, drawing up his legs to a knee bend.

"Maybe," she repeated. Then, "Anything else?"

"Not really, no." Nothing his father had mentioned, and he wasn't ready yet to divulge anything else, no matter how believable it was all beginning to appear. "The only thing I do recall—and this will probably sound crazy— was his saying that kidney transplants were a bit too late."

"Kidney transplants?"

"That's what he said. And that they were too late."

FRIDAY, DECEMBER 22

Chapter Fourteen

➔ ✦

"What you're asking me to do, Gran, is be your gofer."

"Yes, dear, I know. Do you mind awfully?" Lavina set her huge red shopping bag down on the steel-slatted escalator step rising up ahead of her.

"Mind! Of course not. I thought you'd never ask me to help you on one of your cases." Susanne stood alongside her grandmother on the same step. "I thought you didn't trust me or something."

"Don't be silly. I just don't want to chance your getting hurt, that's all." She turned and gave the girl a scolding glance. "And this is not, as you like to put it, one of my cases."

Together they stepped off the escalator on the fifth floor—TOTS—and U-turned right to proceed up the next bank of moving stairs to the sixth floor. This section was old, with wood-ribbed threadboards. Lavina stared down at them in amazement as she always did. They had to be the same ones she'd ridden as a girl, ones that would probably outlast the newer steel version. Just another example of the fact that they didn't make things like they used to.

"How come you want *me* to do it, Gran?" Susanne asked as the escalator rattled upward.

"Who do I know who's more qualified to do research than you, may I ask? Aren't you in your junior year at Boston College?" It had taken her a while to sort out B.C. from B.U. but she had finally gotten them straight.

"I knew that much when I was still at the Mount," Susanne said with a smile.

Mount St. Ursula. Yes, of course. The Ursulines would certainly have prepared her granddaughter well in advance, as they had her and Tracey before her. "All the more reason," she added.

"I don't know, Gran. Somehow you always manage to have the answer to everything." The girl tossed her short-cropped blond head and laughed as she stepped off the escalator into the bath world of the sixth floor. Her trim athletic figure was hidden now beneath a burnt-sienna leather jacket, her shapely muscular swimmer's calves under matching full-length boots.

Lavina smiled alongside her. "Stick with your old grandmother and it will wear off on you," she said. "If it hasn't already."

"Do you think I'll be able to find both those things at the Forty-second Street library?" Susanne asked, switching the cords of her shopping bag from one reddened palm to the other.

"I don't see why not. Just ask the librarian for the newspaper directory. *Ayer's,* I think it's called. You'll probably have to view the thing on microfilm or microfiche—whatever they use. But I do want a copy of the article or news item after you find it."

"Nothing less."

"The librarian will probably have to photostat it for you."

"Yes, Gran, I know." Susanne smiled.

"You sure you'll remember the date? I didn't see you write it down."

"Gran, please! This is your granddaughter you're talking to, remember. Chip off the old block and all that." The girl closed her eyes in mock rumination. "I see the *Chicago Tribune,* June 6, 1950. Lower right-hand column, page five." She opened her eyes, pale blue like her grandmother's. "Okay?"

"A veritable Archie Goodwin."

"Gumshoe and legman *extraordinaire.*"

"I guess that would have to be *legperson* nowadays, don't you think, dear? To be politically correct and all that?"

They both laughed and stepped off the escalator at the top of the rise, then turned once more to continue their mechanical climb.

"How's your new addition doing, by the way?" Lavina asked.

Susanne gave a little laugh. "Father loves the cat—no two ways about it. Unfortunately it's a one-sided romance. Sheena keeps hissing and spitting at him." She laughed again. "And all Mom does is keep repeating, 'What's wrong with that woman, anyway, bringing a cat up here?' " She shook her head and sighed. "As it is now, the poor thing practically lives in my room. What will happen when I have to go back to college, I don't know."

"You'll just have to see that she and your father come to terms," Lavina said. "She obviously had a bad time of it somewhere along the line with a male."

"And how am I supposed to do that, pray tell?"

"How about a psychiatrist?" Lavina said with a grin.

"A pussychiatrist, you mean," Susanne said, enjoying her own play on words and setting her grandmother to laughing.

On the eighth floor they proceeded to glassware where Susanne made a final purchase, setting it in the shopping bag she handed over to her grandmother. "You're sure you don't want me to take the bags, Gran? You're going to be awfully loaded down with the two of them."

"No, no, they'll be fine. You couldn't manage with them at the library anyway." Lavina grabbed up the second bag and sampled them together for balance. "I have one more stop here at the bookstore, and then I'll drop everything back at the hotel."

"And then you're going to see more of those people from the party, aren't you?" A pained expression shot across the girl's usually happy face.

"The Hessons, yes. But not until after I've seen my agent." The die was cast.

"Can't I go with you?"

"No, you've got research to do. Important research that might just break this ca— solve this whole mystery."

Susanne managed a faint smile. "At least promise me you'll be careful."

"I promise."

With that they kissed, Lavina dismissing the girl with a loving pat on her rear. "Now scoot." It reminded her of all the times she had sent Susanne off to grammar school when she was taking care of her.

Lavina gathered up the two shopping bags and headed off through the store in the direction of Seventh Avenue.

Audra's death still weighed on her conscience, as it had all night after Bran brought her back to the hotel. When the initial shock had worn off and the realization set in. She had finally fallen asleep saying a rosary, not only for Audra, but for whoever had taken the two lives as well. There was no doubt in her mind which one needed prayers more. Finding that murderer was more important now than ever. It was no longer a question of silencing wagging tongues intent on sullying her name and reputation; that was unimportant. A dear, if almost forgotten, colleague had been cruelly and wrongly killed. And who was to say there wouldn't be another murder? Whoever was responsible had to be stopped before he or she found it necessary to strike again.

After pausing and lowering the bags to catch her breath, she gathered them up again and proceeded through the store. What could have been so frightening that it drove someone to commit two murders? It had to be fear of some type, of that she was convinced. Wasn't that what Audra had been hinting at Wednesday night? Those ghosts from the past again. From her own past, too, come to think of it. It was frightening even to her.

The sight of the glass-enclosed book department up ahead jolted her back to her present mission. Bookstores never failed to tantalize her. To think that her own memoirs might one day be on the shelves to lure buyers almost sent shivers up her spine.

Inside, she gave the open area a wide sweep of her eyes until she spotted the mystery section. She headed over and set down the bags, then slipped on her reading glasses. She chose copies of two hard-to-find David Handler paperback originals for Susanne's stocking—the same big one she had crocheted for her first Christmas—the most recent Jeremiah Healy for the girl's present heartthrob, and the new Bill Crider hardcover for Sean O'Kirk. Winnie wasn't a reader at all, so she didn't rate an additional goodie. Tracey's taste in reading was limited to the bestsellers list, which, as far as Lavina was concerned, was very limited. When she spotted Lillian Jackson Braun's *The Cat Who . . .* series, she grabbed up the four available titles for Damian, hoping they would tide her son-in-law over during the period of adjustment that obviously lay ahead for Sheena.

At the cash desk, she deposited her selections on the counter, informing the cashier she had more browsing to do, then returned to pick up the two shopping bags and proceeded to the health and medicine section. If Hamilton Dane had been able to tell her anything about the history of kidney transplants when she phoned him this morning, Susanne might have been saved the added research. As it was, the Boulder M.D. had merely suggested that she come in for a checkup after the holidays.

She flipped through a few medical titles, searching the index in each for kidneys and transplants. All she came up with was a list of diseases and symptoms. Under other circumstances she might have taken time out to read a few of the more interesting entries. Satisfied that they held nothing that would be of help, she headed back toward the cashier.

She spotted a popular old tome on sale near the counter. And tome it was. She remembered when it first came out. Its title was simply *Chronicle of the 20th Century*. No wonder it was so mammoth.

She set down her bags again and opened a copy at random to four different sections. In layout it seemed to be a monthly reportage of news events, in this case from 1900 through 1986. The brief historical facts were arranged to read like newspaper articles. While it was ridiculous to think she'd find anything, she turned to the entry for June 1950. A careful scanning of the two facing pages proved her right. Nothing.

In the left-hand column was an additional listing of news events for each day of that particular month. After noting nothing at all listed for the sixth, she went back to the top and let her long, slender index finger travel down the narrow column. Her finger passed it the first time and had to retrace its step to the point where her eyes had stopped— (June) 17, Chicago: Richard G. Laoler performs first human kidney transplant.

She looked up and stared at the wall facing her. The seventeenth of June had been too late. What did it all mean?

Lavina surprised herself by actually making it to the IRT by one o'clock. She hoisted the strap of her shoulder bag over her head so that it looked more like an auto seat belt than anything else, took out her paperback, and grasped the bag firmly in her lap. She was no stranger to the New York subway system, and had no intention of becoming one of its victims.

With the police report out of the way earlier in the day, she had time to meet Susanne for breakfast before Macy's opened. Her earlier toasted English muffin and coffee after the seven-o'clock mass at Saint Francis just about tided her over.

She turned now and looked up from her reading as the

sunlight streaked its way across the subway car through
grimy windows. The train nosed its way up out of the hole
in the ground and became elevated. Lavina never remembered exactly where it was that Manhattan suddenly became the Bronx, especially here on the Broadway line. And
while she had never particularly cared for the New York
subway—even back in its cleaner and more efficient
days—it was the only sensible way of reaching Riverdale
short of driving, which, of course, she had no intention of
doing once she was made aware of the newly predicted
snowfall. It would be problem enough trying to get back
upstate tomorrow.

At West 231st Street, she alighted and made her way
down the long flight of ancient steps to street level. On the
corner of 231st and Broadway, she hailed a cab. The bar
names, she noticed when they were under way, were still
predominantly Irish, as she remembered them. She wondered if the neighborhood was the same. She made a mental note to ask Bran the next time she saw him. Later that
night, she hoped.

The route up to the Henry Hudson Parkway was by
way of steep, curving roads, most of them still covered
with packed snow. They passed two stalled buses on their
way, their spinning tires spitting up sprays of dirty slush.
They were on the far side of the parkway in less than ten
minutes, and she was in the lobby of the Hessons' co-op a
minute later. With the unneeded assistance of a young uniformed doorman who had obviously started his holiday
celebrating early, she announced her arrival on the lobby
intercom, proceeded into the elevator and up to the elev-
enth floor.

The green carpet in the long windowless corridor was

like sponge under her rubber-soled feet. Spotting an open apartment door down to her left, she headed down, unzipping her jacket on the way.

"Come in, Lavina," she heard from inside when she knocked on the opened door. "And close the door after you."

Lavina entered, pushing the door shut behind her, then turned to find herself confronting the heavily made-up face of Violet Hesson, her girdled figure in near pain under a tight kelly green dress. She was wiping her ringed hand on a paper towel.

The exchange between the two women was warm and, to Lavina, somewhat surprising, remembering, as she did, a more elusive and reserved Violet. The woman took her coat and hung it on a silk-wrapped hanger in the hall closet, directing her to take off her boots and leave them in the hallway, which Lavina proceeded to do. She stood them upright on the transparent vinyl runner that covered the off-white carpet.

"Where's Cole?" Lavina asked, taking a seat in the middle of a four-piece black sectional that took up the better part of two adjoining living room walls. A circular glass-topped table on a brass base sat in the crook of the inner curve. Lavina lifted off her shoulder bag and set in on the rug under the table.

"Out walking the dog."

"I didn't know you had a dog."

"Yes," Violet sighed, eyeing the expanse of white rug. "He's good company for Cole." Lavina thought she was going to add more, but she didn't.

"As long as you insisted on the phone on not having

lunch," Violet said, "you'll at least have some coffee, I hope."

"Yes, that will be fine," Lavina said, watching the woman as she moved off into the kitchen, paper towel still in hand. In high heels no less. Unlike Jae Patrick, she didn't carry her age at all well, in spite of all her blatant ploys. The shoe-black Dutch haircut, for one thing, was far too youthful, and the makeup something off a palette. The last time she had seen the Hessons before Friday was back in the '50s after their talk show ended—back when Violet was hosting her own interview show mornings from New York. She couldn't recall what Cole had been doing at the time.

"Vi . . . ?" Lavina prompted from the living room.

"Yes, Lavina?" This from the other room amid the clatter of cups and silverware.

"What was it Cole did after your luncheon show ended?"

There was a hesitation from the other room. "When, Lavina?"

"Back in the '50s when you had your interview show."

"Oh. Well, after we came back here from Chicago, he decided to try his hand at writing—something he'd always wanted to do."

"For the soaps?"

"Lord, no. For some of the detective shows that were so popular back then. Not stories . . . those true detective things. I think one of them was called *True Detective Magazine*."

Lavina remembered the genre well. Not that it had ever particularly interested her—it hadn't, no more than it did now in her reading.

"After that," Violet continued, "he went into commercials."

"Writing them?" She undid the buttons of her white cardigan.

"No. Broadcasting. Especially when they needed different voices. He was always good with impressions, doing animals and such. Remember?"

"Yes." How could she have forgotten? That was probably where Cole had made his fortune . . . all those commercials.

"That was pretty much it until we retired," Violet added, returning through the dining room door, a ceramic tray in her hands. She set it down on what was more a cocktail than a coffee table and, still standing, filled the two Limoges cups from a matching coffee server. "There, now," she said, taking her seat alongside Lavina and picking up her small white napkin, which she snapped open with a flick of her wrist. "I seem to recall your liking these brown and white cakes, so I picked some up at the bakery this morning."

"Yes," Lavina said with a smile, picking up one of the flattish, round, chocolate and vanilla frosted cakes she vaguely remembered as duchess cakes. "I haven't seen them in years."

"You know, you could have knocked me down with a feather when you phoned and told me about Audra," Violet said, tipping cream into her coffee.

The cliché was as good as any, Lavina decided, recalling her own reaction when the uniformed policeman at Audra's apartment had informed her of the woman's death. The tiny apartment flashed unbidden across her mind. She saw the highly polished old silver service and the chipped old china. The woman's best for the person who was probably her murderer. A vast difference from Violet's Limoges coffee set.

". . . and all so senseless," Violet was saying as Lavina returned from her reverie to the painted doll sitting straight-backed at her side, cup and saucer in hand, her right pinky crooked out as she grasped the thin handle of the cup with three fingers. "Why would anyone want to kill a harmless old thing like that?"

Not harmless to someone, certainly, Lavina wanted to say. "I was hoping maybe you or Cole might know," she said instead, just to see if it would elicit a reaction.

"I'm afraid not," Violet said, more controlled than she would have expected. "Until the party, we hadn't seen Audra in over twenty years."

"What a shame," Lavina said in all honesty. "I got the impression she was pretty lonely. Outside of Bran Slattery, I don't know anyone who saw her with any degree of regularity."

"How about Will Argon?"

Lavina thought again about the ex-announcer and his somewhat bitter recriminations. Against whom had they really been directed? Himself more than anybody, probably. For not having aimed high enough. "If you don't try, you have no one to blame but yourself," her father had told her. She never forgot it. No matter how old she got, the rule always seemed to apply, with the prospect of her memoirs the most recent case in point.

Lavina shook her head. "Audra said they hadn't been in touch either." She glanced across the large L-shaped room to the corner opposite the dining room. The undressed metal of the aluminum tree shimmered in the rays of sun that streaked through the partially open blinds. Audra hadn't even had a tree, she realized now for the first time. Probably couldn't even afford one. Unless, of course, it was because of Sheena. She smiled to herself as she pictured the natural, eight-foot fir that adorned the Halliday household every Christmas. The cat who . . . indeed.

"Bran is the executor, I know," Lavina said. "Not that she has anything worth worrying about, poor thing."

"How do you know that? He tell you?"

"Yes. Not that he's ever seen the will."

"So he says."

While she didn't particularly care for the insinuation conveyed by the remark, Lavina let it pass. No sense having Violet get the wrong idea if she suddenly started defending the handsome Irish bachelor. That he had never married she finally ascertained before they left the promenade Thursday afternoon.

"What happened in Chicago, by the way?" she asked abruptly, fully aware that the loaded question was nothing more than a disguised form of retaliation for Violet's flippant remark. She had no reason whatsoever, of course, to connect the Hessons with anything untoward in Chicago. Not at this stage, anyway. If Violet thought her a little crazy, she could hardly blame her.

The sudden clatter of china alongside her, however, told her otherwise. The question had struck a nerve. Her only regret was that she hadn't had a chance to read the article from the *Tribune,* which might have given her some leverage.

"What do you mean, what happened in Chicago?"

If she had actually had the copy of the article in her bag, she could have taken it out slowly, unfolded it—whatever it was—and waited patiently, watching the woman squirm. Then she could have begun to read it aloud: "Chicago, June 6, 1950 . . ." Instead, she just smiled to herself at the imagined theatrics.

"You said you were in Chicago after your luncheon show ended," Lavina continued, trying desperately to leave it open-ended, to give the woman the impression she knew something she didn't, maybe even lead her to fill in the gaps.

Instead, Violet took a deep breath, regaining her composure. "Yes, that's right," she said, raising her coffee to take a sip. "Cole and I moved back there for a while. We had a few acting jobs in between—at WMAQ primarily. Nothing big, just enough to tide us over before we came back to New York." She broke off a piece of the duchess cake. "It was only temporary. As a matter of fact, I almost forgot about it. Which, I suppose, is why I didn't mention it." She gave a little laugh and bit into the vanilla frosted section of cake.

"When was that?" Lavina asked, still determined. "When you were in Chicago, I mean."

Violet shrugged, running her tongue across her upper teeth. "In the '50s."

"Yes, I know. But when in the '50s? Right after the luncheon show? In 1950?"

The bright green shoulders went up again. "I suppose so. I think we went right back home after the show was canceled. We were both originally from the Chicago area, you know. And Mama was still living there at the time."

"Your show ended its run in June, didn't it?"

"June or July, thereabouts. It's all so long ago; who even remembers?" She paused, then added, "Why do you ask?

You certainly don't want anything as dull as that for your book." She let out a hearty laugh this time.

Lavina just smiled. "Why *did* they cancel your talk show, Vi? I was always under the impression that it was fairly successful."

"Who knows, Lavina? Sponsors are as fickle as anyone else, I suppose. On the surface they claimed the show was poorly conceived from the outset and wasn't getting the audience response they'd hoped for. We were hardly in a position to argue. After all, we were both only in our early twenties at the time, don't forget."

It was hard to believe that it had all been almost forty years ago. Who could remember, indeed.

Cole Hesson was at the door and his wife up on her feet with a big smile before Lavina could pursue the subject further. The Irish setter was around the couch and at the stranger's knees before his master could undo the leash. Unabashed, Lavina lavished her usual affection on the canine, rubbing his ears, neck, and chest.

"He'll let you do that all day if you let him, Lavina," Cole said from the open closet where he was hanging up his outerwear. "And how's my favorite actress, anyway?" he added, striding across the short distance to the couch. He bent down and planted a kiss on the cheek that she extended up in his direction.

Lavina laughed good-naturedly. "Still acting up," she said, patting the couch cushion on her left for him to sit down. "Just not getting paid for it."

"What about that book of yours I keep hearing about?" Cole asked, unfastening the dog's leash from the rhinestone collar and taking the proffered seat next to his old colleague. "Oodles of dough there, I bet."

Lavina laughed. "If you're Mary Margaret McBride, maybe," she said, remembering the more famous woman's earlier autobiography, *Out of the Air.* A definite must re-read, if she could lay her hands on a copy.

"Nonsense, it's a sure nostalgia piece. People will eat it up."

"I should make you my publicist."

"Fifteen percent will be just fine."

Lavina laughed again. "I just left my agent, as a matter of fact. I've been running around all morning."

"What do they want?" Cole asked. "An outline?"

"Either that or a few sample chapters. Preferably both."

"Or the finished product," Cole added with a laugh.

"That, best of all," Lavina said, wondering how she'd ever be able to steer the conversation back to Chicago and 1950.

"Will you have a collaborator, Lavina?" Violet asked.

The idea of a collaborator had never crossed her mind. Nor had it even come up. "If I can't handle it on my own, Vi, there'll be no book. Any editing they want to do later is up to them, but I'd have to work alone at my own pace." Visions of another type of ghost made her smile.

"And you'll do it, too, by golly," Cole said.

"I hope you're right."

"I love that gray hair, by the way," Cole said, nodding at what she still, after all these years, liked to refer to as her feathercut, much to the amusement of her stylist. "Makes you look like you're still into acting."

"You're as bad as Bran Slattery with your compliments," she said, smacking him on the knee.

"Are you doing any acting at all these days?" he asked,

reaching in his dress-shirt pocket for a cigarette. "Mind?" He held up the almost full pack of Salems.

"Not at all."

He stuck a cigarette in between his thin, cracked lips, then reached across the table and pulled a round crystal ashtray toward him across the thick glass.

"Wait, I'll get you an ashtray from the kitchen," his wife interposed as she rose and scurried off in the direction of the other room.

Cole lowered his head, like a child who had just been scolded in public.

"As for the acting," Lavina said, coming to the rescue, "no, I'm afraid not. Not since I gave up my short-lived fling with TV back in the '60s."

"That's too bad," he said, his head up again. "That's a lot of talent going to waste."

Lavina smiled. "I keep active," she said as she watched Violet return from the kitchen with a kidney-shaped plastic ashtray which she set down on the table, returning the other to its original spot near the artificial floral piece in its white ceramic planter.

"How come you never went to Hollywood like so many other radio actors, Lavina?" Cole asked when his cigarette was lit and his wife seated again. "Agnes Moorehead made it. So did Don Ameche, John Hodiak, Orson Wells . . . plenty of them. And look at Ameche, still working. Terrific!"

It was probably the question people asked her most frequently, which is why it now surprised her coming from someone like Cole Hesson—someone who, like herself, cut his teeth on radio.

She shrugged. "I loved radio too much to give it up, I

suppose. Which is pretty much the reason I never cared for
television either. For one thing, I always enjoyed the live
audiences radio used to have. Remember?"

"Sure do. And what about those long lines waiting outside the studios morning, noon, and night?"

Lavina laughed. "They were worse than the lines for
sugar and nylons during World War Two."

"I bet you'd like stage work, Lavina. The theater, I
mean."

"I know I would, though it's a little late to start thinking about it now." Not that she hadn't in the past, of
course, because she had—many times. There had even
been talk for a time not too long ago of starting up a community theater in Boulder, but nothing had ever come of
it.

Cole lowered his head again and this time shook it
slowly. "It's hard to believe this latest news about Audra,
isn't it? Henry's death was bad enough."

Lavina nodded. "Vi and I were just discussing it before
you came in."

"The police have any idea who killed her?"

"No, not that I know. Whoever it was, though, was
someone she knew very well." She turned and looked at
Violet. "She seemed to have been having coffee with her
murderer."

"Oh, my God—" Violet suddenly seemed on the verge
of passing out, her eyes closed, her body gyrating clock-
wise.

Lavina grabbed the hand closest to her and started rubbing it vigorously to keep the circulation flowing. "Are
you all right, Vi?" Then, over her shoulder, to Cole: "Get
her some water."

Cole almost tripped over the reclining setter as he turned and ran out to the kitchen. The dog jumped up and followed closely at his heels.

By the time he returned, his wife had come around and was patting Lavina's hand with her own. "I'm fine," she said with a wan smile. "It was just picturing poor Audra there. . . ." She gave a little shiver and took the glass her husband extended to her across their guest. With a pair of shaky hands, she took a deep swallow.

"Maybe I should call Dr. Walling," Cole said, checking his watch.

Violet shook her head. "No, dear, I'll be fine."

Lavina straightened her cardigan and sat back again in her seat on the couch. "Are you sure you're up to talking about this, Vi, or should we change the subject?"

"I'm fine. Really. And I'd like to know what happened."

From her other side, Cole touched Lavina lightly on the arm. "How can they be sure she knew her murderer, Lavina?" he asked. "She didn't leave a dying message or anything, did she?" Was that a note of anxiety she detected or just her imagination?

"Hardly anything so dramatic," she answered with a smile. "It's my own deduction, more than anything else. The police haven't said anything on the subject."

"But why? Just because of the coffee?"

Lavina nodded. "And her good china," she said, choosing the adjective advisedly.

"Couldn't someone else have come in and killed her after her guest left?" Violet said.

"Right," Cole agreed.

"Anything's possible, I suppose," Lavina conceded.

Why did the two of them seem so eager to involve a hypothetical second visitor to Audra's apartment, she wondered. "But if so, why didn't Audra clean the cups and things?"

"Maybe she just didn't get to it right away, that's all," Violet suggested.

"Audra was meticulous, Vi. I just can't picture her leaving dirty dishes around for any length of time. Except for the fact that the apartment had been ransacked, it was immaculate." And she still wasn't completely satisfied with that ransacking business either—anymore than she had been with the copy of the *Chicago Tribune*.

"Who do you suppose was with her?" Cole asked. "Not anyone we know, certainly. And why ransack the place? You said yourself that she didn't have anything of value to leave to anybody."

"If we knew that, we'd have it made, wouldn't we?" Lavina said, stealing a glance at her watch.

"I still can't believe she was killed by someone she knew, Lavina," Violet said. "What reason would they have had?"

"The same reason he or she had for killing Henry, I suppose."

"You think the deaths are related?" Cole asked, stubbing out the cigarette that had all but burned out in the plastic ashtray.

"I think so." Lavina waited for a reaction—then when there was none, added, "Audra knew something that someone was afraid she'd tell."

"What did she tell *you*, Lavina?" Cole asked, the note of anxiety in his voice again.

"Actually she didn't tell me anything. She just hinted

that she knew something. Unfortunately she wasn't willing to share it with me."

The sighs of relief were clearly audible on both sides of her. Under the circumstances they sounded downright tactless.

"But I do have a lead," Lavina added, unwilling to let them completely off the hook.

"A lead?" Cole again.

"Yes."

"Like what?"

"I'd rather not say. Not right now, anyway—not until I check it out and see if it holds water." She was probably mixing metaphors, but at that point she didn't particularly care.

"And after that, what?" Cole asked.

"Well, if I think it means anything," Lavina said, "I'll pass it along to the authorities . . . to Detective Sergeant Packard." The personal note somehow added to the official tone she wanted to convey.

"Yes, I suppose you'd have to," Cole agreed.

Lavina reached down to the setter, who was sprawled out at their feet and stroked his silky brownish-red head. "You know, it's a shame the two of you never had any children," she said, looking back up. The remark was the upshot of a long personal debate she'd had with herself ever since Garrett had put the notion into her head. That it might have been callous, she had no doubt. On the other hand, it was the one sure way she had of getting an honest, on the spot reaction in the event that the Blaine rumor had been correct. The look that Cole shot past her now in the direction of his wife told her everything she wanted to know on that score. Henry Blaine's remark years ago in the presence of his young son had been right on the mark.

"How about more coffee, Lavina?" Violet asked, taking the tack Lavina probably would have taken herself.

The three of them spent the next hour and a half reminiscing about old times, Lavina's only wish being that it had been under less onerous circumstances. More than once she could feel the tension as either or both of them measured their words before speaking.

The sun at the window made an early departure somewhere around three thirty, prompting Violet to get up and light a few lamps. "How about a nice cold buffet, Lavina?" she said when she sat down again. "Nothing fancy. Potluck."

Lavina begged off, using the impending inclement weather as her excuse. "I'd really like to start back before it starts." If the truth be known, she was more than a bit leery of the Riverdale roads.

As it turned out, the taxi ride downhill was more nerve-racking than the earlier one. It put Lavina in mind of her youthful sledding days on Snake Hill in the East Bronx. She supposed all kids had a Snake Hill of one sort or another where they did their daredevil sledding away from the watchful eyes of their mom and dad. Theirs—hers and her brothers'—leveled off right smack in the middle of 188th Street and two-way traffic. Every time she thought of it now, it gave her goose pimples. Ah, the innocence of youth. And thank God for guardian angels.

Once they reached Broadway, she heaved a deep sigh and sat back in the soft leather seat. She decided on the spur of the moment to continue the ride all the way back into Manhattan, in spite of the ominous, if majestic, pewter sky that hovered overhead, shrouding the borough below. It both frightened and awed her, something only God in His creation was able to do.

The ride south under the elevated only added to the darkness that crept into the cab. Reading was out of the question; she could barely make out the shoulder bag alongside her. She turned, instead, and looked out the window.

The sidewalks were as crowded as they had been downtown earlier. A line of Christmas trees leaned precariously against a taut stretch of rope strung up along the sidewalk between two lampposts. While the streetlights themselves had not yet been turned on for the night, bare bulbs dangling at set intervals along the supporting rope did their best to light up the outdoor tree market and the seasonal hawkers that stood about stamping their feet or blowing on their bare hands against the cold. It reminded her that her own potted tree was still out behind the house on the lake waiting for her. Something else she had to do when she got home.

She spotted the first flurries against the background of the fluorescent lighting inside a passing supermarket. Even at that distance, they looked big and wet and eager to smother the city in their soft, crystalline beauty. A symphony in white come down from heaven to lull man's pain. Peace on earth, good will to men.

She turned and stared past the driver's head through the windshield. Somehow that longed-for peace had been shattered, first by Henry's murder, then by Audra's. Good will—on somebody's part at least—was sorely lacking. The thought would have been difficult anytime, but all the more so during Advent, that season before Christmas otherwise so full of hope and anticipation.

She closed her eyes. What about today's visit? What had she learned? Besides the obvious fear that for some reason still gripped the Hessons, it was hard to say. They had both protested just a bit too strongly at the suggestion of having seen Audra Mateer either before or since Henry's party. Why? There had to be a reason. What Lavina couldn't figure out was exactly how serious that reason might be. Deep down she was afraid she really didn't want to know.

Chapter Fifteen

➔ ⬅

Garrett Blaine rubbed a sweaty palm over the pebbly vinyl armrest of the chair, his eyes darting back and forth between the aluminum and Lucite fixtures of the roomy reception area and the pinch-waisted secretary intent on her spiral steno pad as she typed away at warp speed. She looked about thirty. Some guys got all the breaks—and then some. How do you end up nursing a bottle, he wondered, when there's so much else within reach? Now if this had been his agency . . .

He jerked his head over to the door as he caught its movement out of the corner of his eye. A not-so-boyish mail boy—they probably had a fancier name for them nowadays but he didn't know what it was—sauntered in and dumped a batch of envelopes in the incoming rack on the secretary's desk.

"Thank you, Bobby," she oozed without removing her eyes from her copy.

"My pleasure, Jane," Bobby said with a less than covert glance in the direction of her cleavage. *Double your pleasure . . . ,* as the commercial said.

As the mailclerk bounced back across the carpeted area and out into the corridor, Garrett stared again at the name on the pebble-glass upper portion of the door: SIMON DOSS & SON, ASSOCIATES, INC. He shook his head. It could never have been Henry Blaine and Son by *any* stretch of the imagination, no matter what the business. Even when they were younger. He had never really been *son* in his father's eyes.

"Yes, sir," Jane said in response to the intercom buzzer that suddenly sounded on her desk. She still had one hand on the IBM keyboard while the other fingered a switch on the desk machine. At the end of a few moments of garble from the box, she said, "You can go in now, Mr. Blaine." The wide smile caught him by surprise; maybe the boss's voice did something for her hormones.

It would have been nice if she had opened the inner door for him and announced him like they did in the movies, but she didn't. Dream on, Blaine.

"You really need all that desk space, Doss?" Garrett asked as he entered the large, bright office and closed the heavy wood door behind him.

Nelson Doss was seated behind a long, uncluttered desk, his leather chair back extending a good eight inches up beyond his curly, burnt-red hair. He was poring over a sheaf of papers clutched in both hands. Light blue vertical blinds on the wall-to-wall window provided the perfect backdrop for his dark gray sharkskin suit and solid midnight-blue tie.

"Mr. Blaine?" The expression on his face was not one of instant recognition, let alone delight.

"Right. Garrett. It's been a long time."

"Please have a seat, Mr. Blaine." Doss made a feigned

attempt at rising but didn't quite complete it before he sat down again, a tapered hand waving in the general direction of the leather chair to his left alongside his desk.

Garrett moseyed over and sat down. Even then, he was a couple of yards from the agent. "Nice place you've got here," he said in honest admiration, looking around. "Must cost a pretty penny to rent space like this on Fifth Avenue. From what I hear, everyone is pulling up stakes and moving down below Twenty-third Street, where the air isn't quite so rarified."

"Give it a few years," Doss said, pushing in the top right-hand desk drawer and running his tongue across his chapped lips.

Garrett briefly wondered where he stashed the hair of the dog. He looked around again. The bar was probably behind the ornate set of hardwood bookshelves. Press a button and *Open, Sesame,* the shelves part and out she rolls. Something like that. "You and Simon must get on pretty good, huh?" he said, looking back. "How is he, by the way?"

"As well as can be expected, I suppose, considering." A slight pause, then, "What exactly can I do for you, Mr. Blaine?"

Garrett grinned. "Couldn't get me a nice cushy job here at the agency, could you?" Then, after a little laugh, he added, "What's with the Mr. Blaine bit? Heck, we were practically brought up together." It wasn't true, of course. For one thing, Nelson Doss was at least three years older, not to mention how many millions richer. Oh, he'd been to old Simon Doss's house, all right—several times. But always with his father, whenever the man had business he felt couldn't wait, which usually meant at night after regular business hours. Each time he was scooted off to join Nelson in his playroom. God, even back then the guy had it all. The proverbial silver platter.

"I heard you were up at my father's farewell bash," Garrett continued, "and . . . well, I wanted to thank you, for one thing. You know, of course, that he's dead." He had no difficulty saying it at all.

Nelson Doss stifled a yawn. "Yes, I read about it."

You might not even have had to read about it, you bastard. Maybe you're the one responsible, Garret thought.

"Yeah, I guess you did."

"Look, I'm sorry to hear about your trouble, Blaine"—Nelson suddenly lost the Mister there somewhere along the way—"but surely that's not the reason you came to see me." He swept a hand across the length of his desktop. "I've got a lot of work here, and a big day ahead of me. So if you'll just tell me what it is . . ." He left it up in the air, up to Garrett Blaine.

Garrett shifted uncomfortably in his chair. "I was wondering . . . I mean, now that my father's gone, I was wondering if he had any money coming to him from your agency."

"Money?" Doss stretched his hand in the direction of the right-hand drawer, then just as quickly pulled it back again, folding it into the other one on the edge of his desk.

"Yeah. You know—residuals, royalties . . . things like that."

Doss took a deep breath of stale air, then let it out. "I'm sure you don't know what you're talking about, Blaine. Our agency doesn't owe your father—or his estate—anything."

"He was with your advertising agency though, wasn't he?"

"The past few years of his career, yes."

"And you represented his sponsors, right?" He remembered his father talking about it often enough—complaining more often than not.

"That's how it worked in radio in those days, yes."

"So my father actually worked for you rather than for any of the radio stations he appeared on."

"Right again. The radio shows are products—*were* products—of the agencies. We actually created, owned, wrote, and cast our shows—or our sponsors' shows, if you like. Is that what you mean?" He ran a thin finger inside the narrow white collar of his dress shirt.

"Yeah. And you still don't owe him anything?" Granted it had been a shot in the dark to begin with, but what the heck . . . what did he have to lose? There might have been something outstanding that was still owing.

"Nothing whatsoever. Why? Do you have proof of some type to the contrary, Mr. Blaine?" The title was back again. Maybe the guy was getting nervous. Maybe there *was* something he was hiding after all. Maybe Garrett's visit was rousing some sleeping dogs. The only problem, of course, was that he didn't know where to run with the ball now that he had it.

"Well . . ."

"Would you care for a drink?" Doss asked, unwittingly coming to his rescue. Without waiting for an answer, the agent went over and pushed a button under one of the shelves in the library. Two sections parted in the middle, revealing a bar that suddenly blinked to life under fluorescent light.

While alcohol at that hour of the morning was the farthest thing from Garrett's mind, it at least provided him with an excuse to hang around. And Doss certainly needed something, that was for sure. "Sure," he said, watching as Doss moved behind the bar.

"What'll it be?" the agent asked, bending down and scooping up two rocks glasses in one hand, then lifting down a bottle of Beefeater from the lowest of the mirror-backed shelves.

Blaine would have preferred a simple beer, but hesitated doing anything that would only have added further to the gap between then. "Bourbon will be fine," he said. "On the rocks."

"Your father didn't say anything in his will about any money that was coming to him from us, surely," Doss said, leaving the bar open and returning around the desk to his executive swivel chair. "Because, if he did, he was in error. Our lawyers—"

"No, no, nothing like that," Garrett said. "As a matter of fact, I haven't even seen the will." He managed a little laugh. "And unless my father was pulling a fast one, I don't even expect to be named among the beneficiaries."

Doss put down his drink after a healthy slug. "I don't understand. Then why—"

"Look, I'll be perfectly honest, Nelson, okay? I need the money. It's as simple as that. I was hoping for the property up on the lake, but . . ." He tossed up his palms, then reached for the drink the agent had set on the edge of the desk near him.

"I had no idea things were that bad." Doss furrowed his brows, as if he couldn't imagine such things happening between father and son. "Why would he cut you out of his will?"

Garrett took his first sip of bourbon. It bit the tip of his tongue and burned all the way down his throat. "It's a long story. Suffice it to say he hated my guts."

Doss shook his head and again ran his tongue over his lips. During the brief silence that ensued, Garrett could make out the spidery red lines running down the sides of the man's nose. He wondered how far gone the guy's liver was. Come to think of it, maybe Doss wasn't the lucky one after all.

"That might have been so much talk, you know," Doss said. "When the chips are down, don't forget . . ." He paused in midsentence and looked down into his glass as if it were some sort of crystal ball, then raised it and took another swallow. He looked up again. ". . . blood is still thicker than water."

If that had been the case, Garrett's relationship with Henry had long been in need of a transfusion. He smiled to himself at the thought. "I hope you're right."

"Look, Blaine, why don't you go down to Personnel and fill in an application," Blaine said, jotting something on a monogrammed pad on his desk and then ripping off the page. "Give this to whoever's in charge there. I can't promise anything, mind, but you never know . . . we might be able to find a place for an old friend of the firm." Doss smiled for the first time as he handed across the sheet of paper that he had folded neatly in half.

"I appreciate that, Nelson." Actually he was of two minds about the sudden and totally unexpected gesture of good will. Was the guy trying to soothe his own conscience, or was there really a Santa Claus after all?

"What are old friends for, huh?" Doss said, looking at his watch and then rising to his feet.

"By the way," Garrett said, still nursing his drink, "did you know there's been another murder?"

"If you mean Audra Mateer, yes," Doss said, his slender fingers splayed on the desk blotter. "I remember my father talking about her." His eyes suddenly became slits. "I hope you realize that Henry did most of his business with my father, before he became ill. I only got to know him in the later years, when he was . . . at the end of his career."

Yeah, why not say it? Washed up.

"This has been some week," Garrett said, sucking in his paunch as best he could and pulling, unthinking, at his thick, full beard. "First my father, then Audra. Meeting people I barely remember from my misspent youth." He laughed. "And unless one of them is careful, she's likely to end up victim number three."

"Who's that?"

"Mrs. London. Lavina London. From the phone conversation I had with her, it sounded like she's rushing in where angels fear to tread. You know her at all?"

"Only by name and reputation. Why do you think she might be in danger?"

Garrett took another sip of bourbon. It wasn't quite so bad this time around. "Think a minute. If these murders are connected in some way, the killer is probably one of the people at my father's party. Lavina was Johnny-on-the-spot after my father and the Mateer woman were killed. And now she's going around asking questions."

"I see."

Garrett set his unfinished drink down on the desk, then inched his weight forward on the chair. "Well, I guess I'd better let you get back to whatever it is you do around here, and go down to Personnel and offer my services. Such as they are."

Doss just smiled as he extended his hand across the desk.

Out in the reception area, Jane had the phone up to her left ear under a cascade of soft brown hair. Her pointed pencil was going full speed in the steno pad.

"Thank you, Jane," Garrett said in a louder than usual tone of voice as he grabbed for the doorknob.

The secretary looked up and smiled, then went back to her pad.

That, Garrett, is what they're looking for in Personnel. Company dedication. At thirty-eight he wasn't quite sure he was up to it. Or wanted to be, for that matter.

Chapter Sixteen

→ ←

As usual, Lavina overtipped the cabbie. Hoisting up the strap of her shoulder bag, she stepped out of the cab, which the uniformed doorman held open for her. He'd be next when she finally checked out of the hotel.

One prolonged shiver ran through her body as she made her way, head down against the wind, toward the main entrance to the hotel. Once inside, she chose the escalator rather than the stairs that flanked it up from street level to the main lobby. Her feet hurt. She then proceeded across the marble floor, straight back to the bank of elevators opposite the concierge's desk and up to her suite.

The phone inside stopped ringing even before she closed the door and switched on the wall light. Susanne, most likely. Or Bran.

She doffed her jacket and hung it in the closet, then sat on the edge of the bed and pulled off her boots. A soak in the tub would be sheer joy—once she got everything else out of the way so she could relax and enjoy it. The phone rang again while she was slipping into her white furry scuffs. She reached over to the end table and picked up the receiver.

"Gran, it's me."

"Hello, me. Did you just call?"

"Just now? No. But I did earlier. You just get in?"

"Yes. Did you get the information?"

"I'm fine, Gran, thanks. How about you?"

Time for fun and games. Lavina shook her head and smiled, running a hand across the floral, quilted bedspread. "Sorry, dear. How are you?" She turned on the lamp near the phone. It was a little past four forty-five.

"Fine."

"And how was your afternoon?"

"Fine, too. I—"

"And your dear father?" Lavina wasn't about to let her off the hook that easily—not after she had started it.

She could detect a muffled laugh at the other end. "He's hard at work, poor man, what with having to support a spendthrift wife and wayward daughter and all in the manner to which they've become accustomed."

"A sorry plight, indeed. And how is the spendthrift, now that you mention her?"

Susanne giggled. "She's climbing the walls."

Lavina shook her head. The predictable Tracey. "And the kitty?"

"She's the reason Mother's climbing the walls." Susanne laughed out loud this time. "Mother's furious we can't use tinsel this year because of her. Claims the tree looks anemic without it." For once, Lavina could sympathize. It was one taste, at least, her daughter had somehow managed to acquire at her mother's side. If very little else. "Aren't you going to ask me up?"

"You're downstairs?"

"Uh-huh."

"You ninny! Why didn't you say so? Get your buns up here."

After she hung up, it dawned on her that she hadn't mentioned the room number. When she thought about it, she laughed. An obstacle that simple certainly shouldn't faze a granddaughter of Lavina London.

The knock on the door came just as she sat down on one of the straight-backed chairs around the oval walnut dining table.

"Come in if you're good-looking," she half shouted, borrowing one of Ken's favorite expressions. She smiled at the thought that the person on the other side of the door might have been Bran Slattery. Not that he'd ever show up unannounced, of course.

"Hi! It's only me again," Susanne said. "In the flesh this time." She locked the door behind her and moved across the suite to the table. After removing her leather jacket, she hung it on the back of the chair facing her grandmother and sat down, stretching out her feet in their full-length boots under the table. "You land anything on your fishing trip uptown?" she asked.

"Nary a bite." Or nothing she could sink her teeth into, anyway.

"You should have waited until your gofer reported in." Susanne grinned this time, and with both hands gave a little tug at the bottom of the black and red vest she was sporting over her white blouse.

"Oh?"

"What happened to that snow, by the way?" the girl asked, slipping a small manila envelope out of her bag.

"I don't know. Fizzled out all of a sudden."

"I was hoping for a White Christmas." Susanne feigned

one of her little-girl pouts that endeared her so much to her grandmother.

"And I'm hoping for a dry trip home," Lavina said, facially mimicking her granddaughter.

The two of them laughed.

"So what have you got?" Lavina asked, nodding in the direction of the envelope.

Susanne undid the metal fastener and slid out a bunch of folded papers which she opened out on the table. "First, about the kidney transplants . . ."

Lavina was about to blurt out what she had learned by sheer accident on her own at Macy's, but bit her tongue. After all, you didn't go around biting the hand of the gopher that fed you. "Go on."

"Well," Susanne began, looking up from the sheets, "the first human transplant of a kidney took place— Are you sitting down? Yes, of course you are—in 1950."

"Really!"

"Yes."

"June, by any chance?" Oh, Lavina, you'll be an actress till your dying day, she thought.

"Right. The seventeenth. In Chicago. By one Richard Laoler."

Middle initial G. She'd have to be careful she didn't inadvertently let that one out later in front of Susanne. "And does it connect up in any way with that clipping we're missing?" Lavina found herself almost crossing her fingers.

"It's not missing anymore, Gran." Susanne snapped the sheet of white paper in her hand. *"Ta-da!"* she trumpeted, reminding Lavina of the angels in Rockefeller Promenade. The girl handed the sheet across to her grandmother. "A photostat, as requested, Your Granship."

With a broad smile, Lavina slid her glasses on her nose, taking the proffered sheet at the same time. "Did you have any trouble getting it?"

"Are you kidding! I followed your instructions to the letter. What trouble could I have?"

Lavina held the article out in front of her and read:

The five-year-old son of nationally known daytime radio talk-show hosts, Violet and Cole Hesson, died late today at Northwest Hospital.

John Hesson suffered severe head and internal injuries, apparently as the result of a fall sustained sometime earlier in the day and was admitted to the hospital at 10:11 P.M. Attending physician Dr. Nathan Bronca mentioned in passing the possibility of acute renal (kidney) failure. An autopsy has been ordered to determine the exact cause of death.

The child's parents were absent from the home of the actress's mother, Mrs. Joanna Deladae, at the time of the accident. The boy's father, Cole Hesson, told reporters the boy had apparently fallen down the steps leading to the cellar and was not found until the parents returned from an earlier business appointment. The boy's mother was not available for comment. An investigation is continuing. No action is presently being taken against the child's parents or grandmother.

Lavina shook her head and then looked up at her granddaughter. "Sad," she said. "Very sad."

"Poor little thing," Susanne commiserated. "How could parents leave a five-year-old alone like that?"

"His grandmother may have been there. The article

isn't quite clear on that point." The thought of the agonizing grandmother hit close to home, making her feel even worse.

"At least it answers your question about Mr. Blaine's reference to kidney transplants."

"Does it?" Lavina wasn't so sure.

"Sure. If the boy had the accident on the fifth, and the first transplant wasn't until the seventeenth . . . well . . ."

"Yes, that part's right, certainly." She tapped the sheet of paper with a manicured nail. "And I suppose if it was renal failure that Henry Blaine might have assumed such a transplant would have saved the child's life."

"You don't think so, Gran?"

"If recollection serves me correctly, those early kidney transplants were not very successful in the long run. I think the first one that actually took was between a pair of identical twins. I'd have to look it up, of course, to be certain, but—"

"Maybe *that's* what Henry Blaine was referring to," Susanne said, her eyes lighting up.

"What?"

"Identical twins. Maybe little John had a twin."

Lavina was having enough trouble dealing with the one child she hadn't even known existed without having to think about the possibility of two of them.

"Personally I think you're out in left field with that one, Susanne. But even if you're right, I don't think it makes much difference at this point. The important thing is that the Hessons considered it serious enough to lie about."

"Oh, how so?"

"They told me—no, that's not quite true—they led me to believe they'd never had any children."

"I thought you knew them back then."

"I did. Beginning in 1945. But if John Hesson was five at the time of his death in 1950—"

"He was born in '45."

"And obviously before I met them, because Violet certainly wasn't in a family way at the time."

"Pregnant, you mean."

Lavina glanced at her over the tops of her glasses.

"We didn't use that word back then." Another of those euphemisms she'd been collecting recently. She smiled.

"And when they say the child was five, of course," Susanne said, following her own train of thought, "he could actually have been closer to six, right?"

"Of course! Susanne, you're cooking with all burners this afternoon."

"But with nothing in the oven." The girl giggled.

"Let's hope not," Lavina said, her brows up in a mock arch. "Where did you learn that old expression?"

Susanne shrugged. "Listening to you probably, somewhere along the line."

Lavina shook her head. The girl was probably right.

"But why did the Hessons let you think they had no children?" Susanne asked. "I mean, if it was an accident and all."

"If . . ."

"They weren't arrested, were they?"

"Not to my knowledge, but if Henry Blaine knew something, or thought he knew something, and started blackmailing them—"

"Gran, do you think they killed the boy?"

"I'm not saying that, no. But they might have been hiding something." Child abuse, maybe?

"Henry's knowing would be important, wouldn't it?"

"I think so, yes."

"That, plus the fact that this clipping was cut out of that old paper at Miss Mateer's apartment."

"That, too."

Susanne canted her head. "You haven't figured it all out yet, though, have you?"

Lavina sighed and smiled at the same time. "Hardly." She picked up the article and read it through a second time. The heading, she noted now, said simply CHILD DIES IN FALL. Succinct, if premature. After all, they hadn't even performed the autopsy yet. She lifted off her glasses and held them in her hand on their chain, staring vacantly across at the young girl opposite her.

"How would Henry Blaine have known, do you think, Gran?" Susanne asked, her elbows on the table, her chin in her hands.

"A good question." If only the Hessons had opened up. Maybe they would, now that she had more facts.

"What about the son?"

"Garrett?"

"Yes."

Lavina let her glasses drop back again against her breast. "I wonder . . ."

"What?"

"Garrett said he was talking to Jae Patrick." She tapped her nail on the sheet she'd laid on the table.

"So?"

"It was right after their meeting that he brought up the Hessons."

"As if they were fresh in his mind, you mean."

"Right."

"You think she knows something?"

"At this point nothing would surprise me. Everyone down here seems to know something except your grandmother."

"But little do they know . . ." Susanne laughed at her own intended play on words.

"Garrett did seem hesitant about something," Lavina said, only half listening. "Maybe Jae does know more than she's admitted. It wouldn't surprise me, seeing as she's lied to me once already."

"When?" Susanne bent as close as she could across the table.

"She told me she'd never been to the Blaine house upstate, but Garrett mentioned meeting her there on more than one occasion after his mother died."

"A little hanky-panky, do you think, Gran?"

"Either that or—"

"Worse?"

"Yes."

"Maybe whatever Miss Patrick told Garrett about the Hessons was done with the express purpose of diverting suspicion from herself. You ever think of that?"

"Unfortunately, yes."

"Would Garrett have gone along with her if she told him something and asked him to keep her name out of it?"

Lavina nodded. "He's just gallant enough to buy something like that, yes. Nor do I think he would have questioned her on the matter."

"What about Garrett? Maybe he's been running around making up his own stories."

"That wouldn't surprise me either. I almost caught him

in one outright lie already—about telling his father he wouldn't be at the party."

"Could he actually have killed him, Gran?"

"I really don't know, dear. I'd have to find a sufficient motive first, I think."

The motive was the all-important thing at this point. Which brought her back to the *Tribune* clipping. She had been convinced from the outset that it hadn't been taken by the ones it purportedly involved—in this case, the Hessons. If they had seriously wanted to hide the clipping, why cut it out? Why not just get rid of the whole paper? No, the only reason the paper had been left on Audra's coffee table with a gaping hole where the article should have been was to bring it to someone's attention by its absence—that someone being the police. Sergeant Packard had put the idea in her head when he hinted at a clever killer who might have left a dirty coffee cup behind deliberately. Only in this case it was the excised newspaper article. An outright red herring.

"What about this Bran Slattery you mentioned, Gran?" Susanne suddenly asked out of the blue.

"What about him?"

"Well, you haven't told me anything about him at all—not really. Maybe *he's* the one we should be looking at. Still waters and all that."

"No, Susanne," Lavina said with a slight break in her voice, lowering her eyes, "I think you'd be barking up the wrong tree there."

Susanne met her eyes when she looked back up, then narrowed her own. "Or maybe it's Lavina London who's the quiet one—trying to hide something from her granddaughter."

* * *

The call came about fifteen minutes after Susanne had finished grilling her and left, and about a minute before she set foot into the warm, inviting tub.

"Lavina London, you are without a doubt the most exasperating woman I have even come in contact with, even if I can't contact you when I need to."

Lavina inched the receiver away from her ear for a few seconds before the tirade subsided to a dull roar, then sat down on the edge of the bed and tucked her chenille robe around her bare legs, holding it closed between her knees. "No need to shout, Tod," she said. "I can hear you just fine."

"Yeah? Well, I don't know how many messages I left for you at the hotel. Don't they give them to you, or do you just file them in the circular file?"

She had gotten them, all right. "I'm fine, Tod, and how are you and Polly?" she asked, borrowing the same tactic Susanne had used so successfully on her.

"Don't hand me that, Lavina. I'm wise to your stalling tricks. Have the police down there been in touch with you yet?"

"Not since I made my statement at headquarters, no. Why should they?"

"I asked them to keep an eye on you, that's all." He wasn't shouting anymore. As a matter of fact, Lavina had all she could do just to make out his words.

"Why? I thought you had our murderer up there in Boulder."

"That was before Audra Mateer was killed, Lavina, you know that." He sounded almost apologetic.

"What about that videotape?" she asked, more interested in developments than in making Tod eat crow.

"We didn't find it. In the car or anywhere else."

"You checked the garage?"

"No, Lavina," Tod said in obvious exasperation. "We decided to wait until you got home to do that— Of course we checked the garage!"

"You're shouting again, Tod."

"That's my blood pressure you hear."

"Well, keep it down."

The groan was unmistakable. Then, "But you were right, there was a taping all right. The folks at the Seventeener verified it. It wasn't done by any of the listed professionals up this way, though; we checked that first."

"Probably an amateur," Lavina said, stating the obvious. "You see them listed all over the place nowadays. Even in church bulletins. And knowing Henry, I doubt he'd have paid professional prices for anything like that. He probably hired some young kid to do it and then took it home after the party."

"If that's the case, where is the damn thing?"

Lavina shook her head. He knew the answer to that one as well as she did. "Might I suggest that our murderer took it along after killing Henry?"

"You might. And might I then ask why?"

"If we knew that, Tod, we probably wouldn't have any need for the tape, now would we?"

Tod heaved a deep sigh.

"What about Henry's will?" she asked. "You learn anything there?"

"This may come as a surprise, Lavina," Arthur began. "In addition to a tidy sum in his savings and checking accounts—more that *I* expected he'd have—everything goes to his son, Garrett, including the unsold house and property."

If Lavina knew how to whistle, she would have. Instead, she settled for an appreciative *hmmm*.

"What was that?"

"Just thinking aloud. You know, Garrett is under the impression he's been cut out of his father's will."

"That what he told you?"

"It's the story that's going around, let's put it that way." No sense dragging Bran's name into it if she didn't have to.

"A mighty convenient little alibi if he really knew he was the heir, wouldn't you say?"

Lavina couldn't fault the logic. "Did you check to see who stayed at the Seventeener the weekend of the party?" she asked, sidestepping the question.

"Now you know I did, Lavina," Arthur said, obviously annoyed. "Why do you ask such damn fool questions sometimes?"

"Just to give you the chance to show how smart you are, Tod." She smiled, sure her tone conveyed it down the wire.

"Yeah, sure. Big macho buildup. Make them feel superior. I watch Donohue and Oprah sometimes, too, you know."

"So tell me. Who?"

"Okay, let's see. . . ." She could picture him at his desk reading off the names from a sheet of paper. "The Hessons, Nelson Doss, and Will Argon. All of whom, I might add, were on Blaine's list I told you about earlier." He gave a little cough, then went on: "Argon checked in Thursday, left Saturday morning very early. The Hessons came late Friday and left Saturday morning. Doss, Friday afternoon till Monday A.M."

"Not till Monday," Lavina repeated aloud.

"What was that?"

"Nothing. No one else?" She crossed her legs, rearranged the robe, and began waggling the furry scuff on her right foot.

"Except for the ones from out West and whatnot, no. And no, none of them stayed anywhere else in the immediate area either, in case you were going to ask."

"No need to be sarcastic."

"It's called being realistic, Lavina. Keeping one step ahead."

"None of it tells us much, though, does it?" she added, ignoring the remark.

"Not in itself, no. And what about you? What have you learned down there?"

Lavina let out a little sigh, then proceeded to fill him in on everything she had done and learned since their last telephone conversation—everything that wasn't strictly personal, that is.

"You sure haven't let any grass grow under your feet down there, have you?"

"Must be all this snow."

It was Arthur's turn to do the ignoring. "So you think the ransacking of the Mateer apartment was a put-up job to mislead the police."

"I do. And what's more, I think there was a lot of staging done in that apartment."

"Staging, huh? One of your actor friends, maybe?"

Since there was only one outstanding name that fit into

that category, Lavina quickly added, "I was speaking figuratively, Tod, referring to someone who was very clever, as Sergeant Packard suggested earlier."

"This Packard hasn't told you what *they* think, I suppose—the New York police, I mean."

"Nothing more than I've already told you."

"No, I guess not. After all, they can hardly be expected to know your credentials yet."

She couldn't miss the laughter he attempted unsuccessfully to hide behind his dry cough. "More sarcasm, Tod?"

The silence spoke for itself. "Anything else, Lavina?" he finally asked.

"Yes, now that you mention it, there is. Now it's my turn. Tod Arthur, you're an A-1 louse. Do you know that? L-O-U-S-E. And you can count your blessings that my mother raised a lady."

Again, no answer.

"Are you listening?"

"I'm listening."

"It took me a while, but it finally sank in. Your pumping me now is really what did it." She paused and took a deep breath. "You deliberately let me come down here, knowing full well that I'd do your work for you." She thought about Susanne. "Your unofficial legman."

"Deputy sounds better, Lavina."

"*Bolshoi!* You knew full well I'd start asking questions of all my old colleagues down here, didn't you? They were your main group of suspects all along. That business about suspects in Boulder was all hogwash. Admit it."

"Now, now, Lavina, you said yourself you wanted to help."

"Help, yes. Be made a fool of, no. You preferred to let

me come down here without your blessing, knowing all along I'd tell you everything I learned."

"I knew I could trust you, that's why."

"That's more than I can say for you, Tod Arthur."

"Come on, Lavina, don't be like that," Arthur said after a long pause. "I'm sorry. I felt you'd be more at ease on your own than if you thought I was expecting something of you."

It sounded believable, and certainly more like the Tod Arthur she thought she knew. "I wish I could believe that, Tod," she said.

"You can, Lavina. Honest."

"Well . . ."

"Truce?"

Now that it was off her chest, it was a thing of the past. She was psychologically incapable of holding a grudge. "You promise to be more honest in the future?" She managed a little smile, knowing full well that any promise he made under duress would go only so far. But at least she could always hold it over his head if she had to.

"I promise, Lavina."

"We'll see," she said. "In the meantime, all is forgiven."

"Thank you."

"You've been in touch with the police down here all along, haven't you?" she asked, sure she'd get the truth.

"Yes."

"From the first day, I bet."

"Even before you left Boulder."

She sighed. "Sneak."

"Just doing my job, Lavina. Protecting your hide."

"I hope you don't mean that I have a shadow"—there

was that word again—"down here, a plainclothesman following me." She didn't relish that picture at all.

"They didn't promise to go that far, Lavina, no."

"Good thing for you."

"I don't know, Lavina. I think it's kind of nice to know there's a man in blue around in case you need him—even out of uniform."

"Or if he wears gray like you."

"Better yet."

"Well, I'll let you know the day I need a backup, Sheriff."

"*Sheriff* now, huh? About time I got some respect."

"Enjoy it while it lasts, Tod." She laughed and was glad to hear him join in.

"Seriously, Lavina, I hope any call for help doesn't come too late."

"Why do you say that? You think I'm in any danger?"

"That depends. You've been going around asking questions, haven't you? You might be getting close to the truth."

"As far as I see it, I'm nowhere near the truth."

"As far as *you* see it, yes. Maybe someone else sees it differently."

"Thanks for telling me."

"You owe me one."

"By the way, there's something you might pass along to your newfound friends in the NYPD down here now that you're all so chummy."

"What's that?"

"Have them check out any scissors they find in Audra's apartment for possible prints. That newspaper clipping was cut out with one, and it's not easy to do that using gloves. Besides which, I doubt our killer thought we'd catch on to his cleverness. It might just be his undoing."

"I don't know what kind of prints they'd get from a pair of scissors."

"You never know. If they're shiny and stainless . . ." She left it up in the air.

"And we're still not sure the killer cut out that article to implicate the Hessons, like you say. After all, you're—"

"Yes, yes, I know. My intuition again. Okay, I don't deny it, but we'll know soon enough once I confront Violet and Cole with the facts. The two of them are stretched to the breaking point, believe me."

"Do I have a choice?"

Lavina smiled. "There is one thing, though, that has been bothering me more than anything else."

"What's that?"

"The simple reason why—if the killer is one of these people out of Henry's and Audra's past—he waited all these years. Why now?"

"Maybe he—or she—was stretched to the breaking point, too, Lavina." A pause. "It happens, you know."

Lavina sighed.

"Now that we're talking about the past, did you come up with any ideas for the reason behind that Shadow message on Blaine's answering machine?"

"Personally—yes, I know, more intuition—but personally I think it's another red herring. Like the missing newspaper clipping."

"In what way?"

"The same as with the clipping—to throw suspicion on someone. In this case someone directly connected with the golden age of radio. One of those in our immediate little group."

"Someone like the Hessons again, you mean."

"Precisely. Only this time I think our invisible voice out of the past is using the Shadow *to cloud men's minds* in a different way entirely—to the truth." She paused for a reaction. When there was none, she went on. "The only problem, of course, is that it would still have to be someone fairly knowledgeable in his own way, yet still on the periphery."

"And therefore not likely to be suspected, you mean."

"Exactly."

"Someone like Garrett Blaine."

"Someone like Garrett Blaine," she repeated.

"Then you don't think the Shadow message was a warning to Henry Blaine at all."

"On the contrary, Tod. It most certainly was. And a nasty one at that. It was intended to let Henry know he was about to get his comeuppance."

"It served two purposes, then."

"From where I'm sitting, yes. But then, I told you our killer was very clever."

Arthur heaved another deep sigh. "It's a long shot, Lavina. I hope you realize that."

"You have any better ideas?"

"No."

"Then keep an open mind."

"A closed mouth is probably what you really mean."

Chapter Seventeen

→ ←

He propped the wooden cane against the wall and dug the red beret out of the pocket of his tweed overcoat. Stretching the band between two hands, he cupped it over his mass of white hair like a shower cap, then flattened it down with a cocky tilt to one side. With his narrow velvet collar turned up, he retrieved the cane, pushed open the glass door and exited the nursing home.

He stood a few moments on the top step and let the icy wind bite at this ears and nose. Then, head lowered, he descended the short flight of concrete steps to the sidewalk.

The holiday lights in the darkened city only added to his pain and emptiness. He still couldn't decide which had been worse: the long-postponed confrontation or the frightening prospect that a similar institution might one day be home for him as well.

At the corner of Eighty-seventh and Lexington, Will Argon came to an abrupt halt at the red DON'T WALK sign facing him from across the street. His rubber-tipped cane was already planted in the gutter ready to proceed without him. The cab that sped by with its horn blaring narrowly missed turning it to splinters. It could well have been him. He breathed in the cold night air and thanked God for his independence: *Please, Lord, when the time comes, if it be Your will, let me die at home in my own apartment.*

He couldn't be sure, of course, that the Lord was even listening, especially after everything that had happened. But was it really his fault? Should he have been able to foresee it all? Prevent it? Even more important, should he have acted differently at the outset when he'd had the chance? If he had to do it over, what . . .? It was all so long ago. There was no fast and easy answer, even knowing, as he did now, where it would all lead.

No, that was wrong; he was being too hard on himself, as usual. He *had* done the right thing; he was sure of it then and he was equally sure of it now. The decision had hurt, but it was the only decent one to make. For her sake as well as the boy's. What happened, happened. *Lord, why must I constantly wrestle with this ghost? Let it be put to rest once and for all.*

When he reached the opposite side of the street, he turned and headed south on Lexington, the stars barely visible against the wintry night glow from the city. A surprising number of empty cabs were headed south as well, most of them straddling the white lines, prepared to move right or left at the first beckoning arm. But they were not for him; he felt like walking, as he always did. Winter, summer, the season made no difference. His heart kept pace with the beat of the pavement beneath him—with the pulse of the city. Maybe only native New Yorkers felt it—he didn't know. Somehow it was his own God-given pacemaker. Take it away and he'd be gone soon after. The city was his life support.

Images of Henry Blaine and Audra Mateer crowded his mind, their strident voices vying for his attention over the din of the late-evening traffic. He blinked his eyes several times to ward off the onset of salty liquid that threatened to mist his vision. It was his fault, dammit, no matter what anyone said. He could have prevented it if he had only taken time out to give it the thought it deserved. After all, he knew Blaine well enough; he should have known what the man would do given half the chance.

But what if he was wrong? It was possible. After all, he did have a bad habit of always projecting the worst, didn't he? He shook his head. Not knowing for sure was probably even worse.

Undeterred, he straightened up, the rhythm of his long strides unaltered. He swallowed hard, clearing his parched throat. For a few minutes he had managed to forget the other problem that was always with him. In a way it was one of the things he was learning how to handle. He didn't dwell too much on the progress of the cancer anymore, or how long it would take before it got the upper hand. *Please, Lord, just let it be in my own bed.* There he was again. As if the Lord hadn't heard him the first time. Further treatments were out of the question. All they'd do would be to confine him to some strange bed in a forlorn, antiseptic hospital wing. His final punishment for having thrown back in God's face one of His most precious gifts. *But I didn't do it for myself, Lord, You know I didn't. Hasn't it caused me enough suffering already?* And now . . . to think what it may all have led to— He swallowed hard again, then rubbed his eyes, one at a time, with his free hand.

If only he could talk to someone, someone who could be objective. Not like what he'd just gone through. How could he really tell that poor old man everything? He was suffering enough as it was. If only they'd talked earlier, not wasted all those years, hadn't lived in their own private little worlds, afraid the truth would somehow rear its head. But, then, people always seemed to wait till it was too late—one of man's saddest shortcomings. Like never saying I love you until there was no one there to hear it.

He was wallowing in self-pity and knew it. It was like reliving one of the old soaps, and Lord only knew, he'd announced enough of those tearjerkers for the Blaines over the years. That was *his* big career boost back in '40. *Whoop-de-do!* Other announcers landed things like *Captain Midnight,* with its great premium toys and fabulous decoder badges—*Broughttoyoueveryday . . . MondaythroughFriday . . . by the makers of O-val-tine!* Lucky Pierre André. And that show lasted till '49! Or *Superman,* which went just as long. He knew he should have switched to Mutual when he'd had the chance. Of course, his stint in the army hadn't helped any—not his career, anyway. He let out a deep sigh. As usual, no one was around to empathize.

At Eighty-sixth he was tempted to turn west again and walk along the wide, busy thoroughfare bustling with holiday shoppers, but changed his mind and crossed instead, continuing south on the avenue.

Midpoint in the block he checked his watch. Almost five thirty. Audra's wake didn't begin until seven, or so Bran Slattery had told him when he called. Of course, he could always wait until morning and go in time for the final service before they sent her body down South for burial, as she'd requested in her will. So she'd had a will, after all. Maybe Slattery was the person to talk to. Audra had obviously thought so. Here he was just about taking care of everything for her—clearing out her apartment, setting up her wake and service, seeing to her bills. The man was a possibility, certainly. He'd just have to give it a little more thought.

By the time he reached Seventy-seventh Street, he realized he was never going to make it to Twenty-third by foot—and he'd still have to head east after that if he intended going to the funeral home. Maybe he should stop for a bite to eat. Maybe even a little nip. He smiled. That's all he needed. The last time he let himself relax like that, he'd ended up opening his big trap in front of Lavina London. He wondered again what she must have thought of him. He still wasn't sure he hadn't said more than he remembered. Well, if he had, he could always laugh it off. Not that it really mattered at this point. So why the hell was he worrying about it? He was thinking like a blithering idiot.

There was really only one thing that mattered, anyway. If only he knew what to do. No, that wasn't quite right; he knew what he had to do—he had to protect, as always. The question was *how*. By continuing to remain silent? Or by speaking out? Maybe even going to the police, if necessary. But before he could do that, he'd have to be sure. Which would mean a confrontation. There just might be some other possible explanation he hadn't thought of. "Damn you, Blaine, why did you have to start in again, anyway!" he muttered.

What still puzzled him was why Audra had been killed. Maybe others were in danger as well. He really hadn't considered that possibility until now. If it were true, that would certainly narrow his choices. If no one else was doing anything, it would have to be up to Will Argon. No matter what the cost, it had to stop.

His decision made, he stopped in midcourse and moved over to the curb. He raised his cane at a mass of oncoming yellow vehicles.

"Citicorp Center," he directed as he pulled the cab door shut behind him. A little linguini and clam sauce at Alfredo's was definitely in order. After a little something to bolster up his courage.

Chapter Eighteen

→ ←

"Go ahead, honey, let it out," Cole Hesson said as he stretched his arm around the shoulders of a sobbing Violet, pulling her to him. She turned and buried her face in the broad lapel of his dark gray double-breasted jacket.

Lavina, alongside them, clutched the photocopy of the *Tribune* article in her hand and waited.

The basement lounge of the eastside funeral home was empty except for the three figures seated in velveteen-upholstered metal folding chairs against the wall farthest from the staircase. NO SMOKING signs had replaced the earlier ashtrays on the hardwood tables, which was only one of the reasons for the nearly empty lounge.

"We wanted to tell you, Lavina," Cole finally said, bringing his free hand up to stroke the head pressed against his chest, "but just didn't know how. God, it's been a nightmare." Tears welled up in his eyes. "For a while there we figured it was over—the blackmail, I mean—until Henry phoned us last month to tell us he was resuming."

"I don't understand," Lavina said, wanting to make sure she had all the details.

"Henry started with the blackmail back in '50, and we paid every month for a couple of years. Until he married Hildy, as a matter of fact. First, two hundred a month, then the second year he upped it to five. This time around he wanted seven fifty. For starters. You know what that meant."

Lavina shook her head. "But why, Cole? I'm assuming this"—she waved the photocopied article—"was an accident, as you said. So, why pay him?"

"Oh, Lavina, you don't understand," Violet interposed, raising her head and pushing aside a fall of black straight hair from her face. Tears were still streaking down her heavily blushed cheeks, the mascara running in the wrinkles no amount of makeup could hide. "He was so awful. He knew I had a temper. Don't forget the three of us— Henry, Cole, and I—started out together in Chicago. He'd seen me take it out on John on more than one occasion, I'm sorry to say—" She caught at a sob. "Especially that last year when the boy was getting harder to handle."

"Your son continued to live with your mother all this time?"

"Yes."

"Why didn't you ever tell any of us?"

"Our careers, Lavina," Violet said. "We didn't want to chance losing the talk-show contract we signed in '45. John had just turned six months at the time, but we had seen it coming. It was our first real break. If the sponsors had any inkling that we were a couple of young parents, it might have ruined everything. We couldn't chance it."

Lavina understood, even if she didn't quite approve. Who knows what she would have done under similar circumstances? She'd learned long ago, thanks to Father Cernac, not to be so quick to judge.

"Henry was convinced Vi used to abuse the boy, Lavina," Cole said. "He had a one-track mind. In the end he accused her of pushing John down the stairs."

"What *did* happen that day, Cole?" Lavina asked, watching Violet's pained face.

"It was just like the article—"

"Cole, please! No more lies! Oh, God, no more lies," Violet protested, the tears starting again.

"Hush, Vi." Cole closed his hand over the one she had placed in his lap. "If that's what you want . . ." Then, turning back to Lavina after a quick glance in the direction of the staircase: "Are you sure no one will come down, Lavina?"

"Trust me, Cole. We won't be interrupted." The second reason for the deserted lounge. Lavina had stationed Bran Slattery at the head of the staircase with a friendly command: "No one comes down till we're through." Fortunately for all concerned, the Mateer wake was the only one booked at the home.

"Henry was right," Cole began, reassured. "Or partially right, anyway. He was there when it happened, so he wasn't second-guessing. We'd all just come back that week to Chicago; Henry's show had gotten the axe that year as well, if you recall. He and Hildy weren't married at the time. And we—"

"I did hit him, Lavina, I did," Violet broke in, overriding her husband's preliminaries. "He was carrying on something awful, stamping his feet, screaming. I told him to shut up and go play in his grandma's cellar. Either that or go to bed. When he saw that the temper tantrums weren't working, he started holding his breath, defying me." She paused to catch her breath. "I couldn't stand it when he got like that. I just hauled out and hit him. Harder, I guess, than I realized. He stumbled and . . . and . . ."

"The door to the cellar was open, Lavina," Cole resumed, finishing the story. "He went down backward. As simple as that. It *was* an accident. When we realized how bad he was, we rushed him to the hospital."

"What about Vi's mother?"

"Joanna was up in bed. The story in the paper we agreed to on the way to the hospital. Even Henry went along with it at the time. It was late and the boy was probably overtired to begin with. And we'd . . . well, we'd been out drinking, I won't say we weren't. We had invited Henry back to the house." He looked again at his wife and squeezed her hand.

"What time was this?" Lavina asked.

"Just after ten. They . . . they pronounced him dead shortly after our arrival at the hospital. Henry said later that we wasted time, but that's not true. We were probably stupid to have lied about being out, but we were afraid, what with the alcohol in our systems and all."

"And Henry started blackmailing you over the incident later," Lavina said, stating the obvious.

"That September. After we'd all returned to New York."

Lavina shook her head. "Didn't it dawn on you that Henry would have been charged as an accessory if he'd said anything?"

Cole nodded. "We discussed all the possibilities, believe me, Lavina. Knowing Henry, he probably would have ended up plea bargaining and gotten off scot-free. And even though we'd lost our show, there was no saying we mightn't have been offered something else. After all, we had five years of experience under out belts with that show. If the story got out, it might well have been the death of our careers." He paused. "We were young, Lavina. And selfish."

"Did they ever tell you why you were canceled," Lavina asked.

"The usual excuse. Poor ratings."

Lavina merely nodded. "I gather you were never charged with negligence or anything, am I right?"

"No," Cole said, his gray hair now the color of pink lemonade in the subdued, artificial lighting of the funeral home lounge.

"Thank God," Violet added.

"You realize, of course," Lavina said, "that you'll have to tell this to the police. They'll have to know what sort of person Henry was if they can be expected to come up with any type of honest profile of the man. You know as well as I do how important the personality of the victim is in the apprehension of his killer."

"Look, Lavina," Violet finally said after a few moments. "I know you're probably right, but won't our story be tantamount to admitting we killed him? Or worse yet, that we killed Audra?"

"Nonsense. You didn't, did you?"

"No." This, almost simultaneously, from both of them.

"Then don't worry about it. If they found out on their own—which they probably would—you'd be in worse trouble."

"That's true," Cole agreed with a sigh of his own.

"Now, another important question. And don't start holding anything else back on me. One of you did go to see Audra the day she was killed, didn't you?" It was only a hunch, of course, but by far the most satisfactory answer if her theory concerning the newspaper article was correct.

Violet stared her. "How did you—?"

"Yes," Cole interrupted. "*I* went down to see her that afternoon." He lifted his wife's hand in both of his own and began rubbing it briskly, as if to restore circulation. "She phoned and said she was very concerned about Henry's death and that she wanted to talk to us about Chicago. Needless to say, that's all we had to hear. Vi wanted to go down with me, but I wouldn't let her."

Violet managed a weak smile and lifted the fall of black hair off her face with a toss of her head.

"We had coffee as soon as I got there," Cole continued, "but she didn't beat around the bush. She had that article"—he pointed to the one still in Lavina's hand—"out on the coffee table. Not a photocopy like that, though. She had the whole section of the *Tribune*.

"Audra confronted me with it, much as you did a little while ago. She seriously believed we had something to do with Henry's death, that we—or at least one of us—had actually killed him. All because of that stupid article."

"Poor Audra," Lavina said, staring into the man's eyes, and seeing there the image of the woman whose bluntness might well have been her own undoing.

"She gave me an ultimatum. Either we went to the police, or she did."

"She had the paper all those years, I imagine," Lavina said.

"So she said. Claimed she'd read the story when it first

appeared." Cole shook his head as if he still couldn't quite believe it.

Lavina smiled. "She collected everything in those days, Cole—magazines, newspapers, digests, you name it. She still had them all, too." Remembering the thick files in Audra's bedroom, Lavina made a mental note to raise the matter of their disposal with Bran. They'd certainly prove invaluable if her book ever managed to get beyond the talking stage.

"She said she'd never once believed we'd intentionally hurt John, but that Henry's murder got her to thinking. She had long been convinced he was blackmailing someone over the years. Don't ask me how; she didn't say, and I didn't ask. I was too concerned for Vi and me, if you want to know the truth."

"Did she say whether Henry had been in touch with her at all for any reason?"

Cole shook his head. "The subject never came up, no."

"And what was your answer to her ultimatum?"

"I told her I'd have to discuss it with Vi—which, of course, was true. This was something we were in together." He gave his wife's hand a little squeeze. "She wanted to believe me, I know, but deep down . . . well, she was just too confused and upset, I guess. But she finally agreed to wait."

"Did you take the news article yourself," Lavina asked, "or did Audra give it to you?" She found herself childishly crossing her fingers in her lap, hoping she was right—that the clipping had never left the apartment with Cole Hesson.

Cole stared across at her, his brow furrowed. "Neither.

The newspaper was still there when I left, article and all. Why do you ask?"

Lavina let out an inner sigh of relief. While he could be lying again, of course, she didn't think so.

"Because someone cut it out," she said, "and left the rest of the paper behind."

"Why?" Violet asked.

"Obviously to throw suspicion on us, Vi, what else?" her husband said, quick to realize the implication Lavina had suspected all along.

"Is that what you think, Lavina?"

"I'm afraid so, dear," Lavina said, more convinced now than ever.

"The lousy bastard . . ." Subdued and succinct. And even accompanied by a smile on his face as Cole mouthed it.

"Did the New York police contact you yet?" Lavina asked.

"Shortly after you left," Cole said, nodding. "We have to see them tomorrow after Audra's service. Bran Slattery called, too, with the particulars. Which is the only reason you caught us here tonight, by the way."

"And a good thing, too," Lavina said, "I was worried when I phoned you and got no answer. I wanted to get this whole business out in the open and the air cleared before I left in the morning."

Cole just nodded.

"By the way, you said you had coffee at Audra's," Lavina said. "Both of you?"

"Yes. She was very gracious, in spite of the whole ugly mess that was obviously weighing on her mind."

"Was there anything else?" She checked her watch. "I suppose we've monopolized the lounge long enough."

"Just one thing, Lavina," Cole said, looking up at the actress who had already vacated her folding chair and stood towering above him. "We weren't the only ones Henry Blaine was blackmailing." Violet nodded agreement, first in her husband's direction, then in Lavina's.

Lavina had certainly suspected as much, but until now had very little by way of confirmation.

"How do you know?" she asked.

"Just a little slip Henry made when he called about the seven fifty—our 'subscription to security,' as he called it." Cole smirked. "Anyway, he inadvertently said something about '*all* of you.' "

"Maybe not quite as inadvertent as you think," Lavina said. "Henry was something of a braggart as well, as I recall."

"I never thought of that. Certainly makes sense."

"Do you have any idea who that someone might have been?" Lavina asked.

"None whatsoever," Cole stated flatly without giving his wife a chance to speak.

"And no one ever mentioned his blackmailing to you in the past, either, I suppose."

"Not to me, they didn't, no. But who in his right mind would admit to such a thing if he didn't have to?"

From the foot of the staircase, her hand on the wooden newel cap, Lavina looked up and gave a deliberate little cough. At the top Bran Slattery turned and looked down, acknowledging the signal with a silent nod and then moved off out of her range of vision.

"It's about time," Lavina heard from somewhere on the floor above. Jae Patrick's bell-tone voice sounded more like brass than silver. Annoyed was probably a better word for it.

The combed-out, dirty-blond curls bobbed with every step as the woman made her way crabwise down the mauve-carpeted stairs in pointy black high heels. The expensive black dress, Lavina knew, was not prompted by the occasion. A gold and onyx brooch was pinned to one side below the narrow Nehru collar. There were probably matching earrings, but Lavina couldn't see them from that distance. The pantyhose were black on black, rosebud design. Lavina fell in love with them on the spot.

The two women embraced warmly at the bottom of the staircase.

"What's all this secrecy?" Jae asked, waving in the direction of the seated Hessons.

"Like a James Bond movie," Garrett Blaine said behind her, a grin on his black-bearded face.

"You remember Garrett, don't you, Lavina?" Jae asked.

Lavina had guessed the man's identity even before hearing his voice, which she recognized from their phone conversation. "I certainly do," she said with a smile. "Garrett."

The young, heavyset man wore a drab herringbone suit, a wrinkled white shirt, solid-red tie, and lackluster, black-laced shoes. He leaned over and kissed the actress on the cheek. "It's been a long time, Mrs. Lon— I mean, Lavina."

Lavina laughed. "Glad to see you remembered. Come and sit down."

They proceeded in the direction of the Hessons, where

they exchanged warm greetings, then on to the row of chairs along the adjacent wall.

"Put this in your bag before I forget, will you, Lavina?" Garrett said, handing her a small white bag fastened with a couple of thick rubber bands.

"What is it?" Lavina asked automatically, looking down at the lightweight, rectangular package now in her hand. Too big for a paperback, she thought, and too narrow for a hardcover.

"The note inside will explain," Garrett said. "When you get home." He gestured for her to put it in her shoulder bag, which she did without further question, shoving it into a side pocket.

"And where have you been, Jae?" she asked the younger woman, sitting between them. "In town all this time?"

Jae shook her head. "Only Wednesday night. I went home Thursday after a full day. I do work, remember. Even if it is only a few days a week. When are you heading home?"

"Tomorrow morning after the service."

"It looks as if you got more than you bargained for this trip, doesn't it?"

Lavina nodded. "Unfortunately." She signaled with her head in the direction of the floor overhead. "Did you go into the chapel to see her yet?"

"Yes. Poor thing. Though, from what I hear, she's probably better off."

It was a moot point at best, and one Lavina decided was best left alone.

She watched as the Hessons rose and headed for the staircase, with Cole in the lead. Obviously the man's nicotine craving needed to be satisfied, with a quick trip outdoors his only recourse. Bran, she noticed, was on his way down. They exchanged a few words in passing.

Lavina smiled as she watched Bran cross the lounge and plop down on the empty chair to her left, then turned back to face the newcomers. "Where was it you said you first met Jae, Garrett?" she asked, feigning forgetfulness.

"Up at the lake. At my father's."

"Hemlock Lake?" This time with disbelief in her voice. Once an actress . . .

Garrett stared at her across the agent between them, a puzzled expression on his face. "Yes."

Caught in the middle, literally and figuratively, Jae lowered her head, closed her eyes a few seconds, then let out a ripple of laughter. She patted Lavina on the knee, shaking her head at the same time. "Okay, so I'm not as good an actress as you are, Lavina, and now you've caught me out. But what will poor Garrett here think?"

From the blank look on his face, Garrett wasn't thinking anything—except maybe that he was dealing with a couple of old loonies fast on their way to the funny farm. Lavina smiled at the notion. There were actually times she wondered, too.

"So you *have* been to Henry's place," she said, all attempts at pretense gone.

"A few times, yes." She raised a halting hand. *"After* Hildy's death, mind you. The only reason I lied, Lavina, was that I didn't want you to get the wrong idea. Henry and I went back a long ways, don't forget, and I felt I owed him that much after Hildy died."

"You don't have to explain to *me,* Jae," Lavina said.

"But I might have to explain to the police, if they knew. That's what you're saying, isn't it? And they might get the idea something more serious was going on, something they might see as a possible motive for Henry's murder, maybe."

"That's for them to decide," Lavina said. "When was the last time you were up there?"

"The beginning of the summer sometime. You were down in Atlantic City with your next-door neighbors. Or so Henry said."

Lavina remembered it well. It had been Winnie's idea; it seemed like the only way to get the first-time gambling bug out of her system. Unfortunately she had made a surprise killing at one of the one-armed bandits, and was already driving Sean and Lavina crazy for a return bout.

"You didn't kill him, did you?" Lavina asked. It was a silly question, and she felt even sillier for having asked it.

"No, Lavina," Jae said, lowering her eyes after a quick look over at Bran. "I wouldn't have hurt Henry for the world." She raised her eyes again, and Lavina thought she could see tears beginning to well up, but in the poor lighting couldn't be sure. "Not that he probably didn't deserve it," she added. Then, turning to Garrett: "Forgive me, Garrett, but your father could be pretty unkind when he had a mind to be. Oh, I don't mean to me; we were always close friends—except for one brief period after his show had been canceled." She dug a hanky out of her purse and wiped her nose.

"That's what I was trying to tell you last night about the Hessons." She lowered her voice, as though she had forgotten that the couple had already left the lounge. "Your father had something on them—don't ask me what— something to do with their little boy." She turned back to Lavina and Bran. "I don't know if you know it or not, but the boy died back in Chicago when he was very young. Henry would never tell me exactly what happened or what he suspected, but he somehow blamed them for the boy's death. I have a feeling he was blackmailing them over it back before he married Hildy."

"And started in again," Lavina added, "last week."

Garrett's jaw dropped, while Jae Patrick's face registered no reaction at all. Bran, whom Lavina had filled in over dinner, merely looked on.

"I'm sorry, Garrett," she added.

"That's all right, Lavina," Garrett said. "After what Miss Patrick told me last night, I'm really not all that surprised."

"And don't start blaming yourself, either," she added, feeling the young man somehow seemed ripe for the self-inflicted role of luckless heir to the sins of the father.

Garrett just stared down between his legs at the scuffed black shoes planted firmly on the rug.

"Henry certainly had a thing for the almighty dollar," Jae said, shaking her head. "And, come to think of it, he probably enjoyed picturing himself in the role of avenger as well. Righting the wrongs of some of his less fortunate associates."

The word gave Lavina a little jolt. If what Jae intimated was true, maybe the Shadow message had been significant after all. One avenger to another, so to speak. Maybe it even had a double purpose—to mislead the police, as she originally thought, and to speak to Henry in his own language as well—one he fully understood.

She looked again at the young-looking woman next to her. How much of what she had just said could be taken at face value? Hadn't Lavina already caught her in one whopper? And if Jae had still been in love with Henry after all these years, any number of reasons might have prompted her to kill him. If Audra knew or suspected, that would have been reason enough to dispose of her as well. After all, hadn't Bran told her that Audra phoned several of their crowd after Henry's death? She sighed. Jae had probably been only one of them.

There was also the fact that Jae—admittedly—knew something about the Hessons, which could have made that little clipping incident a natural follow-through. And if her supposition was correct, somebody had seen the article sitting on Audra's coffee table after Cole's departure and was knowledgeable and clever enough to make quick use of it for his or her advantage. Why not the clever businesswoman? No, Jae Patrick was far from in the clear as far as Lavina was concerned.

Susanne was standing outside Chapel A facing the staircase, her starry eyes looking up into the handsome, if drawn, face of a man Lavina recognized at once as Nelson Doss. The girl took time out to give her a tiny wave as Lavina reached the top of the stairs, then turned back to her companion. That she hadn't signaled her grandmother to join them told Lavina all she needed to know. She smiled, wondering what a certain young Marty Knappe would have made of it all. In a way it amused her to think of her granddaughter "playing the field," as they used to say in her own heyday. The child was far too young to be getting serious—and no one "went steady" in this day and age anyway. Not that Nelson Doss was her idea of a suitable date for her granddaughter, of course. The man was twice her age, for heaven's sake.

Through the milling crowd in the front vestibule, Lavina spotted Will Argon standing just inside the chapel behind the last row of folding chairs. A muted buzz at the front of the chapel prompted her to look briefly beyond him to the deep bronze casket in the long, amber-lighted room. She felt a little tinge of pride that someone had placed her spray of white carnations on top of the closed section of the lid.

As she was about to move away, Argon turned and caught her eye, signaling for her to wait. It took only a few seconds before he was at her side, a broad smile on his weather-reddened cheeks.

"Will," she acknowledged, as he leaned forward on his cane to place a kiss on her cheek. "Shouldn't you be sitting down?"

"I'm all right," he said. "But I certainly would never have guessed anything like this the last time I saw you." The thick head of curly white hair seemed bristly, Lavina thought. She could still picture the auburn tresses that had once been his pride and joy.

"To tell the truth, Will," she said, "I'm beginning to feel like I'm living out some horrifying *Suspense* script." She shook her head in disbelief at everything that had happened.

"I know what you mean."

"Hi, Mr. Argon," she heard behind her before she could add anything else. She turned to look over her shoulder to see Garrett Blaine.

"I didn't know you knew each other," Lavina said.

"Oh, sure," Garrett said. "I think I've known Mr. Argon all my life."

"Yet he still insists on calling me Mr. Argon." Will smiled.

"Remember when you used to take us to Rye Beach?" the younger man asked.

"I could never get you off that slide in the Fun House. How could I forget?" He laughed.

Lavina tried to figure out where Hildy and Henry fit into this idyllic scene. "Who's 'us'?" she asked.

"Mom and me," Garrett said. "Dad was always too busy to go anywhere, so Mr. Argon used to take us a couple of times a month to Rye. He knew how crazy I was about all the rides."

"A typical youngster, that's all," Will said, dismissing it.

"And you a typical father." A flush shot across Garrett's face as soon as he had said it. "Sorry, Mr. Argon, but you were sometimes more of a father to me than my own—and I don't mind saying so."

"Did you get things straightened out upstate yet?" Argon asked, clearly changing the subject.

Garrett nodded. "They're releasing my father's body today. He's being buried up there with mom at Evergreen."

"She'd like that," Argon said, sadness visible in his tired, aging eyes. Lavina wanted to say or do something to relieve the pain she saw, but didn't know what.

"Who's that talking to Doss, by the way?" Garrett asked, motioning with his upturned chin in the direction of Susanne and her interlocutor.

"That's my granddaughter, Susanne," Lavina said with unabashed pride.

Just then someone came up and tapped Will Argon on the shoulder, whispering something in his ear.

"Excuse me a few minutes, will you, Lavina? I'll be right back. Don't go away."

"Go on. I'll be here."

"She's very pretty," Garrett said, ignoring their exchange.

"Another one who kissed the Blarney Stone," Lavina said, amazed how they had all seemed to crawl out of the woodwork at the same time. Not that she was complaining, of course. It wasn't something she ran into every day. Not in Sullivan County, at any rate.

"He's a little old for her, though, don't you think?" Garrett said, a wry smile on his lips.

Susanne's beaming face, Lavina realized, was an open book—maybe even an illuminated manuscript. She couldn't remember when she had last seen her so bubbly.

"Don't take it seriously, Garrett. Susanne's a natural flirt, I'm afraid." After she said it, she wondered just how deep that "natural" went. Had *she* been one in her younger days? If she had, she wasn't quite ready to admit it, even to herself.

"He may be getting me a job at his agency."

"Nelson?"

"Yeah."

"Well, good for you." She gave credit where it was obviously most needed.

Garrett sighed. "If I only looked half that good in clothes." He looked down from the couple to his own less than presentable attire.

Lavina patted him on the stomach. "Lose a little of that, and you will, believe me."

Garrett smiled. "Sure, from ugly duckling to swan prince in three easy sessions at Nautilus."

"I think you left a frog out there, someplace," Lavina said with a little laugh.

"You know," Garrett said, ignoring the pleasantry and looking back in the direction of Nelson Doss, "seeing him here in a social setting, I can understand what Dad meant."

"And what was that?" Lavina asked.

"He used to say that he had it all handed to him on a silver platter."

"I think you're mixing your metaphors," Lavina said with a smile. "Born with a silver spoon in his mouth is more like it."

"Funny you should say that. That's what I thought, too, but when I corrected him, Dad just said, 'Bullshit!' Excuse me, Lavina."

"Not one for corrections, your father, I'm afraid."

Garrett gave a little laugh. "You can say that again."

Lavina gazed across the wide vestibule of the funeral home at the man with her granddaughter. Whatever had led to his drinking, she didn't know. The silver spoon she had just mentioned, maybe? She had met enough recovering alcoholics in the course of her volunteer hospital work in Boulder to know that most alcoholics had to hit bottom before they even admitted they had a problem. Obviously Nelson Doss hadn't yet reached that stage. And tonight, of course, he looked just fine. Maybe a little drawn, but otherwise fine.

She canted her head, first left, then right as she continued to watch him, almost as exuberant now as Susanne. There was something about him she couldn't put her finger on. It wasn't *déjà vu,* or anything like it. He just reminded her of someone. An actor, maybe? One of her neighbors his age on the lake—late thirties, early forties. There weren't too many that age among her acquaintances. No, it had to be someone else. That nice young man who worked with Tod Arthur, maybe? What was his name? St. John? No, St. James. That was it, Chad St. James. She couldn't picture him clearly, but, then, she didn't know him all that well either. Not that it mattered.

She heard Will's frightful cough and turned to find him back at her side. "That was someone wanting to know about the funeral and whatnot," he managed from somewhere deep down in his throat.

"Has anyone looked at that throat of yours?" Lavina asked, throwing caution to the winds.

"It's just a cold, Lavina. Get them this time every year."

That's no cold, Will Argon, and you know it, Lavina thought. He was either hiding it from her or denying it to himself. Either way, she was shut out from pursuing the matter. "Whatever you say. I just hope you're not being foolish."

"You know, I didn't even recognize Patricia's daughter before," Argon said, changing the subject and nodding in the direction of Susanne, "or I would have spoken to her. Let's go on over."

"Oh, I don't think—"

Argon paid her no heed but instead led her by the elbow across the room toward Susanne and her male companion.

"Well, well, young lady," he said when he reached his quarry and released Lavina's arm. "I guess you don't recognize Uncle Will, do you?" He cleared his throat and gave her a big smile.

Susanne looked from the older man to her grandmother, then back again. "No, I'm sorry, I—"

"Will Argon, dear," Lavina said, coming to her rescue. "Many a time he used to rock your mother to sleep at the studio. He was the Blaines's announcer on their soap opera—among other things."

"And my mother used to call you Uncle Will?" Susanne said, a smile on her face.

"No, I can't really say that she did," Argon said. "She was too young at the time to call me much of anything." He laughed. "I was just about everybody's uncle in those days."

Another one who had never married, Lavina thought. He and Bran both. And the two of them would have made wonderful husbands and fathers.

"I see you've latched on to this handsome chap," Argon said, nodding in the direction of the agent. "I don't know that any woman's got him hooked yet. How about it, Nelson?"

Doss just smiled. Lavina was sure he was more than a little embarrassed by the remark, even if the telltale pink on his face was undetectable in vestibule lighting.

"Leave the poor man alone, Will," she said. "Young people these days don't need us for matchmakers. They can probably do better on their own than we ever could."

"Oh, I don't know about that, Lavina," Argon said. "I could tell you a thing or two about my own salad days, if I had a mind to. Just because I let *you* get away"—he winked in the direction of Garrett Blaine on Lavina's right—"doesn't mean they all did, you know." He let out a heartier laugh now than Lavina thought proper, given their surroundings.

"You're full of malarkey, Will Argon, and you know it," Lavina retorted.

"People are getting married later nowadays, too, don't forget," Doss finally managed to add, breaking through his reserve. She wondered what he had been so voluble about earlier with Susanne.

"That's certainly true," Lavina agreed. "Though it does seem to pose a little problem in raising a family. Especially for the older woman."

"I wish I—I mean, I wish we had waited," Garrett said. "Sometimes things don't work out when you're both too young."

"It takes the old Two-to-Tango is what you mean," Argon added, looking beyond their group to the casket in the chapel. It gave Lavina cause to wonder—though, of course, she'd never know.

"How's your father, by the way, Nelson?" Lavina asked, in an attempt to change the subject. "I meant to ask you Friday night at Henry's party, but, well . . ."

"I know, Lavina," Doss said. "I wasn't in the greatest condition, I'm afraid. I hadn't eaten all day, and the drinks just went to my head." Unlike Garrett, Doss had no difficulty addressing her by her Christian name. Was it a matter of social grace on his part, a product of his upbringing, she wondered, or did he just consider her one of his inferiors? A silly thought, but there it was.

"My father's in a nursing home, as you probably know. I really couldn't keep him home. And actually they're excellent up there. He's far better off."

"I understand that, Nelson, but how *is* he?"

"Mentally he's fine, I suppose," Doss said, "but, well, I'm afraid the stroke's taken its toll on his body. I visit him whenever I can, of course, but while he recognizes me, he doesn't say anything. Or can't, I should say. The doctors there don't recommend visitors for that reason."

"What a shame," Lavina said. "But one never knows with strokes." She again thought briefly of Ken, then, to put it out of her mind, turned to Will Argon. She was about to say something totally irrelevant to get off the subject until she saw his face. While he was still looking at Nelson Doss, it had become totally drained, almost completely white, even in the amber lighting.

She glanced back at Nelson Doss, who had suddenly become silent. Then again to Will Argon. It was eerie, and for a moment or two she thought maybe she was beginning to hallucinate. Then, like Homer's rosy-fingered dawn, it began gradually to emerge—by way of a strange and totally unforeseen voyage into the past.

SATURDAY, DECEMBER 23

Chapter Nineteen

→ ←

With a slightly shaky hand, he stabbed the tietack into the center of the tiny white fleur-de-lis and secured it to its little anchor behind the shirt placket just below the third button. He then stood back to appraise his handiwork in the full-length mirror on the back of his closet door. His usual morning hangover stared back at him in silent recrimination. He smoothed the tie, shifted the knot to the left, then slipped into his dark blue serge jacket. Satisfied after a final check in the mirror, he swung the closet door closed, left the bedroom, and headed for the outer hall.

For a businessman of Nelson Doss's stature, Saturday was no different from any other day of the week as far as wardrobe was concerned, with conservative the keynote. Today's funeral service had nothing whatsoever to do with it. As a matter of fact, the only reason he was going at all was for appearance's sake. "I'm standing in for my father," he had told a few of them last night at the funeral home. It hadn't killed him to show up, and neither would a few more hours this morning. That Audra Mateer had been almost a stranger to him was unimportant. *Noblesse oblige,* and all that. He smiled to himself as he dug his dark English worsted overcoat out of the hall closet.

He had been overjoyed to hear that Blaine would be buried quietly upstate without any fanfare. He wasn't sure he could handle another trip to the boondocks of Sullivan County. And one of these maudlin things was more than enough, anyway. Well, pretty soon the bunch of them would be out of his life altogether—all except Garrett Blaine. But that was all right; he owed the man that much. And since the job he'd arranged for would keep the guy on the road most of the time anyway, it was unlikely their paths would cross on any but a highly infrequent basis.

He closed the closet door, shrugged into the coat, then turned and gathered up the car keys from the hall table, where he always left them. He slipped them into his outer pocket, taking a final look at himself in the mirror above the table. He smoothed down a few recalcitrant strands of dark red hair, then took his black suede gloves out of his pocket and tugged them on. Today, for Nelson Doss, was just more PR, the thing he was best at.

"I'm afraid, Cole."

"There's nothing to be afraid of, I keep telling you that."

"That's easy to say." Violet Hesson turned to peer briefly out the cab window at the icy Hudson off to her right. She gave a little shiver.

"What can they do?" Cole said. "We were exonerated in Chicago, weren't we?"

She turned back to face him. "But now the whole thing's out in the open again—including the blackmail mess this time. As far as the police here are concerned, we're suspects. What if they suddenly decide we're guilty?"

"Will you listen to yourself, for Pete's sake. Weren't you the one who told me a few days ago that I was worrying about nothing when I heard Lavina was coming down?"

"Well, I was wrong. I didn't think she could latch on to so much information in such a short time—or even be that interested, for that matter. That business with the *Tribune* article scares the daylights out of me." She paused. "Are you sure you told me everything that happened, Cole? You're not keeping anything from me, are you?"

"Vi, let up, will you. Yes, I told you everything. Just like I told Lavina. What more do you want me to do, get out a bible?"

"Lower your voice," Violet said, nodding in the direction of the cab driver beyond the partition.

Cole sighed.

"You realize that means somebody else knows about John besides Lavina," she added.

Cole shrugged, at the same time grabbing the strap hanging alongside the window. "That's hardly surprising. This whole damn business might as well be in the papers, for all the good our secrecy's done us."

"You don't think it will, do you?"

"Will what?"

"Appear in the papers. Oh, Cole, I couldn't go through all that again." Tears welled up in her eyes as she turned again to face the river that ran parallel to the drive.

Cole grabbed her hand and held it between both of his. "I don't think that's likely, Vi. Now, will you stop worrying? When they ask—if they ask—just tell them truthfully what happened in Chicago. As well as about the black-mail. That's all we know."

"If anything happens to separate us, Cole, I couldn't go on. I hope you know that."

"And why should anything separate us?"

"I don't know," Violet said, turning to face him again. "I mean, if anything did . . ."

Jae Patrick exited on the New York side of the Holland Tunnel a little after 7 A.M. and headed north on Hudson Street. Two red lights in a row was not her idea of the perfect way to start the morning. Her temples throbbed, and she could almost hear the palpitations thumping away in her chest. She was projecting again, of course, and hoped the Valium would tide her over the morning once it kicked in. Why hadn't she come up with a logical excuse not to attend? Because her subconscious told her it would look bad, that's why. Just as her conscious mind now agreed. And besides, she wanted to hear what Lavina might have to say before she left town.

She had been stupid to lie about never having been at Henry's place on the lake, which only made things look worse for her now that the truth was out in the open. Damn Lavina and her memoirs! If it hadn't been for that, the woman would probably still be back in the mountains where she belonged. And her own secret would have been buried with Henry.

The black limo in front of her came to an abrupt stop, forcing her to jam on the brakes, just narrowly missing its rear bumper. *Idiot!* When she finally realized that the driver had decided to double-park, she almost had a con-niption. "Asshole!" This time it was out loud. She checked her side-view mirror, waiting for the oncoming traffic to pass, then backed up and pulled out, only to reach the corner in time for another red light. It just wasn't her day.

Just as it was no one's business how she felt about Henry, she mused, as she waited for the light to change. It was her life, and she'd damn well do as she pleased with it. She always had, and was not about to change now for anyone. Her fingers drummed a rapid tattoo on the steering wheel as she waited. She should have had her usual morning coffee before she left the house. Why she was in such a hurry to get into the city, she didn't know.

And what was she so upset about? After all, she was simply going to Audra's funeral service, then bidding farewell to the rest of them—for another forty years or so, she hoped—and then back home. That would be the end of it. What could be simpler?

She shook her head, setting off the tiny bell earrings she had donned for the season. Audra wouldn't think them out of place, certainly. The thought of Audra started her mind going all over again. What if the woman had told Lavina she had phoned with innuendos about her—Jae—and Henry? Maybe she should mention it now before Lavina did, just in case. No sense giving the police more fuel than they already had by letting them find out secondhand. She didn't kid herself—she had to be one of their suspects, no matter how you looked at it. Audra had certainly seemed to know a lot for a woman who didn't get around. The dangerous silent type, that's what she'd been. Jae would hate to imagine what her monthly phone bill must have been like. After all, she had to have gotten her information some way.

She accelerated as the light changed and crossed Spring

Street—then, suddenly realizing how careless she was being, she checked in the rear-view mirror for a patrol car. There were none in sight. She let out a deep sigh of relief. That had probably been one of her main problems all her life—leaping before she looked. She hadn't always gotten off so easy.

Will Argon walked past Union Square Park with more than a little nostalgia. It was a park he used to love to sit in any hour of the day or night, or even just stroll through. During the weekly "Sweet Sounds of Union Square" concerts, he hadn't even minded standing when he had to. But that was all changed. The druggies had long since invaded, establishing unspoken squatters' rights, and while the politicians of the '80s pretended to have reclaimed it from the enemy camp, Will knew otherwise. He would never feel comfortable here again. As far as he could see, the city was fast losing ground on all sides, giving in to the marauding scum, parasites that were gradually sapping the city of its life's blood. The cops had just about given up hauling them in. What was the use when they only met them again coming out the justice system's revolving door at the end of the day? Judges and lawyers conspired against them, and against every decent citizen in the city. Every time he thought about it, his blood started to boil.

He continued uptown until he reached Madison Square Park. He crossed Twenty-third Street and collapsed onto one of the benches fronting the wide street, the triangular Renaissance-style Flatiron Building to his right. He leaned his cane against the outer slat of the wooden bench and stretched out his long legs. Even now in December, the morning sun was warm on his face. He remained with his head back and eyes closed, thoroughly enjoying its wintry rays. He stayed that way for a good five minutes, until a tickle caught in his throat, setting up a fit of coughing that brought him back down to earth.

When the coughing subsided, he whipped his handkerchief out of his back pocket and wiped his eyes, then raised his arm to check his watch. Still a good two hours to go before the start of the service. He wondered briefly what form it would take. A minister? Priest? He knew Audra wasn't Jewish, so not a rabbi. Maybe just someone from the funeral home with a neat, prepackaged, nondenominational farewell prayer. Dammit, why hadn't he thought of that yesterday when they were all together? It was certainly too late now.

He turned to look around. With the exception of a woman rocking a stroller back and forth from her seat a few benches down from his, this side of the park was deserted. From time to time a few joggers or runners—and some not quite so sure which they were—passed by, but not much of anything else. Saturday morning, with few, if any, on their way to work. In this area, at least.

He thought back again to yesterday's events at the funeral home. It was something he would not forget. For one thing, other than at Henry's party, it was the first time he'd seen his old colleagues together like that in decades. The warmth of the memory was better even than the sun he'd been enjoying so much this morning. It was just too bad it had all been marred by the reality of the situation, a reality that had proved more horrible than his worst fears. After what he'd heard last night, there were no more doubts in his mind. He pretty much knew what he had to do now. He had tossed in bed half the night before mak-

232   *James R. McCahery*

ing up his mind—it was only a matter of waiting until after the service, when they'd all be gone their separate ways. Then, he'd simply force the confrontation. It would probably take what little strength he had left, but there was no turning back. A sob caught in his throat. Everything he had done, everything he had given up, had been for naught. Incredible as it was, it was nonetheless a reality he now fully accepted. Not that it could be allowed to go on, of course. He had, after all, been its immediate source—so in a way he was responsible as well. It was up to him to put an end to it. One way or another.

Bran Slattery sat forward in the brown tweed lounge chair in the living room of his Central Park West apartment, his morning coffee on the drum table to his right, a hunk of cinnamon toast stuck in his right cheek.

"Mm-hm, mm-hm," he managed at various intervals into the receiver held up to his ear. He grabbed with his free hand for the mug on the table and took a swallow of the hot black coffee, then set it down again on the glass tabletop.

"The scissors? Sure, what about them? . . . Hmmm, you really think anyone will swallow something like that? . . . I don't know. . . . It sounds a little strange to me. What about the New York police? Wouldn't they have done something if that were the case? . . . They might buy that, I suppose. . . . Depends how you present it."

He raised the mug again, then set it back before taking another sip. "But I'm not sure I like the idea for another reason—it's too dangerous. If it pans out the way you hope, you know what could happen, don't you? Someone could get seriously hurt. . . . No, of course I'll go along with you—that's not the point. But I hope you realize you're really not giving me much of a choice. What if I said no? . . . That's what I thought you'd say. But remember, I don't like it, no matter what you think. And this is what I was afraid of all along. I worried about it all Thursday morning on the ferry. . . . Don't tell me not to worry. . . . Okay. But I'm not promising to just sit back and do nothing. That I can tell you now. . . . That's for me to know and for you to find out. . . . No, of course I won't louse up your plans. I promised, didn't I?"

After he hung up, he sat back in the lounge chair and reached again for the coffee, only to find that he couldn't keep it from shaking in his hand once he'd lifted the mug.

For once at least, he was glad Rho had stayed in bed. This morning he didn't mind fixing his own breakfast in the least. Fixing his breakfast? What was he talking about? After what he'd heard last night, it was time to start celebrating. Beginning with breakfast in town. Eggs over easy, a side of silver-dollar pancakes, sausage, home fries, a tall OJ, and lots of coffee. He stopped and stayed his jubilation and daydreaming just long enough to dig his frayed leather wallet out of his pocket to check his resources. Satisfied, he smiled. Heck, he could have breakfast and lunch both, if he wanted to.

Garrett Blaine hadn't been able to believe his ears when the sheriff told him. The message, as usual, was on the kitchen table when he came in last night from the funeral home, propped up against the sugar bowl: *Call Sheriff What's-his-name upstate,* and the phone number. *Don't wake me up!* The last part he knew without even reading it. He should have a rubber stamp made for her, for heaven's sake. He laughed to himself at the thought. With her sense of humor, of course, she wouldn't find it funny at all.

So he'd inherited the house after all. He still couldn't believe it. Not after all the bull his father had handed him. All the way up to that last night at the party when he'd gone up expressly to beg him. How could his own flesh and blood have been so cruel when he knew all along he was leaving him the house. *And* the money. That, he never would have suspected. How much did the sheriff say was in that savings account? Something over eighty thousand, was it? Maybe he meant eight thousand. No, it couldn't be; he'd asked him to repeat it. Eighty. *Wow!* Plus stocks and bonds the sheriff wouldn't even go into over the phone.

Sleep away, Rho baby, sleep away, he thought. It was a distinct pleasure not to have to share this with her. Maybe she'd never wake up. No, he didn't mean that—he didn't wish her any harm. He just wanted to be alone to enjoy his unexpected blessings.

As he left the kitchen and headed out through the dining room, he thought more and more about the possibility that had suddenly crossed his mind. Why even let on to her? At least about the money and stocks and stuff. It would serve her right if he let her go on living the way she was. Maybe one day she'd even up and leave him as she'd so often threatened to do. Who knows? It was something that would take some thought. Divorce, after all, was out of the question—at least for him. On practical as well as moral grounds. She'd expect—and probably be granted by some half-assed judge—a chunk of the inheritance.

He picked up his pullover from the captain's chair at the head of the dining room table and slipped it over his head. One thing he didn't want to do was make a false move. Not now. What he'd do, if it panned out, would be to take the job at Doss's agency, and then just work it out carefully from there. What she didn't know wouldn't hurt her. He chuckled silently to himself. Not much it wouldn't.

One thing he could do, though, was sell the house. It wouldn't do him any good anyway, unless it meant getting away from her a few weekends a year. It was hardly worth it. Besides, knowing her, she'd probably only suspect something. Maybe even think he was seeing somebody. He chuckled again. Imagine Garrett Blaine seeing somebody. Who'd even look at him? Unless, of course, the job did eventually make a difference. That, and losing a few pounds. Maybe Lavina was right. The more he thought about it, the more intriguing it sounded—until his conscience started in. Okay, so let it go for the time being. It would be enough for a while just managing to keep it a secret. Meanwhile he'd get hold of the real estate agent upstate, who he knew had listed the house before his father died. The sheriff would know which one it was. They could handle it up there—only this time for *Garrett* Blaine.

He grabbed his overcoat off the chair, where he'd dumped it last night when he came in. It was a little tight over the pullover, so he left it unbuttoned. He then tiptoed across the living room linoleum in the semidarkness and quietly let himself out.

He was down in the apartment building courtyard when a second thought struck him—this one not quite so happy. What if his father *had* intended cutting him out of his will, as he'd said? Maybe that *was* his plan, and he just didn't get around to changing it, what with his moving and all. The only one who'd really know would be the old man, and with him gone, who'd ever believe it? Maybe that's why the sheriff sounded so aloof on the phone last night when he'd finally returned his call. As he turned the corner, he lowered his head and bucked the sudden gust of wind. It, and the idea struck him almost simultaneously. Did the sudden inheritance mean he now became a prime suspect in his father's death? Was there a possibility the old man was going to win out again after all? He shook his head, a near-numbed hand holding closed the collar of his overcoat. No, that wouldn't be fair. God wouldn't do that to him. Not after getting all his hopes up like this.

Passing the neighborhood video rental outlet reminded him of the tape he'd passed on to Lavina at the funeral home. Talk about driving a nail through your own coffin. Granted he wasn't on the tape; still, having had it in his possession was tantamount to admitting he'd been at the house after the party. Dammit, how could he have been so dumb? He should have waited until everything was sorted out. Why had he been so eager to confide in Lavina in the first place? The note he'd left with the tape merely said he'd explain when he got a chance, which is exactly what he'd planned to do. But that, of course, was back when things were looking up for him, when owning up to a little white lie might have made him look good. But now . . . well, now it was a different story altogether. And what was or wasn't on the tape was completely unimportant.

What was it the sheriff had said before he hung up? "I'll see you up here tomorrow, right?" Up in his neck of the woods, he meant. His jurisdiction. It sounded far more ominous now than it had last night, that was for sure.

* * *

Lavina stood outside the funeral home on what was obviously a newly repaved sidewalk, her feathercut sport to the occasional gust of wind backing in from the direction of the East River. The CBS radio weatherman had promised warmer weather for today and tomorrow both, with a probable drop in temperature again on Monday, Christmas Day. With no chance of snow. What was in store for Sullivan County, of course, might well be something else again. Personally she could do without a white Christmas.

The service for Audra was still in progress; only the stifling heat in the chapel had forced Lavina outside. A few of the others had made a move to follow her out, thinking something was wrong, but she had waved them back with a smile. She knew now how Audra had felt that first evening at the hotel.

She turned to face the building as another gust blew a mass of gray hair across her eyes. When it died down, she smoothed her hair and checked in the side pocket of her shoulder bag to make sure the videotape was still there. While she hadn't actually had a chance to view it, she knew it had to be the missing tape of Henry's party. What Garrett had been doing with it, she could only guess. All he'd written in the accompanying note was that he'd fill her in. She didn't want to call him last night at home and chance getting his wife again—there was definitely something wrong between them—so she had waited until this morning, expecting to catch him here before the service. Unfortunately he arrived late. But no matter. It would still add a little something to her scenario. Whatever was on it, she was somehow convinced it had nothing to do with Garrett Blaine. Nothing incriminating, that is. She just hoped she didn't scare him needlessly with her trumped-up theatrics.

The sun beat down on her face, and she unzipped the quilted, dark brown jacket. Her cardigan was buttoned over her yellow blouse, her brown wool skirt tight below her knees.

She went over the lines again briefly in her head—the ones she'd written this morning propped up in bed. It had been a long time since she'd actually had to memorize anything. That was one of the extra benefits to radio acting. No matter how many times they changed the script prior to a broadcast, it was always quite literally ready at hand.

She checked her watch. It was nearly ten thirty. She still wasn't sure when she'd get another chance to call Tod to fill him in. Unfortunately when she phoned this morning, he was out at Al's Diner having breakfast, and while that nice officer, Gwen, had offered to contact him, she thought it better to wait. Until after her all-important final visit—the one she hoped would clinch one of her suspicions. After that, it was only a question of which of the two had actually found it necessary to go as far as murder to keep their secret. The why, she was pretty sure of. Money. And all that went with it.

Lavina turned her head toward the street. The black and gray hearse was waiting in the no-parking zone directly outside the funeral home, its rear door opened. The liveried chauffeur was sitting in the front, a copy of the *Daily News* spread out across the steering wheel in front of him.

It was another two minutes before six of the establishment's trusty hands wheeled out the casket and slid it into the rear end of the vehicle, closing the wide door behind it. Without a word, one of the six moved up and joined the driver in the front seat, and the hearse pulled out into the light morning traffic and drove off. With the body being shipped South, there'd be no cortege to the cemetery.

By the time she turned back to the door of the building, the once close-knit group was already filing out, with Bran Slattery in the lead, holding the door open for the Hessons behind him. At the sight of his striking, robust figure confronting the wind, Lavina decided he would have made as good a seafaring man as his sainted namesake. He was smiling as he approached her with long, brisk strides.

"You sure you're okay?" he asked. "You look a little flushed."

"Flushed? No, that's just the cold."

"I hope so."

Lavina smiled. It was nice having someone like this concerned about her. "Lots of blood and good circulation," she said jokingly.

"And plenty of healthy country living, I suppose." His smile met her own.

Jae Patrick and Nelson Doss joined them before Lavina could make her next move in their private little word game.

"I thought that was very tastefully done," Jae said. "Don't you think? Especially since the poor man probably never even knew Audra when she was alive."

"Yeah," Doss said, prompting Lavina to wonder whether he'd been listening. He looked oddly better this morning than yesterday. Maybe he could take the alcohol or leave it after all.

"I don't know about that," Bran said. "I didn't hear mention of an afterlife."

"They probably don't want to offend nonbelievers," Jae

said. "The sermons must be pretty standard, don't you think?"

"Maybe so," Bran conceded, "but it's nothing I'd care to have for a eulogy, I can tell you that."

"Well, I'm certainly glad that's over with," Violet Cole interposed as she and her husband joined the burgeoning group that had moved out toward the street. "And I'm glad they had the casket closed when we arrived. I can't bear the thought of final farewells like that." She gave a little shiver, hugging tight to her husband's arm.

"I told you it would be closed," he said, looking down at her heavily made-up face, the Dutch cut hidden now under what, to Lavina, was vaguely reminiscent of a '20s cloche.

Will Argon and Garrett Blaine were the last of their immediate group to join them after Argon managed to separate himself from a few fellow announcers. Was she just imagining it, Lavina wondered, or was he leaning more heavily on his cane than when last she'd seen him? He cleared his throat as he wedged himself in between her and Bran.

"Audra would have approved, I think," he said, without waiting for anyone to elicit his opinion of the morning service. From him, Lavina knew, it was praise indeed.

"What about her apartment and all her things?" Garrett asked. "Did I hear someone say you were taking care of it, Mr. Slattery?" He still held on to the old formalities, Lavina noticed. Another year from now, if they didn't see each other in between, she'd probably be Mrs. London again.

"Yes, Garrett, I am," the actor said. "Everything's been fairly well boxed—whatever wasn't thrown out, that is—

and Goodwill is coming the day after Christmas to pick everything up."

"You did all that yourself in the short time since Audra died?" Garrett asked. "You must work quickly."

Bran laughed. "Well, not quite by myself. A couple of the sisters from Gift of Love came over to help out."

"That's Mother Teresa's house on Washington Street, isn't it?" Lavina asked, intrigued by this latest bit of information.

"Yes."

"They must be the same ones who were here early this morning before you all arrived," Jae said. "They just came and went like lightning bugs."

"Probably," Bran said. "They used to help Audra out in the apartment from time to time when she couldn't manage on her own."

Lavina was becoming more intrigued by the minute.

"Audra wasn't Catholic though, was she?" Garrett asked.

"No."

"That wouldn't make any difference to Mother Teresa's Missionaries of Charity, Garrett," Lavina clarified. What bothered her most was the fact that the sisters should have been there at all. After all, the order's guiding principle was in helping "the poorest of the poor." Which would have made Audra much worse off than she had imagined.

"I thought I recognized their blue-trimmed habit," Jae said, stamping her unseasonable heels in an obvious attempt to restore circulation to her feet. Lavina wondered if she wasn't also subconsciously recalling the nuns' all-season sandals.

"Something you don't see too much of anymore on

American nuns," she said before reining in her tongue lest she fall prey to a few of her own less than charitable thoughts on the subject.

"What about all of Audra's tapes and magazines and things?" Argon asked. "Those weren't thrown out or given away, I hope. I mean, they must be pretty valuable. At least to a collector."

"No, Will, of course not," Bran said. "Since Audra asked me a few months ago to be her executor with full rights of dispersal of real property—what little there is—I took it on myself to pack them up and store them. After probate, I thought we'd give them to Lavina. In view of her upcoming book and all. They might come in handy." While he looked around at the individual faces forming their little circle for their reactions, Lavina couldn't help but chuckle inwardly at his clever use of the "we."

"An excellent idea," Violet said. "I don't know anyone who deserves them more."

"Definitely," Jae agreed. "Especially since Lavina is such an avid collector."

Lavina laughed as she tugged her jacket closed. "Well, I don't know that I'd quite say avid, Jae, but I do have a lot of old broadcasts on cassette and reel-to-reel. But it's really all those newspapers and radio digests that will be most valuable, I think, if the book ever actually gets off the ground."

"You didn't get too much done this trip by way of re-search, did you?" Cole said. "What with the two murders and all."

"Oh, I don't know about that, Cole," she said. "I at least got to see my agent and started the ball rolling. How it goes from here is anybody's guess. But I'm determined to give it a go once the holidays are over." Actually the two murders had been the impetus she needed to get her moving. If she could manage it tastefully, she might be able to weave them in as an added thread in the overall narrative. It was something to keep in the back of her mind.

"Good for you, Lavina!" Argon pronounced with an appropriate thump of his cane on the sidewalk.

"Well, if you folks will excuse me," Doss said, "I think I'd better be moving along." The cuff of his camel's hair coat, Lavina noticed, never quite made it above the watch he purported to consult. She reached over and lifted off a few loose hairs she spotted on the sleeve. "Believe it or not, I have a business appointment for lunch," he added.

"No rest for the weary, eh, Nelson?" Cole said with a faint smile. "Even on Saturday."

"I'll see you soon again, I hope," Lavina said. "And that goes for the rest of you as well. But at least I'll be able to see you all on the tape from time to time." With that she slid the videotape out of the pocket of her shoulder bag, brandishing it in front of them with a wide grin. "Henry's tape from the party."

"What tape?" Cole asked, the worry lines above his nose deepening.

"That's right," Jae said. "Someone *was* taping that night. I'd almost forgotten."

"Where did you get it, Lavina?" Violet asked, separating herself from her husband's arm.

"Well, I suppose I really shouldn't have mentioned it," Lavina said. "Our sheriff in Boulder would have a fit if he knew." She had always loved playing the role of gossip, and now more so than ever. "But he sent it down with me to lend to the New York police so they could make themselves a copy."

"Why would the police be interested in it?" Bran asked.

"Search me," Lavina said. "I suppose they want to get a firsthand look at all of us suspects in action. Especially since the tape was made just prior to Henry's murder."

"Are we all suspects, do you think, Lavina?" Jae asked, still drumming her feet in rapid little beats on the sidewalk.

"I should imagine so," Lavina said.

"I hope they didn't tape me doing the Hula Hop," Violet added out of the blue. "I'd die."

"It couldn't be very valuable evidence if they didn't rush it back and forth through official channels," Argon said, an incredulous sneer on his weather-reddened face that Lavina found utterly foreign to his usual winsome countenance.

"Well, that's not saying much for yours truly, now, is it?" she said with a little laugh.

"I didn't mean it like that, Lavina," Argon said. "It has nothing to do with you."

"I wouldn't mind having a copy myself," Doss added, obviously reluctant to leave.

When Lavina caught Garrett's questioning look out of the corner of her eye, she gave him a playful, conspiratorial wink, hoping he'd play along and not challenge her little fiction in front of the rest of them. If she had only had a chance to take him into her confidence earlier . . .

"Did you remember to take the other item I gave you, Lavina?" Bran asked, lightly touching the sleeve of her jacket to get her attention.

"The scissors? Yes."

"What scissors, Lavina?" Violet asked.

"The ones I found in Audra's kitchen drawer."

"What do you want those for?" Garrett asked, obviously eager to get into the act, after having said nothing about the tape.

"I want to give them to Tod Arthur—that's our sheriff—to have examined at the county police lab."

"I thought Audra was asphyxiated," Doss said. "She wasn't stabbed, too, was she?"

"Good Lord, no," Lavina said, horrified by the thought. "It's just that I think our killer might have used them to do a little clipping at the apartment, that's all. With a shiny metal surface like that, there'd be any number of good fingerprints, if he did."

"And the New York police just let you take evidence like that for you sheriff friend?" Cole's brow furrowed. "That doesn't make sense."

"They were still there after they unsealed the apartment," Lavina said. "So they obviously didn't consider them important."

"But you do." This from Cole.

"Most definitely."

"What you're really saying," Argon added, "is that you're keeping something from the police down here."

"Not at all," Lavina was quick to respond. "I told them my suspicions right off, but that nice Sergeant Packard thought I was trying to play Jessica Fletcher and just humored me along. When Bran and I returned to Audra's apartment after it was unsealed, the scissors were still there, as I already told you, and Bran let me have them."

"You told me you wanted them for your sewing box," Bran said.

Lavina gave a little smile to accompany her shrug. "I didn't want to have you worrying, thinking you were doing something wrong by giving them to me."

"Is this sheriff of yours likely to pay any more attention to your notions than the New York police, Lavina?" Doss asked with a little laugh.

"I'll have you know that Tod and I are like that"—she crossed two fingers of her right hand—"when it comes to murder investigations. This won't be the first time I've worked with him." Fighting tooth and nail all the way, of course, Lavina failed to add.

"Don't things like that have to be marked for identification and bagged or something by the police?" Argon asked hoarsely, leaning with both hands on the crook of his cane. "If they're to stand up in a court of law, I mean?" He turned his head and attempted to clear his throat with a series of little coughs.

He was right, of course, and it was a challenge Lavina hadn't foreseen. If she were to pick up the gauntlet with any sort of panache, she'd have to think fast. Personally she could have clobbered him. Instead, she smiled and leisurely tucked the videotape back into her shoulder bag. "But it was," she finally said, looking back up into Argon's face, which in the wind was fast approaching the color of his beret. "I told you Sergeant Packard humored me, didn't I?" She gave a little laugh. "What I hadn't expected, of course, was for him to later toss it back in the kitchen drawer. Thank heavens the bag was still sealed, with his private identification mark and time and date and whatnot still on it. No one else had a chance to touch it." As she listened to herself babbling on, it sounded utterly ridiculous—even to her—so there was no way of telling just how much of it her number-one suspect was likely to swallow. Unfortunately it was the only thing she had to bait her trap with. By now, of course, she had fairly ruled out her second candidate for murderer as highly unlikely. But even if she was wrong, the bait would still be the same.

"You've got gall, Lavina, I'll say that much for you," Jae added. "Is there any specific reason you think the killer's fingerprints might be on those scissors? I mean, you must have told that sergeant something for him to go to all that trouble, even if he was only humoring you."

"Oh, most definitely, Jae. It's a matter of a little newspaper clipping." She shot a glance in the direction of the Hessons, both of whom were intent on her every word, with Violet again clinging to her husband's arm. "But I'd really rather not go into it right now, if you don't mind. There are other considerations involved." She hoped she was the only one to detect Violet's audible sigh of relief. "If I'm right—which I think I am—you'll be reading about it soon enough in the papers."

"You will be in touch with us again for your book, won't you?" Cole asked after planting a kiss on her cheek.

"Definitely. I'll be hounding each of you until it's in final draft. You all promised to help, and I'm going to hold you to it." She made a pretense of checking the time. "But right now I've got to get back to the hotel and pick up the car. Tonight is ritual up at the lake, and I can't miss it."

"Ritual?" Bran's eyebrows shot up. "In what way?"

Lavina laughed. "Tonight's the night I decorate the tree."

"Not all alone, surely."

"All alone. Or ever since Ken passed away, that is. I put on a few of my holiday tapes after dinner and work till I'm done." She shook her head. "And from the looks of it, this year's tree is taller than usual, so I'll probably be at it until the wee hours. But it has to be finished before the family gets here tomorrow—which is another ritual I won't go into right now." She laughed again at what she knew was pure pigheaded insistence on family tradition. Even Susanne had tried unsuccessfully to get her to bend a little.

"Wouldn't it be better if you had someone with you for a thing like that?" Bran asked.

"Not for this job, no. It's the one thing all year long I insist on doing alone. Not that I really consider myself alone, you understand. Suffice it to say that anyone who knows me knows better than to disturb me this one night of the year." She laughed.

For better or worse, the little scene was set. Now it was only a matter of time to see if her pigeon would take the bait.

They separated a few minutes later, with Bran insisting on escorting her back to the Southgate. Much as she hated seeing him leave, she had too much work ahead to start weakening now. They parted at the main entrance to the hotel on Seventh Avenue, where she made her way up the escalator and through the lobby, exiting again on Thirty-first Street. She had two final stops to make before heading back upstate—one at a hosiery store on West Thirty-fourth, and the second at a nursing home on East Eighty-seventh.

Chapter Twenty

→ ←

So Bobbie Burns was right again. *The best laid schemes o' mice an' men gang aft a-gley.*

In Lavina's case it all fell apart with her call later that morning to Sergeant Packard. From what he had told her, her little trap would have been a waste of time. To be perfectly honest, she was relieved. She hadn't particularly been looking forward to setting herself up again as a decoy. She had done it once before and had come precariously close to meeting her Maker before her time. The more she thought about it—seeing herself all alone decorating her tree in the dead of night waiting for a deadly killer—was not exactly her idea of a holiday *ho-ho-ho* either.

Actually it was the visit to the nursing home that had gotten her to rethinking in the first place.

When she had entered the front door and found herself in the lobby of the home, she was almost overcome by depression at the sight of the meager, institutional Christmas decorations. It had saddened her more than if they'd had nothing at all. It was all she could do to follow the nurse down the long, vaulted hallway to the private room that was now home to the wealthy Simon Doss. She hadn't known quite what to expect, of course, because she was acting on her intuition, fueled though it may have been by a few astute observations.

Simon Doss was propped up against a skimpy feather pillow in a wheelchair alongside the single curtained window that looked out on a planted yard that may well have been very pretty in spring and summer. He was positioned in front of what looked like a large, white drafting board with a clamp-on swivel light. His left arm was tucked firmly against his chest as if in an invisible sling, the other painting away meticulously with light, airy strokes. Lavina had neared the board before he looked up from his work to see her. She would never forget that smile of instant recognition. It amazed her that he should remember her after all those years. It certainly would not have been the other way around. After all, they had barely known each other even back then.

It was Hildy, he admitted, after they had exchanged warm greetings, who had first pointed her out to him. And, then, of course, he had seen her several times at the studios, not to mention her photos in the numerous radio digests and papers. After all, she was Lavina London, wasn't she? He made her sound somewhere between Alice Faye and Lauren Bacall. If nothing else, the visit would serve to boost her ego for years to come.

She wasn't surprised to find that there was nothing wrong with Simon Doss's mind, which she had suspected after Nelson's insistence to the contrary in his obvious attempt—to her, at least—to deter visitors. It was Nelson's fear that had gotten her thinking along paths her mind had trod earlier, back when she was still trying to isolate pieces of the puzzle.

Simon spent much of the visit talking about his wife, Laurie. It was a shame she had never met the woman; from the way he spoke of her, he'd obviously loved her very much. Everything Lavina knew about Simon had come from Hildy in one way or another, including—strange to say—the long forgotten innuendo regarding the man's possible sterility. Since it had never amounted to more than that, it was only natural she should have put it out of her mind, and it had only come back to her during her visit to the nursing home. If she had remembered it earlier, it might well have added more substance to her intuitive gleanings.

Yes, she learned, he knew all about Henry's and Audra's murders, though he couldn't for the life of him understand why they had been singled out. Or so, at least, he claimed.

She learned something else, too. Not only had the insinuation about his sterility been true, but he, too, had been approached early on by Henry Blaine for hush money. "But I'd be damned if I was going to pay that . . . that scoundrel a bloody cent, no matter what he threatened," he told her. "His actions proved him far less of a man than I was, sterile or not." And, to his knowledge, Henry had backed off and never followed through with his threats of exposure. And no, he had never let on to Nelson that he wasn't his real father. As far as he knew, the boy had never learned otherwise. Since he seemed so obviously blissful in his ignorance, Lavina saw no reason to burst his little bubble. His sufferings seemed bad enough already.

From what he had jokingly told her, his whole left side was paralyzed from the shoulder down.

After the onset of the stroke, Hildy had wanted him to come live with her and Henry. Poor, unsuspecting Hildy. She had obviously never suspected her husband's penchant for blackmail. For Simon, of course, it ruled out the possibility from the start. By now it no longer mattered; he had long since come to the realization that he was better off at the nursing home than anywhere else. He had just taken his memories of his wife, Laurie, along with him. No, everything he wanted and needed was right there at the home, including new friends.

So she had been wrong. The big, rambling, seemingly impersonal home had a heart all its own. And Simon had even discovered a new side to himself after all those years at the agency. He had a decided talent for painting. The poster he was preparing for an upcoming athletic event for the handicapped was excellent by any standards. Even Lavina had been able to see that.

While she left the nursing home in a brighter mood than she expected, she also left with the now fully substantiated conviction that Nelson Doss had murdered both Henry Blaine and Audra Mateer. What was an even sadder note, however, was the realization that the murders were more senseless than she had originally envisioned. The only thing that remained was concrete proof.

After she left the nursing home on East Eighty-seventh Street, she stopped off at a phone booth and placed four calls. If there had to be a new plan of action, this seemed as good as any. Only time would tell. If the luck she had finding everyone in held out, she could return home with a clear conscience, knowing she had done everything possible for both Hildy and Audra. Not to mention the wonders it would do for her somewhat sullied reputation on the home front. And not whitewash either.

The first call was to Tracey to see if she could stop by to view the videotape Garrett had dropped in her lap. After fending off brunch, lunch, and early dinner, she managed to view the tape quietly in her son-in-law's den and leave. But again only after placing another call to see if she had the final green light necessary to put her new plan in operation. Again, success. She could hardly believe it. Someone up there had taken things out of her clumsy hands and was guiding her step by step.

The tape had proved pretty much of a bust as far as evidence was concerned, but it didn't throw a monkey wrench into her envisioned solution to the murders either.

After a fairly lengthy blank lead-in, obviously left for later titling, she viewed the subsequent goings-on at the party, fast forwarding several times, and stopping at various spots to verify a few of her earlier observations. They *had* caught Violet in the midst of her Hula Hop after all, which gave her a chuckle or two. Somehow, watching her on tape, she found it nearly impossible to picture Violet as a cold-blooded child killer. She and Cole should never have paid that blackmail to begin with. Maybe now, by going to the police, that ghost, too, would finally be exorcized.

In several of the close-up shots, Will Argon was staring off at someone, his eyes intent, if not actually worried. While she couldn't see the person, she was sure she knew who it was. Without the red beret, Will's thick, white mane came across on the color tape like angel hair. How it could have changed so drastically from its earlier auburn shade was one of nature's many wonders. And for a while, nature had led her astray. Fortunately her memory was as sharp as it had always been. And there was nothing wrong with her powers of observation either, even if she had to say so herself.

Jae, she realized, following her every recorded move, was being as attentive as the proverbial mother hen to Henry. The woman, she was convinced, was obviously still in love with him, even after all those years. Another of God's strange and wondrous gifts of nature—attraction.

After a few pans of the camera, the lens finally stopped to focus on Nelson Doss. He was leaning against a circular table, an untouched drink in his hand. The only people she saw talking with him in any of the footage were the Hessons and Bran Slattery. In this one close-up, he was alone, except for whatever malevolent demon was gnawing at his soul. The look of hatred on his face frightened her. Poor Laurie Doss. It was just as well she wasn't still alive to see what she had wrought.

By the time she left Tracey's, it was almost one thirty. As she sat in the cab caught in crosstown traffic, she could picture her tree sitting out back behind her house on the lake. How was she ever going to get it up before the family arrived tomorrow?

Chapter Twenty-One
➤ ⬅

"You killed the two of them in cold blood!"

Will Argon stood in the tiny living room of his equally small brownstone apartment brandishing his cane, his face a close colormate to the red beret he had earlier tossed onto the bulky, turn of the century armchair alongside him. His voice crackled like shaved ice underfoot.

"Is that why you asked me over her—to accuse me of killing two of your old cronies?" Nelson Doss hadn't even bothered to remove his camel's-hair coat. He shook his head at the older man facing him. "You're off your rocker."

"If you only knew how I wished that were true," Argon said, his voice now almost a whisper.

Doss raised his arm to check his watch. "I suppose you have proof for this ridiculous accusation?" When Argon didn't answer, he went on: "That's what I thought. You're as bad as Audra. Or Lavina." He gave a little laugh. "Her and her stupid scissors. She'll never find fingerprints on those, that's for sure. The woman doesn't even use common sense. If anyone used them to cut out that article on the Hesson kid's death, he'd hardly be stupid enough to forget to wipe them off, now would he?"

"Is that what you did, Nelson?"

Doss gave a start, then spun around to face the bedroom behind him.

Lavina London stood in the doorway, her clear-framed glasses dangling from their chain over her gray wool knitted dress.

"Well, well, so you've got yourself a nursemaid, I see," Doss said, a forced smile on his cracked lips. Then, to Lavina: "I thought you went back home to 'deck the halls.' "

"You hoped I went home, you mean," Lavina said.

"Personally I couldn't care less one way or the other. I just hope you're not here to act out another one of your charades."

"You're referring to the scissors, I suppose."

"What else? I mean, give me a break."

"What makes you so sure there were no prints?" she asked, picking up on his earlier comment.

Doss just smirked and ran his tongue over his parched lips.

"I'll tell you why," Lavina added. "Because you wiped them off yourself." A fact she had learned that morning from her call to Sergeant Packard. The all-important fact that had caused her to alter her original plan. The prints had either been wiped off or—less likely—gloves had been worn. In either case it meant the killer would have known there was nothing to fear on that account.

"This was after I supposedly cut out that article?"

"Precisely."

"Then they're hardly evidence of anything, are they?"

"Not physically maybe, no." Lavina glanced past him to Will—who, as they had agreed on the phone—was content to let her take the lead. He moved now and sat down on the brocade sofa against the wall, waiting for his cue.

"You were trying to lay a trap at the funeral home, weren't you?" Doss said. "You thought that the person who killed Audra would follow you home and try to get them off you. While you were supposedly there all alone decking your halls. And all the time you'd have that hick sheriff in the wings waiting to pounce. Ho, ho, ho."

"Something like that," Lavina admitted. Hearing him describe it out loud made it seem even more ridiculous than it had sounded in her head. She was grateful she hadn't been forced to act it out. But, then, she had never for a minute questioned his cleverness.

"You're as gaga as the old man here."

Lavina was growing more furious with every belittling remark to the former announcer. "If that's the case," she said, "why is it you're the one making all the mistakes?"

"Mistakes!" The surprise on Doss's face was an honest one.

"That's what I said."

"You lied about Simon, for one thing," Argon sputtered, this time poking Doss in the side with his cane.

"Will you get that damn thing out of my ribs!" Doss stared down into the older man's eyes again, this time as if trying to see someone or something. Lavina wondered if this was the first time they'd ever been this close. "And leave my father out of it, okay?"

"How I wish I could," Argon said, looking back across to Lavina. "How I wish I could."

"So if that's it, Lavina," Doss said, tugging the camel's-hair coat around his chest, "I'll leave you to your little games. I still have a business to run."

"And that's what it comes down to, doesn't it?" Lavina said. "The business."

"If that's supposed to have some kind of deep meaning," Doss said, the smirk back again on his face, "I'm afraid you've lost me."

"I'm afraid we lost you a long time ago," Argon said, his cracking voice trailing off.

"Another sphinx heard from. If I hang around you two much longer, I'll be Looney Tunes myself." He turned, headed for the door, "Invite someone else to your riddle game next time, will you?"

"There you go making another mistake, Nelson—assuming people aren't quite as clever as you are," Lavina said.

Doss spun around on the uncarpeted floor to face them. "What's with all this 'mistake' crap, will you tell me? The only mistake I can see I made was listening to this geezer and coming over here in the first place."

"That clipping nonsense, for one," Lavina said, ignoring the new insult to Argon. "Your attempt at misdirection, to lay the blame on the Hessons. It was just a bit too obvious."

"I don't know anything about that clipping."

"There you go with another mistake."

"What are you talking about?"

"If you didn't know anything about the clipping, how come you were able to describe it to Will a little while ago as dealing with—how did you put it?—'the Hesson kid's death'?"

Doss shrugged. "I read it in the papers, I guess."

"It wasn't mentioned in the papers. As far as I know, the New York police haven't even looked into that aspect of the case yet." Which, of course, wasn't entirely true because Sergeant Packard had mentioned it to her during their phone conversation that morning.

"Then I must have heard it from you," Doss insisted, a little too strongly.

Lavina shook her head, toying with her glasses as she did so. "Not from me, you didn't. Nor from anyone else. The only way you could have known what was in the clipping was if you had seen it yourself. And the only place you could have done that was at Audra's. You saw it on the coffee table, where she had left it after showing it to Cole Hesson."

"The Hessons. They're the ones who mentioned it. Somebody did." Beads of perspiration formed now across the man's brow.

"Hardly, Nelson," Lavina corrected. "You're the only one who's mentioned it. Just now in this apartment."

"This another one of your little traps?" The attempt at a smirk this time fell far short of its mark.

"More like one of *yours* that backfired, wouldn't you say?" Lavina said with a smile.

"So maybe I did cut out the article, so what? It's just the word of two old codgers against that of a reputable young businessman. And even if the cops did believe you, it's hardly proof that I murdered anybody." He yanked a handkerchief out of his pocket and moped his brow. "Why would I kill Henry and Audra in the first place? I hardly knew either of them."

Lavina nodded. "A fact that worked to your advantage, certainly," she conceded. "But, nonetheless, kill them you did. Poor Audra—to keep her quiet once she guessed, I suppose. Why else would you have gone to her apartment? And Henry—well, Henry brought it on himself in his attempt to blackmail you with exposure."

Doss shot a glance in the direction of Will Argon, then back again at Lavina. After a brief pause, he raked a hand through his dark copper hair and laughed. "And what, pray tell, is this deep, dark secret in my past that Henry was supposed to be holding over my head? Did I beat up some innocent little kid, too? Molest him, maybe?"

Lavina sighed. "Henry seems to have been blackmailing, or attempting to blackmail, a number of people until the time he married Hildy, at which point he stopped. Why, exactly, we'll never know." She looked over to the sofa at Will Argon, then back again.

"What's that got to do with me? How do we know he wasn't blackmailing you? Maybe you killed the two of them."

Lavina ignored the expected attempt at self-defense. "You know, that was really the one thing that had me confused for a while," she said. "Why had someone waited all these years to kill Henry? Why not earlier?

"The answer, when it came, was, of course, really quite simple. When Henry first began blackmailing, you were too young to be one of his victims. This time around you were an entirely fresh target, ripe for a killing. Unfortunately for Henry, you weren't about to sit back and let him get away with it. He'd met his match."

Doss let out a long, low whistle. "That's rich, Lavina, really rich. Now all we need is a little sense behind your accusations. You still haven't come up with this motive you keep referring to."

Lavina looked back again to Argon, who had raised himself up so that he now sat on the arm of the sofa.

"Damn it, boy," Argon began "I should take this cane and thrash you within an inch of your life." The voice, stronger and more resonant than it had been, was still brittle. "Or maybe just break your damn neck and have done with it. . . . To think that my own flesh and blood . . ." Sobs cut off anything more he might have said.

"Easy, Will," Lavina said, moving over to his side.

"What the hell's *he* talking about?" Doss said, eyeing the two of them at the sofa.

"Don't stand there and pretend you don't know that Will is your father, Nelson. You've done it deliberately at least twice since you've come through that door. You've done nothing but insult Will. You should be ashamed of yourself. What you've done to him is worse than what you did to Audra and Henry." When she finally managed to control her sense of outrage, she looked down to see that Will was squeezing her arm. She smiled and pulled away.

"You had to open your mouth, didn't you?" Doss said, staring over at his natural father. The boy Lavina seemed to see in him so often was gone now, replaced by his own personal demon. Mood swings, she supposed they were called nowadays. Whatever they were, she found them frightening.

"Will didn't tell me, Nelson," she said, trying to calm him.

"Then who did? Henry, I suppose. The bastard."

"You didn't know before he told you, did you?" she said.

"No."

"And he tried to blackmail you over it. Told you Simon didn't know about Will and your mother, Laurie."

Doss began to breathe more heavily, as if he had just rushed up a flight of stairs. "He said he'd tell my father—Simon, I mean. I couldn't believe it. Will . . . my father. What a bummer. You wouldn't believe . . ."

She wanted to smack his smug little face, but instead just let her nails sink deeper and deeper into the palms of her fisted hands. She couldn't bring herself to look at Will at all.

"When did you make up your mind to kill him?" Lavina asked.

"The day I received the invitation to his farewell party. What could be more ideal, with all his old cronies Johnny-on-the-spot? From what I'd heard about him, enough of them certainly had motives to kill him."

"Very clever."

"I thought so."

"And that's why you came up with the idea for the *Shadow* message, too."

He laughed. "You even know about that, huh?" He shook his head in obvious appreciation of a worthy opponent. "Let's see how good you really are. Why that particular message? You must have given it some thought."

She had, of course. On more occasions than one. She sighed. "I think you chose it mainly to throw suspicion on one of the members of our little group—as I said—someone directly connected with early radio." Doss nodded periodically as she outlined what she had formed in her mind earlier. "Of all the people who had, or could have had, copies of those old shows, you were probably the least likely. You, and maybe Garrett. Because of your age more than anything else, I suppose."

"Right, but you've already said that. Why the *Shadow*, though?"

"Well, you probably became enamoured of the Avenger idea as well. It gave you a feeling of power, of getting even. Tit for tat. Henry'd tried his little blackmail game, so you thought it only right to bring him to justice—however distorted that view of justice was."

"Even your noble Shadow wasn't all that moral in his interpretation of justice, Lavina," Doss said. "Sometimes it was just an eye for an eye, with no particular concern for the form of punishment. I've listened to many of those old shows from my . . . my father's collection."

"Maybe so, but at least his motives were never selfish, for personal gain."

"And mine were, is that it?"

"Weren't they?"

Doss looked down at his shoes, then back up again. "Is it wrong to want to keep what you've always had? The money, the life-style?"

"Not in itself, no," Lavina said.

"I couldn't chance losing them. And I had no intention of spending the rest of my life paying blackmail money to Henry Blaine just so he could live high on the hog up in Canada."

"But you forgot something very important, Nelson."

"What's that?"

"It's called love and trust. And communication."

"You've lost me again." He ran a hand through his hair.

"We had a nice little visit, Simon and I—"

"You *what!*" On his forehead, beads of perspiration replaced the ones he had wiped away earlier. "You didn't say . . . I mean, you didn't tell him anything?"

"You killed in order to keep your secret. So you wouldn't chance losing all that money. Which probably amounts to quite a fortune by this time, knowing how well the agency has done all these years. You were afraid that if Simon ever found out that he'd disown you, isn't that it? Maybe even have you thrown out of the firm?"

"Certainly. Wouldn't anyone?"

Not quite anyone, Nelson, no, she thought. "You're missing the whole point, Nelson," she said. "All your plotting and killing were for nothing."

"You think he would have forgiven and forgotten." Doss shook his head. "I'm afraid you don't know my father."

"I'm afraid you're the one who doesn't know him, Nelson. Either of them. Simon or Will here. You see, Simon has known all along that you weren't his real son. He loved you too much to ever want *you* to know. He and Will both. I can't say that I agree with them, but that's the way they wanted it."

"He couldn't have known," Nelson protested, speaking now more to himself than to her, the look on his face as frozen as the condensation on the poorly insulated windows.

"I suspected as much before I went to see him," Lavina continued. "Which is why I made my little visit in the first place. I had to know for sure. I had no choice but to ask him about you. You see, Hilda Blaine had told me something many years ago about Simon, something he had to have known himself. He could never have believed for a minute that you were his natural son."

"He knew . . . all this time he knew." The lips moved, but that was about all. Lavina and Argon might just as well not even have been in the room.

"The one thing he doesn't know," Lavina added, as if to ease the man's pain, "is that you're the one responsible for the two deaths."

"If he knew that, he'd probably give me the heave for sure, right?" The little boy in him didn't seem quite sure.

"Somehow I find that difficult to believe," Lavina said. "Simon is too much of a man."

Doss looked off in the direction of the kitchen, staring a few minutes at the stove. Lavina wondered briefly if he was contemplating death by gas again, but somehow didn't think so.

"If what you say is true—about how he feels, I mean—then it probably wouldn't make any difference what he hears or suspects. Is that what you're saying?"

"Yes."

The smirk was back, cockier than ever.

"If you were so sure Simon didn't know the truth about you," Lavina resumed, "why did you lie about his condition, not want anyone to see him? It was one of the things that made me suspicious."

Doss gave a little shrug that was barely visible under the overcoat. "I didn't know who else might have known besides Henry and . . . and Will here, for one thing." He motioned with his head in Argon's direction, obviously still uncomfortable with the situation. "With two of his old friends dead, I didn't want people stirring up the past and possibly rattling old bones. I was worried about you once I heard you were out dredging up the past for your book. I should have realized you'd check things out for yourself." His shook his head, his eyes bright even in the artificial light of the small apartment.

"Isn't there something you forgot, though, Lavina?" he finally said after a few moments of silence. "What about your other little trap?"

She looked to his coat, then back into his face. "Other trap?"

"The videotape."

Lavina let out a little sigh of relief. "Oh, that."

"Disappointing, wasn't it?"

"Not completely," she admitted. "If nothing else, it showed me you hadn't had quite as much to drink that night as you'd led us to believe. You barely touched the full drink in the video sequence you were in."

Doss nodded in obvious appreciation. "I did exaggerate a little. I had just enough to make sure I didn't back out at the last minute. I celebrated when it was over. Once Henry was out of the way, well, Audra was easier."

Lavina closed her eyes, trying to wish away both the man's callous inhumanity and the picture of the dead woman it brought to mind. Maybe the demon in him hadn't quite had its fill.

Doss looked again from Lavina to the pathetic-looking figure of the former announcer, who was leaning on his cane. "If everything you say about Simon is true," he said, "I think I'll just sit back and take my chances. Anything that went on here is your word against mine. And I think I can trust old Simon will take my word over yours, if it comes down to that. After all, you still don't have any *concrete* proof of anything."

"There, I'm afraid you're wrong," Lavina said.

Argon shot her a glance of disbelief.

"Don't tell me there was a video camera rigged up in Henry's garage, too, Lavina. That would be a bit much, even from you." The laugh somehow matched the smirk.

"Nothing quite so rigged, Nelson, I assure you," Lavina said with a laugh of her own. "You see, there was something I couldn't help noticing this morning at the funeral home, something that didn't really sink in until much later, as a matter of fact. I could have kicked myself for almost missing the obvious."

"And what was that?" He didn't seem quite so sure of himself now, Lavina noticed.

"Those cat hairs on your camel's-hair coat," she said, pointing to the telltale strands.

"What about them?" Doss strained his neck to look down at the lapels of his overcoat.

"I'll wager you anything that when the police lab checks, they'll find they belong to Sheena."

"Sheena?"

"Audra's Siamese." Lavina smiled. "Isn't it ironic? Her own personal avenger. And she didn't even have to pick up any mysterious secrets in the Orient either. Just do what comes naturally. Shed."

For a few brief moments she thought he was going to strike out in some way, like a trapped animal. Then the flush passed from his face as quickly as it had come. He let out a deep sigh, then set up the smirk again. "And what will keep me from doing the same thing, Lavina? Shedding, I mean? Getting rid of the thing? Thanks for the tip." He pulled the front of the coat together across his chest and headed toward the door.

"You'd be tampering with evidence, if you did, Mr. Doss," Sergeant Packard said, emerging from the bedroom, followed by two officers. "So, if you'll just come along with us . . ."

"How did you know cat hairs were distinctive, Lavina?" Tod Arthur asked, passing her the last handful of tinsel.

"I didn't," she said, adding the final touches to the tree that now stood in her lakefront living room and then standing back to admire her handiwork. "I just hoped they were. In any case Nelson was in no position to argue the point. Not once Sergeant Packard lent his authoritative voice to my claim, anyway."

"Thanks for calling me, by the way, after you left the nursing home," Arthur said, his eyes following the twinkling lights on the pine tree.

Lavina grinned. "As your deputy I felt I owed it to you to let you know what I planned to do, and get your feedback."

"You don't have to rub it in, Lavina." They both laughed.

"I just hope they can get a conviction," she said. "Nelson certainly had no reason to be at Audra's in the first place unless he intended to keep her quiet. That's premeditation, isn't it?"

"It looks like it to me," Arthur said.

"Still, with all these loopholes nowadays . . ."

"Well, you did everything you could do, Lavina, that's for sure."

Lavina nodded. "I think Hildy would be satisfied."

"And Audra," Arthur added. "Don't forget you also provided her cat with a home." He shook his head. "Poor Damian."

"Listen, Sheena was responsible for providing us with

the concrete evidence we were lacking, wasn't she? How many animals do you know who can say as much?"

They both laughed, and Lavina moved back closer to the picture window to get a better view of the tree. "Beautiful, if I say so myself."

"I thought for a while there this afternoon that you weren't going to get it up today," Arthur confessed.

"You and me both."

And such would have been the case, except for sheer determination. That, and the aid of two fiftysomething neighbors from the lake whom she sweet-talked into bringing in the tree and anchoring it to her metal stand after she'd arrived back at the lake a little after six. The time-honored damsel-in-distress call. She had detained them only long enough to turn the tree this way and that twenty times or so until she was satisfied that its best side was facing out, then treated them to some of her laced, homemade eggnog.

Then, she had gone to work. First, unwrapping and mounting the aging silver star atop the tree, then stringing the multicolored lights and hanging the ornaments, and finally draping the tinsel, piece by piece. Tod Arthur had arrived somewhere between the lights and the ornaments with his yearly gift of pine wreaths and Polly's fruitcake.

Lavina stood in stocking feet, bathed in the twinkling show of color before her—the red, white, green, yellow, blue, orange—not too many orange; she didn't particularly care for the glare they gave off.

"Well, I guess you've pretty much filled me in," Arthur said, reaching for his jacket, which he'd thrown on the sofa.

"You'll have to admit I kept you pretty much up to

date," Lavina said, giving him a mock scowl. "As you knew I would all along."

"How did you know," Arthur asked, ignoring the dig, "that Will Argon was the boy's real father? Or did you?"

"I can't honestly say I knew for sure until Simon confirmed it, though I was pretty certain in my own mind. You see, Nelson reminded me of someone—I just couldn't put my finger on who it was until I saw Nelson and Will standing together at the funeral home. That's when it hit me. The resemblance was just too close to be anything else."

"Provided you were looking for one to begin with, you mean."

"Probably, yes. Of course, thinking back, I remembered that Will had had a gorgeous head of curly auburn hair, and while it was never quite the same shade as Nelson's, still, it helped me put two and two together."

"Well, I'm just grateful you didn't decide to do anything foolish this time. What you did was bad enough."

"How? The police were in the apartment, weren't they? Not to mention Will with his handy cane." She didn't for a minute dare tell him what her original plan had been. What he didn't know . . .

Arthur rubbed a meaty hand across his balding pate, then down the back of his thick, sinewy neck, replacing his wide-brimmed, gray trooper's hat on his head when he'd done so.

"I don't know why it is," he said, reaching for the doorknob, "but I have a sneaky feeling you haven't told me everything."

Lavina reached to grab the opened door. "I don't know why," she said. "I can't think of anything."

"Maybe I'd better have a talk with Susanne."

"Susanne! Whatever for?"

"Maybe she'll tell me all those things about this Slattery guy you managed to sidestep so carefully." He gave her a wide, knowing grin and passed out the door.

MONDAY, DECEMBER 25

Chapter Twenty-Two

→ ←

Long strands of tinsel shimmered with the reflection of the colored lights that flickered on and off in alternating patterns on their separate blinkers, lulling Lavina into a near semitrance as she stood in front of the seven-foot-high tree. It was the mounting clatter of china and glassware from the kitchen that finally summoned her back to the reality of the living room.

From her position in the middle of the homey room, she looked down under the tree to the old wooden stable that had been her parents'. The only plaster survivors of the original crèche were the Virgin Mary, Saint Joseph, the Child Jesus, two Wise Men, an equal number of little sheep, and one sleepy-looking camel—all of which were bathed in the blue light emanating from a single bulb that pointed its nose through an aperture in the side of the rustic structure. Courtesy of Lavina London. She let her eyes travel across the expanse of white sheet under the tree, covered with already opened gifts neatly arranged on display, past the sheet-glass, snow-sprayed lake with its metal figure skaters, to the beige-colored IBM Correcting Selectric. She shook her head—not for the first time.

Watching her from the kitchen doorway, a dinner plate and terry-cloth towel in her hand, Susanne smiled. "I told you I had something special that would help you with your book, Gran," she said, continuing to dry.

"I know you did, dear, but I hardly expected anything like this. And all that money . . ."

"Not all that much, Gran. It's a discontinued model now, don't forget. But it's still brand new. And I was sure you're prefer it to a word processor or computer."

"Heavens, yes," Lavina admitted, recognizing her own limited concessions to modernism.

"And you certainly couldn't use that old manual you've been holding on to all these years. It must be a collector's item by now." Susanne laughed.

"Not quite that, dear," Lavina said. "I bought it in '48 and it still works fine. I'll pass it on to someone, certainly."

Susanne groaned. "Not that, Gran, please. Unless it's to the garbage man."

"You know it's going to find its way back into her closet, Susanne," the girl's mother said from the kitchen sink behind her, where she and Winnie O'Kirk were attacking their end of the after-dinner cleanup. "So what's the use of talking?"

"Will you stop picking on my poor mother-in-law," Damian Halliday protested from the dining room, which, together with the kitchen, extended across the rear of the house. As was their wont, the men—in this case Damian, Sean O'Kirk, and Bran Slattery—were leisurely digesting their meal at the table, awaiting their coffee and usual assortment of holiday postprandial goodies.

"I still can't get over those pantyhose, Gran," Susanne said, obviously siding with her father as she returned to the dish rack for another plate. "I never thought I'd see the day. I absolutely adore them."

"You would, Su," Tracey said, rubbing an itchy nose with the finger of a dripping rubber glove. "You and your grandmother are two of a kind." At that, grandmother and granddaughter exchanged conspiratorial winks. "Green on green, of all things. And with Christmas trees, no less." She shook her head. "I don't know, Mother, it must be second childhood creeping up."

"At least you can't say they're not in season," Lavina said with a little laugh.

"That's for sure," Tracey added.

"I picked them up in New York before I went to see Simon."

"Sort of a spur-of-the-moment thing like those culottes you treated yourself to a while back," Winnie said over her shoulder with a knowing smile.

"Sort of, yes," Lavina agreed, returning the smile. "Keeps me young." She stuck the tip of her tongue out at her daughter again, turned back, then laughed.

"And beautiful," Susanne added, choking back the laughter.

"Thank you, dear," Lavina said, bending down to gather up a few strands of tinsel that had slipped off their branches, and then placing them back on the tree, one at a time. After Tod's departure Saturday night, it was almost two in the morning before she had finally gotten to bed; the wrapping had to be finished in time for the family's arrival for Christmas Eve, no matter what. It was only the body's insistence that had gotten her back to bed for a two-hour nap after Sunday mass. Later that night, after opening their gifts, they had all gone together to Saint Michael's in Monticello for midnight mass. Then it was up again at the crack of dawn to stuff the bird and get it in the oven. Hectic as always, but she loved every minute of it. As usual, there was the one fleeting fear that this might be her last Christmas with the family, a thought that had no lasting effect other than to do as much as humanly possible to make this one the happiest ever.

Also as usual, they refused to let her near the kitchen during cleanup detail, and it was only after they were almost finished that she was allowed back into the dining room to help her granddaughter, who was already at the china cabinet handing out cups, saucers, and dessert dishes to her father. Polly Arthur's annual fruitcake was already on the table along with three pies—pumpkin, apple, and pecan.

Sean O'Kirk was digging the meat out of a cracked walnut with a nut pick as Lavina passed behind his chair. "We were just talking about your escapade, Lavina," Sean said, turning his white-fringed head to look up over his left shoulder.

"Still?"

"The New York cops didn't leave those scissors in Audra's apartment, did they?" he asked.

"Of course not, Sean. Or not after they learned about the clipping, that is. Vince Packard picked them up right after Tod phoned him and passed along my suggestion to check them for prints." She moved up to the end of the table behind Damian and took the pile of dessert dishes Susanne handed her, setting them on the red and green linen tablecloth, then reached into the cabinet for the creamer.

"So, it's *Vince* now, is it?" Bran remarked with a smile. "What happened to good old *Sergeant* Packard?"

Headed back to the kitchen, Lavina just laughed.

"And there were really no prints on the scissors?" Damian asked.

"Nary a one," Lavina said, stopping and standing in the doorway. A service wall separated the two rooms. "Wiped clean as a whistle. Which made Sergeant Packard very suspicious, indeed. I really think that's what softened him up so that he agreed to meet us at Will's apartment and go along with my little plan." She halted just as she was about to turn back toward the kitchen and looked instead at her son-in-law. "Where's Sheena, by the way?"

"I'll Sheena you!" Tracey half shouted from the kitchen.

"I don't know, dear, you always wanted a pussycat when you were little, when we were on the road and couldn't have one." She winked at the little group around the table. "I finally get you one, and look at the thanks I get."

Tracey turned and glowered at her.

"She's at a neighbor's, Mom," her son-in-law said, trying to keep a straight face. "And believe it or not, she's finally starting to come around to me."

"Love will win out every time," Lavina said.

"Talking about love," Damian added, "did Doss really believe his father—Simon, I mean—would have disinherited him if he learned he wasn't his real son?" Frown lines marred his handsome face. He had always reminded Lavina of Richard Denning, radio's latter-day Mr. North, not to mention Lucille Ball's "Favorite Husband" between Lee Bowman and Desi Arnaz. Even now, the hair was almost as blond as it had always been.

"I suppose so," she said. "Otherwise why go to such extremes to hide what he mistakenly thought was a secret that his mother had kept from her husband?"

"It would have made more sense all around if Simon had admitted knowing about Nelson's real father," Susanne said, closing the leaded-glass door of the china cabinet. "Then, if he wanted, he could have adopted him legally."

Lavina sighed. "In retrospect, yes. But back then, Simon and Will thought it was in Nelson's interest that it be kept a secret. Or so Will told me, anyway."

"But that way Nelson never really knew either of them—how much they both really loved him."

"No," Lavina agreed, "he didn't. Which only goes to prove again the importance of communication."

"I'm certainly glad we don't have that problem in this family," the girl said, tousling her father's hair as she passed behind him to follow her grandmother on her way back out to the kitchen.

"You know," Lavina said, still in the doorway, "it just dawned on me last night lying in bed that by using the Shadow message, what Nelson was actually doing was trying to 'cloud men's minds' himself. You know what I mean? He was trying to make us all believe the murderer was someone from the old-radio era." She smiled at the connection that, to her at least, was so obvious. "It didn't work, of course. The Shadow still had the last word, so to speak, by catching Nelson in his own trap."

"Kind of stretching the point there a bit, don't you think, Lavina?" Sean said, a wry expression on his face.

"Oh, I don't know, Sean," she said, a playful grin forming now on her own. " 'Who knows what evil lurks in the hearts of men?' "

A chorus of groans rose from the dining room table, chasing Lavina out into the kitchen, her hands covering her head in feigned self-protection. Lucky for her, the creamer in her hand was empty. Winnie passed her with a silent shake of her head on her way into the dining room with the first pot of coffee.

Lavina set the creamer on the countertop by the sink and proceeded out to the living room where she found Tracey, fisted hands on her hips, examining the tree at close range.

"Mother, when in heaven's name are you going to get rid of all these old Christmas ornaments?" she said, seeing her mother enter the room. "Some of them are as old as Jacob." With a long fingernail she flicked the body of a slender blue-gray icicle, setting up a ping in the paper-thin glass.

"Get rid of them!" Lavina paused a few seconds in disbelief. "Susanne," she finally added, turning to her granddaughter, "remind me to add a codicil to my will leaving all my ornaments to you. That way I'll know the poor things will survive. Your mother obviously doesn't remember how much joy they used to give her every Christmas when she was growing up."

"Mother, really!" A flush spread across Tracey's face.

"Come on, Gran," Susanne said, "Mother would never throw them out, and you know it as well as I do. She's just pulling your leg. Deep down, she's as soft and sentimental as the two of us—she just doesn't like anyone to see it, that's all. She likes to pretend she's hardboiled."

Lavina eyed her granddaughter with obvious suspicion, weighing the plausibility of her words. "I don't know, Susu . . ."

The girl smiled at the childish nickname, squeezing her grandmother's forearm. "How could your own daughter possibly be other than you raised her, Gran—tell me that. Deep down, the three of us are all the same, still kids at heart."

Tracey shook her head and stood back up from where she had crouched down to rearrange the chipped, plaster figures around the ancient manger with its discolored straw. She turned to face her mother and daughter.

"That's the way you always insisted on setting them up when you were little, too," Lavina said, the memory ever-present. Tears filled the corners of her eyes.

Tracey took her mother in her arms, holding her tight, then planted a kiss on her cheek. "Dad was the one who broke Melchior," she said, jerking her head back in the direction of the missing Magus. "In all these years you never replaced him. How come?"

Lavina shrugged, her hand unconsciously toying with the green crystal beads around her neck. "We just kept putting it off, and then, after your father died, I sort of liked to imagine that he had assumed the Wise Man's place there at the crib. It's silly, I know, but . . ." She smiled and wiped her eyes with a finger.

"I don't think so, Gran," Susanne said, joining her mother and grandmother in front of the tree, the three of them encircling one another's waist and staring down at the blessed replica before them. They remained there in silence a good minute before Lavina, in the middle, released her hold on the other two and took a deep breath.

"Let's go back inside," she said with a broad smile, "or they'll be out looking for us." She straightened her leather belt and laughed. "I'm going to have to loosen this thing before the day's over, I can see that now."

Back in the kitchen, she filled an insulated pot from the large aluminum coffeemaker on the counter and handed it to Tracey, who proceeded to take it into the dining room to join the Pyrex already on the table. Susanne followed with a bottle of Irish Mist that she dug out of the liquor cabinet and set it down next to the B&B, Courvoisier, and Cherry Herring. "You always forget me," she said to her father.

"From the little you've told us, Lavina," Sean O'Kirk said as the three women took their places at the table, "it seems like poor Hildy was the unwitting source of all the important information. About Nelson's real father and all, I mean." He reached for a cigarette in the breast pocket of his flannel shirt.

"Not at the table, Sean," Winnie said at his side, stretching out an arm and staying his hand. She removed the ashtray he had set in front of him and placed it on the buffet behind them where Lavina's four Christmas cacti, in bloom since Thanksgiving, were just passing their prime. The elongated pink, white, and salmon flowers weighed down the already cascading stems. The picture window facing east presented an emerging dusk against a background of dense evergreens.

"From what Simon and Will told me," Lavina said, "together with what I've been able to piece together myself, it would seem so." With a finger, she motioned to her son-in-law to turn on the dimmer switch controlling the crystal chandelier. "I imagine Simon was the type to have told her about his condition while they were still keeping company." She smiled at her use of the outdated expression. "Certainly before he proposed."

"You think that's why Hildy never married him?" Winnie asked, reaching for the open box of Fanny Farmer creams that Sean managed to slide out of her reach just in time.

Lavina wiped a smile from her face and gave a little cough. She liked to see Sean getting even—it happened so infrequently. "I doubt it," she finally said. "Judging from what she told me over the years, she was never in love with him. She just valued him as a friend." She met Bran's eyes across the table and smiled.

"She would have been the person Henry learned it from, certainly," Damian added.

"No question," Lavina said. "Poor, unsuspecting Hildy—never realizing what such a piece of gossip would bring out in Henry. That was probably before they married, judging by Henry's early forays into the blackmail game. When they were first going together." She heaved a little sigh. "And Jae, in turn, probably learned it sometime later from Henry. Much in the same way as she told me she had learned from him about the Hesson business in Chicago. Which, come to think of it, is probably why she suspected the Hessons of killing Henry. She did seem intent on putting Garrett on to them." She was well aware that part of what she was saying was solely to herself, since she had not had the chance to fill them all in on all the aspects of the case. "I'll have to have a long talk with Jae during the week."

"I can just see your phone bill now, Mother," Tracey said, digging into her piece of pumpkin pie.

"You'd better spend time filling me in, too," Winnie said, motioning for the sugar bowl. "I don't even know most of these people."

"But it was Will Argon and Simon's wife who were Nelson's real parents," Sean said aloud, obviously still trying to get it all straight in his head, names and relationships both. The Blaines were the only ones he and Winnie had known personally.

"Laurie, yes," Lavina said.

Sean shook his head, then started to laugh.

"What's so funny, Sean?" Damian asked, raising his coffee cup in his wife's direction for a refill.

"I was just thinking about our short-lived Hemlock Lake ghost," he said with a broad grin.

"What ghost is that?" Bran asked, leaning his arms on the table. "Don't tell me you have a ghost up here, too." He looked from one of them to the other, the smiles on their faces a clear giveaway that he was the only one not in on what was obviously a community joke.

Lavina laughed. "Garrett Blaine, as it turns out," she said. "It seems two of our youngsters on the lake here saw his shadow moving around Henry's house the afternoon following the murder. Their overactive imaginations did the rest, I'm afraid." She laughed again.

"What was Garrett doing back at the house?" Bran asked, obviously puzzled. "Looking for that videotape?"

"Actually, no," Lavina said. "As a matter of fact, he thought his father had already left for Canada—as, indeed, he should have. He just came back to see what he could scrounge before the agent had a chance to find a buyer. He was short on cash and was looking for anything he could remove and sell. He had a key to the house, don't forget, so he had no trouble getting in." She took a breath and a sip of black coffee. "He found the tape quite by accident in the car. After he found the body, that is."

"And he never told the police?" Winnie said, unthinking.

"He was too frightened, Winnie," Lavina said. "Not that I can blame him. Just imagine how it would have looked, given his situation. He was a prime suspect as it was."

"How did you learn all this, Mother?" Tracey asked.

"I called Garrett yesterday morning before you all arrived. It seems his wife was out and he was in a garrulous mood—especially with his father's murder solved."

"And here I thought I was in for a good ghost story," Bran said when she was through, the beginnings of a smile on his lips.

"Pay him no mind," Lavina said, dismissing the actor with a backward wave of the hand. "It's that Irish imagination of his at work, I'm afraid. He's as bad as the boys, for heaven's sake. You know these Irish storytellers."

Bran laughed this time, enjoying the teasing even more than the rest of them, especially when Lavina winked at him from the other side of the dining room table.

"When's that young man of yours going to get here, Susanne?" he asked as a last resort. "I need some outside support here." He laughed again, and the others along with him.

"Marty will be over after he finishes dinner with his family," the girl said, lowering her small snifter of Irish Mist. "And you're right, by the way. Marty gets teased here all the time, too. Wait and see—Dad will start in on him before he even has his coat off." She smiled down the length of the table at her father.

Damian, in turn, merely feigned innocence. "Who, me?"

The laughter continued against the background of Christmas music provided by Lavina's collection of cassette tapes. It was only Pavarotti's rendition of "O Holy Night" that induced a spontaneous few minutes of silence, instilling in them all again the true meaning of the season.

An hour later they were standing alone near the dock in the semidarkness, just beyond the flood of lights provided by the spots fastened under the eaves on the side of the house. Both of them had their jacket collars turned up, with Bran now in a pair of Kenneth London's boots, and Lavina in her own, in eight inches of snow.

"It appears to be a fine-looking house from here," Bran said after Lavina had indicated the shadowy outline of the Blaine house down the far end of the lake to the right of the community beach. "And certainly plenty of room, judging by the size of it."

"More than you'll need, that's for sure," Lavina said, turning to look up into his shadow-darkened face. "I still can't believe you went and bought it without even seeing it!" she said, shaking her hatless head, the steel-gray hair now almost silver in the faint light. "Whatever possessed you?" If he was going to blush with his answer, she'd never know in the near-darkness.

"Well, I haven't actually bought it yet. I just phoned Garrett, as I said, and told him I was interested. He wants to speak to the agent up here tomorrow or Wednesday to find out what price his father was asking for it. I'll get a chance to see it after that. And, of course, his father's will has to be probated before it's legally his, anyway. But I don't foresee any problem."

"You still haven't answered my question," Lavina said. "What will you use it for? Just the summer, or what? I mean, you have your apartment in the city and all." She was still looking up at him, his features clearer now that her eyes were accustomed to the dim light.

"That depends," he said.

"On what?"

Bran smiled. "You know, Lavina, when you confided in me Saturday morning over the phone about that scissors business, telling me what you wanted me to say after the funeral service, you can't imagine how terrific you made me feel."

"Why's that? Because I gave you a role to play?" She gave a little laugh.

Bran smiled. "What you were actually doing was telling me you had ruled me out as a possible suspect in the two deaths. And without—or so it seems to me—any logical reason."

"My instincts are logical enough for me," Lavina said with a faint smile she was sure he'd be able to detect even in the faint light. "They haven't failed me yet, happy to say. And I don't see them getting any rustier after all these years either."

"That's very nice. Thank you." He lowered his eyes, then looked up again. "And thank you, again, for the beautiful edition of *The Voyage of Bran*. I don't know when you found the time to track it down; it's certainly not easy to come by, that's for sure."

"For that, you can thank Susanne. She's a whiz at such things. I asked her to see if she could find a copy while I was still in the city. She'd even heard of it, for heaven's sake. In her medieval lit course. And while we're on the subject, while I naturally didn't get a chance to read it, I did flip through it. You forgot to mention in your description the section dealing with the sojourn in the Land of Women."

Bran let out a hearty laugh. "We men have to keep some things to ourselves, don't we?"

"You sound just like Ken." She was sorry she'd said it as soon as it was out. Though probably more for the truth it conveyed than for the actual voicing. She wasn't sure she was ready to accept it.

"I'll take that as a compliment," Bran said.

"Thank *you*, by the way, for the beautiful Connemara-marble rosary," she added, changing the subject. "It's something I never would have spent all that money on for myself."

"Then I'm extra glad I thought of it. It still hasn't been blessed yet, by the way."

"I'll see Father Cernac tomorrow after mass and have him do the honors."

She turned to look out briefly toward the lake, then back again. "Well, I suppose we'd better go back inside before they think we've turned into a couple of human icicles out here."

As she turned to face the house, Bran reached out and took hold of both of her gloved hands and held them out between them. "More than anything else, Lavina, I also want to thank you for the invitation to share your family Christmas. I know how much the occasion means to you."

"You've been talking to Susanne."

He smiled and nodded. "Though I didn't really have to. I could see it pretty much for myself."

She looked into his eyes, wishing she could see them more clearly. "I was delighted you were able to come— and wanted to." She lowered her eyes to look down at her boots, half buried as they were in the crystalline snow.

"I carve a wild turkey, don't you think?" Bran said, lightening the mood. He released her hands.

"Like a pro," Lavina agreed. "I never saw it done so fast and so neatly."

"I cut a wild rug, too, I'll have you know."

"I don't doubt it for a minute."

"How about it?"

"How about what?"

"Going dancing?"

"You're not serious," Lavina said, eyes wide.

"Do I sound like Fred Allen?"

"More like Charlie McCarthy."

"Come on, Lavina. I'm serious."

"I haven't been dancing in years, Bran." She didn't even know if places allowed dancing anymore. Outside of at weddings, that is.

"So what? It's like riding a bicycle—you never forget."

"It's not that, it's just . . ."

"Just what?"

"Well, just that I don't think I could."

"I haven't noticed any varicose veins."

Lavina laughed. "You're incorrigible, Bran Slattery. Of

course I don't have varicose veins. I'm just not sure I want to go out dancing at this point."

"That's something else you women never forget how to do," Bran said with a smile.

"What's that?"

"Be coy," he said. "Play hard to get. All you need is one of those fancy fans to conceal your lower face." He grinned.

Lavina let out a howl that sent Bran's eyebrows shooting up about half an inch. "Do I sound that old-fashioned?" she said, calming down. "I certainly hope not."

Bran shook his head. "Just teasing."

"But you're probably right just the same," she admitted, picturing herself the demure heroine of a Jane Austen novel. She smiled and started back toward the house, with Bran at her side.

"You know, you really had me worried for a while there," he said, pushing his scarf up to cover his mouth.

"When?" Lavina stopped in her tracks and stared at him.

"After I heard you were coming down to New York. I figured you'd end up getting personally involved in Henry's murder. Especially knowing the condition Audra was in at the time. I'd heard about your earlier sleuthing, and to be quite honest, I was worried something might happen to you." He paused. "At that point I honestly felt like taking you over my knee and beating some sense into you."

"I'll bet you did," Lavina said with a feigned scowl, setting them both off laughing again.

"Seriously, Lavina," Bran said, when they'd finally

calmed down, "after I saw you at Henry's party, I . . . well, I wanted to see more of you. A lot more."

Lavina looked down again to the tops of her boots, silent.

"I spent half of Thursday morning riding back and forth on the Staten Island ferry, trying to decide what to do. How to approach you." He forked a shock of gray-blond hair off his forehead with the fingers of his gloved hand, all the while aware he was fighting a losing battle with the wind.

"Why didn't you say something the night of the party?" Lavina asked, looking up again. They were in the full shower of the floodlights now. His reddened face, she was sure, wasn't entirely a result of the cold. As a matter of fact, she felt oddly flushed herself, though she was standing in the December night air on the lake.

"It was too crowded, Lavina, and everyone seemed to want to spend time with you," he said. "And then, before I knew it, Audra was asking to go home."

Thinking back, she realized how right he was. At times that evening she had felt more like the guest of honor than Henry Blaine. "Buying the Blaine house wouldn't by any chance have anything to do with me, would it?" she asked, knowing the answer now in her heart full well.

Bran shrugged under his winter jacket and smiled. "I'll let you answer that one for yourself, Lavina."

"But there's nothing between us, Bran," she said. "We're just two old friends."

He smiled again, wider this time, and took her by the hand. "Let's pretend, Lavina," he said, leading her back toward the house. "Let's pretend."